To Bob & Mary
I'll remember a long
term Friendship, Thanks

Paul Kendrick

THE BEAVER
and
THE BEAR

by
Paul Kending

authorHOUSE®

AuthorHouse™
1663 Liberty Drive, Suite 200
Bloomington, IN 47403
www.authorhouse.com
Phone: 1-800-839-8640

© 2008 Paul Kending. All rights reserved.

No part of this book may be reproduced, stored in a retrieval system, or transmitted by any means without the written permission of the author.

First published by AuthorHouse   6/12/2008

ISBN: 978-1-4343-7071-6 (sc)

Library of Congress Control Number: 2008902485

Printed in the United States of America
Bloomington, Indiana

This book is printed on acid-free paper.

Dedication

To Candy, my wife of thirty years, who lost her battle with cancer in May, 2007. She was my inspiration and support for each of my books.

Acknowledgements

I wish to thank John Bray for the cover picture of Chauncey the Bear Hunter's lodge, Mert Warner for providing me with information about Chauncey the Bear Hunter and my daughter Kathy Senn for reading an early draft of the manuscript and providing insightful comments and for her continued assistance with my web page, *lcloud.com*. I also want to thank personnel at Authorhouse for their help in the design and publication.

Preface

The period between the two World Wars saw a sudden influx of new residents to the previously wild areas of Northern Wisconsin. The great depression of '29 forced an exodus from the cities where the manufacturing companies had closed their doors. Many, who had embraced the urban life when they returned from the war, found the farm work in the rural north no stranger. It had been their roots before the conflict in Europe interrupted their young lives. Pay was meager, sometimes only room and board and a little *"tobacco money"*. The farmers they worked for were also suffering from the depressed economy, but on a farm, there was always enough food, a wood stove to provide warmth in the winter and a dry bed to sleep in.

There was one organization in the big cities, especially New York and Chicago, that had been strong enough to withstand the depression. They had enjoyed a thriving business during the "roaring twenties" and while people did not have as much cash to buy the product, they provided, the depression made the demand even greater. Their board rooms did not include a DuPont, Carnegie or Vanderbilt and they were not listed on the stock exchange. They produced and imported alcoholic beverages, outlawed in the United States with the passage of the *Eighteenth Amendment* in 1920. Their migration to the north was not to escape financial hardship.

Al Capone, constantly pursued in Chicago by rival gang leader George Moran found refuge in a palatial hide out in Sawyer County, Wisconsin while brother Ralph bought land for a permanent residence near Mercer in Iron County. Had it only been the pressure of the gang wars Alphonse might have stayed in Chicago, but in 1929, the same year he had struck a major blow to the Moran gang on St. Valentine day, he encountered a new and more formidable enemy. A young treasury agent named Elliot Ness had just formed the Untouchables, a group of agents specifically charged with the job of eliminating the illicit alcohol trade.

The Capones were rarely seen in Northern Wisconsin but the threat to their empire produced a larger outmigration. Shakespeare wrote in Hamlet, "The cease of majesty dies not alone," and rarely was that so clearly demonstrated as the eventual fall of Al Capone. The massive wheel of his influence included an army of body guards, drivers, mechanics, bookkeepers and domestics, plus his customers, the owners if the speakeasies and their employees who also found refuge in the northland.

There was one migrant from Chicago who fell into neither of those categories. He found his paradise in the Northern Wisconsin wilderness, but he had arrived years before any of the others. Chauncey Bottom came to Bayfield County in 1926. Chauncey was not concerned about a lack of money. Though he had none, the depression had little effect on him. He didn't need money. Nor did he need a job, save working for himself to build a lodge on one of the states most remote lakes. He was one of a kind. He called himself Chauncey the Bear Hunter, but few of the anecdotes about his unconventional life involved hunting. Chauncey was not just a character in a story. He was as real in Northern Wisconsin history as he was remarkable, but in this work his persona is revealed as he becomes a central figure in a fictional mystery.

Chapter 1

The year was 1914, the place, Minocqua, a city surrounded by the waters of two beautiful Northern Wisconsin lakes. It was after midnight when Johnny Bearheart scaled the high wrought iron fence intended to keep intruders away from the massive structure centered on the estate grounds. The building was guarded by a grove of pines that stood as sentinels watching over the baron and his family, not a feudal lord from some European country, but a lumber baron, equally wealthy and influential in Wisconsin's richly wooded northland. Johnny Bearheart had found the mansion where he was born.

As he peered through the semidarkness, he wondered about the people who lived in this big house, the biggest house he had ever seen. They might have been his brothers and sisters, shared the blood of the same father. Johnny had never known the man whose name he carried, the man his mother had married. Bearheart was a violent and abusive man who had been killed in a fight with a white settler. In those days there was no question of who was right and who was wrong. He was an Indian. He was wrong. When he died, Johnny's mother had not participated in the wailing, as expected. She had remained in her lodge for a few days then emerged wearing her best clothes. She had braids in her long black hair which she had refused to cut in accordance with Chippewa custom, and she wore her favorite copper bracelet that her father had given to her when he returned from a trip to the Keweenaw. Her late husband's family, especially those more distant who knew nothing of the turmoil in their marriage, were furious. "Why do you come looking like this?" They asked. "Have you no shame. Have you no feelings. You should wear mourning clothes and cut your hair. Why do you adorn your arms like that? Remove the braids from your hair and bangles, that you will have a place of honor at the restoring ceremony next year." She answered them, "how can you expect me to blacken my face or wear the mourning clothes for a husband who beat me and treated me like *ken'abeek*, the snake?" She screamed, "*Ah kaween*, I will not honor such a husband with mourning. Those who will be released from their season of mourning in the restoring ceremony will not find me with them."

She left the tribe and found work as a domestic in the home of James J. Calvert, the lumber baron who had recently been elected to the Wisconsin State Senate. Johnny was born a year later. Mrs. Calvert insisted that Johnny and his mother must go and as far as she was concerned, the senator can go right after them. Her husband disagreed. "I know how you feel and you have every right to feel that way, but think what that will do to my position in the senate, what it will do to us," he said. "Please, for both our sakes, let's keep this quiet at least for a few months, after the election. After that, we can send them away and no one will know a thing about it. Being the wife of a senator won't be so bad, will it?" He cajoled. She reluctantly agreed. Johnny's mother continued to work in the Calvert home and to raise her child there, and by the time he became a toddler, both Mr. and Mrs. Calvert had grown very fond of him.

Johnny's eyes searched the mansion, window by window hoping to catch a glimpse of Senator Calvert the man he now knew was his real father. The night lights were on and he could see the elegant furnishings, the crystal chandelier and paintings hung on the walls in their gilded frames. *That's where I should have lived,* he thought. *My mother told me. They wanted me to stay and live with them.*

It was true. The senator's wife became very fond of Johnny, but every time she looked at the boy, it reminded her of her husband's infidelity. She decided The Indian woman had been living and working in their home long enough. Johnny's mother had overheard Calvert and his wife talking. She heard them say they wanted to keep Johnny but send his mother back to the reservation. They said the boy could go to school and be raised as their son with all the advantages of a white child. His mother did not want to lose him. In the dead of night she took Johnny, the money she had saved from the meager wages they had paid her and what clothes she could carry wrapped up in a blanket. With those few possessions and no way of knowing if they would find acceptance again among the Chippewa, she left the Calvert home forever. She had never told Johnny how she managed the trip from Minocqua. When they arrived at their village, she discovered that her father, Eagle Feather had become chief of the Lac Vieux Desert band and all sanctions for her failure to live up to mourning customs of the Chippewa were forgotten. Johnny Bearheart had grown up Chippewa and only when Eagle Feather lay on his death bed almost a quarter century later did she disclose the events associated with his birth.

When Eagle Feather fell ill, Johnny Bearheart assumed, as the only heir, the tribal elders would choose him to be the new chief. He talked to his mother about it and she told him the elders would not select him. Even if they would accept someone related only on the mothers side, they would not accept one whose father was a white man. She had said that it was only because her father was an old brave many times decorated at the powwow and had been chosen to become the new chief that they were allowed to return to the tribe at all. Johnny was less than two years old when his grandfather took the scepter of leadership. He had grown to full manhood with no knowledge of his real father.

That he had spent hours with his grandfather, trying day after day to become a complete Chippewa, made his recent discovery even harder to bear. He had learned to hunt when he was but five years old and by the time he was eight he was adept with bow and arrow. Even at a young age he had gone into the woods when the snow was deep and sent his arrow into a small deer that provided the food for those in his wigwam. At his grandfather's feet he had learned how to make a snare and catch *wabasso,* the Rabbit, and a stout spear to kill *maskenosha*, the big fish. He became familiar with the woods and knew the spirit of every tree. He learned how to read dreams. He had participated in the powwow and all the sacred rites except, at this he took a deep breath and gritted his teeth, except the naming ceremony. Johnny had never been sent out to find his dream, had never appeared before the namer. His mother had called him Johnny, when she lived with the white senator, and he had received no other name, no Indian name since.

The Beaver and the Bear

Hiding in the darkness near the big mansion, Johnny suddenly thought he knew why he had not received his Indian name. Even his young friend, the white boy Ahmeek, had been given an Indian name by his grandfather, but Johnny was just Johnny. What kind of a name was that for an Indian boy? Having been born the son of a white man, he was deprived of the chance to be a complete Chippewa and having been taken back to the tribe by his mother, he was deprived of all the advantages of being white. He longed for his friend Ahmeek. It had been many years since he last saw the young white man with two names. He couldn't even remember what his white man's name had been.

Suddenly, the lights came on in the house and he saw a door open at the servant's entrance. Johnny jerked from his memories and became alert. A dog came running out into the yard barking. Johnny heard a voice cry out., "Who's out there?" He grasped two spikes at the top of the wrought iron fence and vaulted over. As he crept away, he heard the voices again. "What was it?" "I don't know," came the answer from a second voice. "Looked like an Indian, probably a drunken Indian. No telling what he'd hang around a wealthy politician's house for."

Johnny Bearheart returned to the tribal village determined that he was going to try to fit in, but he could not avoid comparing the poverty of the his people with the affluence he had seen in Minocqua, especially the family of Senator Calvert, That he had no share in that wealth, could not be a part of that life, struck him like an arrow in his chest.

Many tribal lands had been broken up and allotted to individual Indians under the Allotment act of 1887. While some tribal villages like the Lac Vieux Desert continued to be populated by a band of the Chippewa and despite the fact that they still lived according to their tribal culture, aid from the Bureau of Indian Affairs became almost nonexistent. Those tribes that maintained their solidarity and customs by remaining on the former reservation lands were left with little to provide a living beyond the subsistence of an ever shrinking plot of ground. For the Lac Vieux Desert that meant a diet of little more than wild rice and fish.

Johnny's behavior began to reflect his bitterness. He frequently went into town at night where he could ask one of the locals to buy a bottle of whiskey for him, giving that person of course, considerably more than the bottle cost. He worked occasionally in one of the nearby logging camps to get the money. He had learned some rudiments of that work when, as a boy, he had worked with Ahmeek in the Marichetti camp on the south end of the lake.

Whenever Johnny returned to the village, no one felt the wrath of his bitterness more than his mother and his sister, Mourning Dove. They had watched his anger grow day by day. He was never physically violent, as Mourning Dove's father had been, but no one was spared his verbal onslaughts. It was not long before his mother had enough of his brutish behavior and verbal abuse.

"Johnny, Johnny," she cried, "This is not what your grandfather taught you?"

"My grandfather taught me to be Chippewa," he answered, "but now I have learned I am not Chippewa. I am a half breed. You know what that is? Half breed? It is nothing. It is not white and it is not Indian and both hate me. Johnny Bearheart has no people"

"No one hates you Johnny. You hate you, only you. Not anybody else. The people of Lac Vieux Desert have never hated you."

"But I have no honor here," he said, "I might have hoped to earn the honor, but because of you that is no longer possible."

"Me? It is my fault," she replied. "What I did was long ago and the years have taken it from their memories. All they know now is I am Chippewa. Johnny, you are Chippewa."

"I am no longer Chippewa," he shouted. I will be *Wawa*, the wild goose"

And with that renunciation of his Indian blood, Johnny Bearheart left the tribe.

He had little respect for the white man since a store keeper had falsely accused him of trying to steal a knife years ago when he worked in the logging camp with Ahmeek. How could he be expected to accept the news that he was a member of that race?

Chapter 2

Jotham Marichetti had not made the trip from Madison to the Northern Wisconsin timber country very frequently over the past six years. When he was in college and later in law school at the University of Wisconsin, he had visited his father and brother at least twice each year, but after obtaining his law degree he had accepted an appointment as a law clerk for Justice John Barnes, a former resident of Rhinelander. Justice Barnes had been appointed a year before Jotham's graduation. Jotham decided the opportunity to serve a Supreme Court Justice would be a great way to launch a career in law, but the work was intense and gave him little opportunity to travel north. He looked forward to visiting his family and perhaps a few old friends at the logging camp but, this time, those pleasures were secondary.

He had received word from his bother that old Eagle Feather, Chief of the Lac Vieux Desert band of the Chippewa had died, and the boy the old Indian had befriended and given the Indian name Ahmeek was not about to miss the funeral.

ASTRONAUT
CONTINUED FROM A1

shuttle's crew before being picked as the pilot on the Columbia for a mission in August 1989 – the first of his four shuttle flights.

Richards, now 62 and living in Houston, is attending the Association of Space Explorers' 11th Planetary Congress this week in Seattle. The organization, started in 1985 to foster dialogue between astronauts and cosmonauts on opposite sides of the Cold War and open to anyone who has traveled to space, meets about every year so its members can discuss their experiences.

At each event, the astronauts and cosmonauts travel to area schools to encourage interest in math and science. On Wednesday, they fanned out to Puget Sound-area schools, including Sumner, Federal Way, Tacoma and Steilacoom.

But few schools can claim Scobee Elementary's fascination with spaceflight. The school feels like a miniature museum dedicated to space exploration: Near the office, a mural with an astronaut on a spacewalk covers an entire wall. Scobee's flight suit from training hangs down the hall from a display of dozens of mission patches, autographed photos of astronauts and several large models of space shuttles.

The school's mascot is the Challengers. Each year during Scobee Week space exploration dominates the curriculum, Principal Greg Brown said.

About 25 to 30 astronauts have visited the school since it changed its name from North Auburn Elementary School in 1987.

"It's part of this school's identity,"

Former astronaut Dick Ric[...]
in Auburn. "The people w[...]
Auburn resident who died

Brown said. "And it's great [...]
get astronauts to come he[...]
these kids the importance [...]
science. It often means a lot [...]
from someone like an astr[...]
About 380 students ass[...]
gymnasium to listen to Ric[...]
them were members of the [...]
including Dick's father, br[...]
law and niece. Brown sa[...]
many of whom live in the a[...]

'INSULTING TO THE AMERICAN PUBLIC,' HE SAYS

Republican senator says Palin not ready to lead

Sen. Chuck Hagel raises doubts about Sarah Palin's lack of experience in foreign policy. He says it's required in today's world.

BY JOSEPH MORTON
Omaha World-Herald

WASHINGTON — Sen. Chuck Hagel of Nebraska on Wednesday became the nation's most prominent Republican officeholder to publicly question whether Sarah Palin has the experience to serve as president.

"She doesn't have any foreign policy credentials," Hagel said in an interview with the Omaha (Neb.) World-Herald. "You get a passport for the first time in your life last year? I mean, I don't know what you can say. You can't say anything."

Palin was elected governor of Alaska in 2006 and before that was the mayor of a small town. She has cited the proximity of Alaska to Russia as evidence of her international experience. Hagel scoffed at that notion.

"I think they ought to be just honest about it and stop the nonsense about," I look out my window and I see Russia and so therefore I know something about Russia,'" he said. "That kind of thing is insulting to the American people."

A senior member of the Senate Foreign Relations Committee, Hagel has been an outspoken critic of the Bush administration's handling of the Iraq war.

Hagel says he has no plans to endorse either presidential candidate. He offered a couple of caveats on his assessment of Palin: Experience is not the only qualification for elected officials — judgment and character are indispensable.

Washington experience isn't the only kind of experience, Hagel said, and he noted that many White House occupants have been governors.

"But I do think in a world that is so complicated, so interconnected and so combustible, you really got to have some people in charge that have some sense of the bigger scope of the world," Hagel said. "I think that's just a requirement."

The trip is not so long and tedious as it had been during his college years. The modern trains were much faster and the Marichetti logging camp had been moved to Boulder Junction. As the timber began to thin around the Lac Vieux Desert camp, Dominic and his father moved westward to a forest not yet depleted by the woodsman's axe. In addition to the faster train ride, Jotham could remain on the same train all the way to Woodruff where Dominic would have a car waiting. Jotham thought of his trips from Wausau to his father's old camp when he was a child. In those days a horse drawn wagon picked him up for a long ride over rough logging roads.

The engine slowed and Jotham heard the train whistle. He remembered his first train ride to the old logging camp when he was eight years old. Then, the sound of the train whistle had intrigued him. This time he was only conscious of how often it whistled. It occurred to him that this same rail line that crossed through such remote countryside when he was a child was now crossing highway after highway and whistling for each grade crossing. Transportation was no longer limited to trains and horse drawn wagons, but now included the automobile. He had heard of automobiles since 1903 when the Oldsmobile Corporation first developed them for the public to purchase, but for the common man they remained an impossible dream. That changed in 1909 when Henry Ford began to produce the Model T in a quantity that brought the price tag down low enough for people who were not wealthy to buy. Since then good gravel roads began to be developed all over the state and even a beginning barrister might hope to drive on them in the not too distant future.

About the time Jotham formed a picture of himself in a new Ford Roadster the train's brakes screeched. He heard the loud clunk, clunk, clunk as the coupler of each car slammed against the coupler of the car in front of it and finally caused him to lurch forward in his seat as the car in which he was riding joined the thunderous procession. When he raised himself to an upright position again, he saw Brother Dominic waiting on the platform.

"I thought maybe you'd dropped off the end of the earth;" Dominic began as they pulled away from the railroad station. "That big city life don't leave much time to come back and visit country folks," he teased.

"Dominic, I know you don't think what I do as a law clerk is work," Jotham answered, intentionally taking the bait, "but it burns up a lot of time and, believe it or not, I come home as tired at night as I used to when I spent the day hauling logs, especially after all the parties and all those city women."

"Yeah, I know." Dominic feigned sympathy then continued. "But seriously, you gotta be in the middle of that political circus down there on Madison. From what they tell me that's a full time job all by itself. What's happenin' there? I hear some of the fellas that can read betterin' me say that the days of the La Follettes is over. Gotta new governor now. What's his name?" Dominic asked.

"Emanuel Philipp. He's . . ."

"Yeah. That's him." Dominic cut in. "Looks like he's going change all the stuff old Bob LaFollette and that guy from the university got started. . ."

"Van Hise," Jotham prompted.

"Yeah. Van Hise. I hope they'll at least get the government out of the business of running' the river system and tryin' to control how the logging camps operate."

"You don't need the rivers anymore, Dominic," Jotham joked. "From now on you can use your tin Lizzie here to pull wagon loads of logs out of the woods and all the way to the saw mill."

Dominic laughed. "You been gone a long time brother. We don't send many logs to the saw mill anymore. The logging business is mostly pulp wood and we got to get that all the way down to the paper mills south of Wausau. Besides, sometimes when it rains, I'm lucky if I can get this tin lizzie out over these rough dirt roads all by itself without pullin' anything"

Dominic turned onto a road that was no more than two sets of tire tracks through the woods. A half mile later he pulled up beside one of the temporary shelters that housed the loggers at Boulder Junction. Before getting out of the car, Jotham turned to his brother.

"Dominic, I've got a couple of questions to ask. How did you know so much about what's going on in Madison? I never knew you to be interested in politics."

"I can read, Little brother," Dominic said with feigned indignation. "Besides, when I run into something in the paper I can't handle, I get Stanley Rodzaczk to help me. You don't remember, but I went to school for a couple of years. We lived in Land O Lakes then and Dad took the horses from town to the camp every day so Gino and I could go. Gino got all the way to the fourth grade and learned lots of stuff, but I only got as far as reading and some easy arithmetic. Then when Mom died, we both had to go to the camp with Dad and that was the end of our schooling. Now, what's your other question?"

"I was wondering how far the Boulder Junction camp is from Eagle River."

"Oh, I get it. You want to go and find the girl you left behind. I s'pose your next question is going to be can you borrow the car?"

"Yeah," Jotham admitted. "But you'l have to take a couple of hours to teach me how to keep it on the road."

Mourning Dove and Jimmy Little Wind stood near the center of the tribal burial ground beside Mourning Dove's mother. They watched as an automobile pulled to a stop some two hundred yards from the grounds. Jotham and his brother stepped down from the running board on either side and walked toward the crowd. Jimmy Little Wind met them half way and escorted them to the area where his wife and her mother stood. No one made a verbal greeting. Eagle Feather's body lay in a wooden box that had been place in the center of the circle with his feet facing the west. When the drum started beating, the Grand Medicine Man placed a bow and a small quiver of arrows along with a pipe and pouch of tobacco in the box beside the body. Mourning Dove's mother walked slowly forward and added a small kettle, a dish and a spoon. Jotham whispered to Dominic that these were necessary for the four day journey to the spirit world. Then several members of the *Midewiwan* approached and spoke to Mourning Dove's mother and the large crowd of Eagle Feather's family. They assured them of the reality of the spirit world and the ability of the Mide to assist Eagle Feather to make sure he would arrive there. Then as the drums began to beat faster each member of the Mide, in turn, walked past the wooden box, each saying a brief word of encouragement to the deceased. They spoke in their native tongue very rapidly to the beat of the drum and Jotham could not make out any of the words. Later when he asked Mourning Dove about it, she just said "directions."

"Directions?"

"You know, how to get to the land of the dead."

Following the funeral they sat together in the ceremonial ground and, between interruptions from well wishers, talked about all the things that had happened in the many years since Jotham had last visited the tribe. Jotham avoided addressing Mourning

Dove directly. Instead he made his comments to Jimmy Little Wind, not wanting to offend anyone or cause problems in their marriage. If it were a question for Mourning Dove or her mother, he knew Jimmy would redirect it to one of them, then sit back and listen to the answer along with the Marichetti's. While they talked, Jotham noticed that Mourning Dove's mother appeared agitated and, guessing what might be the reason, asked. "Where is Johnny Bearheart? I didn't see him at the funeral."

Jimmy nodded deferentially to his mother-in-law who began, "O Ahmeek, Ahmeek" then broke into a rapid combination of English and Chippewa that Jotham could not understand.

Mourning Dove smiled and addressed Jotham. "She calls you by your Indian name from long ago." Then she explained, "she says she wishes you were here when Johnny left. She says you could talk sense into him. If you were here he might have stayed in the tribe."

"But where is he? Why did he leave?"

"Johnny Bearheart was starting to drink much whiskey," she said. "Find him for us Ahmeek. He will tell you what happened and you can get him to come home. He always listen to you."

On the way back to the logging camp, Dominic let Jotham take the wheel. He had always been well coordinated, but driving a Model T Ford was almost more than he could manage. The combination of three floor pedals, along with an ungainly lever on the drivers left side, to shift the transmission was totally confusing. Maintaining control of a steering wheel at speeds approaching thirty miles per hour was also a major challenge. They decided it was going to take more than one lesson. After several days of close calls, punctuated by Dominic, laughter at having, after so many years, found something in which he bested his younger brother, they decided Jotham might be competent to take the car out alone.

The next morning Jotham slowly and carefully guided the Ford over the trails that people called roads in Northern Wisconsin's timberland and managed, without incident, to get to Eagle River. Rebecca Morgan was impressed with the car, but Jotham felt compelled to tell her it belonged to Dominic and his father. Rebecca still taught at the same elementary school where she had when he left for college many years before. She had been his girl friend then and, though they maintained contact over the years, the lack of frequency in his visits north made that term seem less than appropriate now.

They had lunch and Jotham drove out to the lake and stopped the car where they had a pleasant view of the water. There were still some small log jams on the surface but nothing like Jotham remembered from his youth. He took Rebecca's hand and she leaned against his shoulder. They sat in that position for a long time talking about nothing of importance. The kind of conversation people had already begun to refer to as "small talk." Eventually, Rebecca's expression became pensive.

"Jotham," she said. "What's going to become of us?"

Jotham knew what she was referring to. "What do you mean, Rebecca?" He asked.

She didn't respond, just smiled and gave a look that said, you know quite well what I mean.

"I don't really know, Rebecca, Jotham finally said. "I always thought of you and I being together, you know marriage and the whole family thing, but not in Madison. My work in Madison won't lead to a permanent career. Even if I was willing to continue to be a law clerk, Judge Barnes won't be a Supreme Court Justice forever. In Wisconsin, Justices to the Supreme Court are elected.

He could be out at any election. Besides, I've thought, sooner or later I'd quit clerking for the judge and move back here to start my own law practice and then . . ."

"And then it will be too late Jotham," Rebecca broke in. "Before, waiting seemed all right. Women teachers can't be married anyway and I did want to keep teaching, but now I'm over thirty years old. How long do you think I can wait? A woman doesn't start a family when she's forty, you know."

"I didn't mean that long. Rebecca, you know I love you. I have since we were in grade school, but in these times a man doesn't get married until he's got a good job or is established in his profession. I'll leave Madison soon, then we can start planning for a wedding."

"Oh, Jotham I've wanted to hear you say those things, but we have to start planning now. At least start discussing some of the problems."

"Problems?" Jotham asked. "What problems?"

"Well," Rebecca hesitated, not sure how she was going to broach the subject. "There's the question of religion.'

"Religion?"

"Yes. You know I'm Catholic and you were raised Episcopalian."

"I wasn't raised Episcopalian. I lived with my Aunt Sarah and Uncle Oliver and I went to church with them, but I didn't join the Episcopal church or any other church. I learned more about religion, or at least spiritual things, from Chief Eagle Feather of the Chippewa than I did from Father Smythe at the Episcopalian Church.

"I think that's part of the trouble. Even if my church did allow me to marry a non catholic, there is no way I could accept what our priest says is a savage religion."

"Rebecca," Jotham protested. "I didn't say I believed what Eagle Feather taught me about Indian ways, just that I learned from it. You wouldn't be marrying a religion. You would be marrying a man, a man who cares about you whether you're Catholic, Protestant or, for that matter, a Jew."

"Jotham," she said, "I'll talk to the priest about it. I've heard about people who were catholic and married a protestant, but I don't know if they were able to stay in the Catholic Church."

"You do that," Jotham said, "and I'll do some serious thinking about it, but right now I don't know how I could ever become Catholic. I would have to give up everything I believe in."

As Jotham drove away from Eagle River and turned onto the dirt road that wound through the forest to Boulder Junction he had mixed feelings. He was sad that his visit with Rebecca went so badly but that sadness turned to a vague resentment that she failed to have any understanding of his side of the issue. He heard Rebecca in his thoughts. *There is no way I could accept what our priest says is a savage religion. Has her priest ever heard of the inquisition? Does he know any Indian that burned people at the stake for believing something different than they did?*

The hour had been late when Jotham had dropped Rebecca off at her rooming house and the evening sun was already setting behind the tall trees. The rays of the sunset reflected in deep shades of red and orange from the low lying clouds in the west, but that did little to comfort Jotham or to light the road in front of him. When he reached a wide spot in the road, he pulled the car to a stop so he could get out and light the carbide headlamps the way Dominic had demonstrated. They provided only a dim light for a short distance ahead. He backed off on the throttle. He was familiar with the north woods and knew a deer or a bear could be on the road ahead of him at any turn. The tin lizzie was no match for an animal like that. It meant he would reach the logging camp later than he planned, but he would get back.

The next morning Jotham joined his father and brother in the cook's shanty for breakfast. As soon as he came in, a procession of loggers that had been in the Lac Vieux Desert camp when Jotham spent his summers working there greeted him. They all wanted to know how he like working for a Justice of the Wisconsin State Supreme Court. He answered them all in turn with the same comment. It was interesting and a great place to learn about the law, but he really couldn't wait to get back up north and start his own law practice in some small town. He did not want to be a big city lawyer.

When the loggers finished their meal and went to their various personal chores before starting a hard day's work in the woods, Dominic and his father stayed for a time to visit with Jotham.

"Well, how did it go last night with the long lost girlfriend?" Dominic asked.

"Not too well, I'm afraid. She wants to get married."

Enrico Marichetti winked at Dominic and said with a broad smile, "You better be careful now Jotham. That's what they all want."

"Well," Dominic said, "you knew that didn't you. How long you been stringin' her along now, fifteen years?"

"About that."

"So! What's the problem?"

"The problem is," Jotham said, "she's Catholic."

"And whatsa matter with that?" The elder Marichetti asked. "I'm Catholic. You be Catholic too if we don't live in a logging camp where we don't have a Catholic Church and there's no Priest to baptize you."

"That's right Jotham. We'd all been Catholic if mama was alive," Dominic added. "She would've found a church and a priest even if we lived at the North Pole."

"But that's the point, Dominic. Maybe you and I were born catholic, but we were never baptized, went to a Catholic Church, or grew up catholic. We never had a priest to tell us who we could marry and who we couldn't marry and filling our heads with all kinds of stuff we couldn't possibly believe."

"If priest says you gotta be catholic to marry the girl, you be catholic," Enrico Marichetti said. "What's a difference."

"When I was little," Jotham said, "when I would ask you what I was going to be when I grew up, you always said, 'first you be yourself, Jotham, then you can be anything you want to be.' That's the problem. I have to be myself first and that means I have to be what I believe in."

"OK, but now it's time to go to work," his father answered. "We talk more after supper tonight, yes."

But they didn't talk about it after supper or any other time and Jotham knew that was the way his father wanted it. It was his problem and he was the one who had to solve it. His father would neither help nor interfere and whatever Jotham decided, he would say it was all right.

After supper Enrico Marichetti began the conversation, as he always did. He asked Dominic about the days news. Dominic's reading was not really at the newspaper level, but his father knew he would have talked to Stanley during the day's toil and Stanley, an avid reader, was the town crier and gazetteer of the logging camp. Marichetti was especially concerned when war was being waged in Europe. Since the assassination of Archduke Francis Ferdinand of Austria by a Serbian terrorist on June 28, 1914, precipitating war between Austria and Serbia, the news reading became a nightly ritual. Austria, was backed by Germany and within a year, almost every country of Europe, with an old score to settle had joined on one side or the another. World War I was well underway. Enrico handed the newspaper Stanley had given him earlier in the day to Dominic.

"Dominic," he said, "Read me the news."

"Jotham's a lot better reader than me," Dominic said. "How about we let him read the paper tonight?"

The elder Marichetti nodded in agreement and Dominic handed the paper to his younger brother. Jotham looked at Dominic, obviously confused.

Dominic continued. "He wants the war news, not the whole paper, and just the meat of the story. Ya don't have ta read all the other stuff they put in."

Jotham proceeded to read the news for his father. He was sure, Dominic, in spite of his lack of education was the better reader for this job. He had a hard time skipping over the parts his father wouldn't be interested in and translating the words in the newspaper to those more familiar to the culture of the logging camp.

The newspaper was predicting a victory for Britain and her allies in the war against Germany. The French had achieved a major victory in the Somme River area. The battle of Verdun had held the German advance and ended in a stalemate, but British and French forces had driven a wedge nine miles deep in the German lines. A major contributor to that offensive had been the introduction of a new fighting machine developed in England. Workers had mounted an armored body on a vehicle with caterpillar treads. It looked like containers built for holding liquids so they named it the Tank.

There was a story about the election of David Lloyd George as the new prime minister of England and another on the French selecting General Robert Naively to replace Marshal Joseph Joffre. Finally, and of greater interest to Jotham, Germany fought the allies for control of the sky over Europe. They had developed a machine gun that could be synchronized with the planes propeller making it possible for pilots to get a sight on allied planes directly in front of their own craft. The German air war didn't go as well on another front, however. Count Ferdinand von Zeppelin's fleet of Airships failed to qualify as fighting machines. The huge gas filled bodies made them vulnerable to the enemy and nature. In the course of fifty-one raids with the big ships seventy-seven were lost to aerial combat, antiaircraft fire and storms. The article noted that this was the first aircraft to bomb London on May 15th of the previous year.

Jotham put the paper down and the three of them began to discuss the war. Foremost in the minds of people throughout the country was the question, "Will the United States enter the war? Two years earlier, Woodrow Wilson won re-election against Charles Evans Hughes with the slogan "He kept us out of the war." After the sinking of the *Lusitania* by a German submarine, a British liner whose twelve-hundred passengers included one hundred-twenty-four Americans, opposition to the war was weakening.

"I'm sure we'll join in the war," Jotham said. "The president's promises were just political rhetoric."

"Political what?" Dominic asked.

Jotham laughed, not at his brother, but at himself. "I'm sorry Dominic," he said, "That was a dumb thing for me to say. I meant that those promises were nothing more than speech making, you know, just to get elected."

"Yeah," Dominic said. "I know them politicians do a lot of that."

"People in America," Jotham's father cut in, "They don't want war, not to go to a war in Europe."

"A lot of them feel we should be there," Jotham said. "A lot of aviators have gone to Canada and joined the Royal Canadian flyers so they could go. There are also a lot of Americans aviators in France already. They've been there training for quite a while. They're called the Lafayette Escadrille and according to the papers they're ready to start flying fighter planes against the Germans. I'm not an aviator but I want to be ready when America gets into the fight. I went in last week and filled out papers to join the army."

"No, Jotham, you don't want to do that," his father said. "You remember your brother Gino."

Gino had joined the army during the Spanish American War and had died at San Juan Hill. Jotham remembered it well. He was only fourteen years old when they received the letter from Teddy Roosevelt and it was the saddest day of his life.

"Of course I remember, Papa," Jotham said. "That's the main reason I have to be ready and it's the reason I must go."

He went on to explain that, as a lawyer, he would not be on the front lines. He said, " I won't end up like Gino did," a lump formed in his throat as he finished, "dying on a charge up some hill nobody ever heard of before.".

"You are all grown up, Jotham," Enrico Marichetti said. "I know you will do what is right for you to do."

Chapter 3

Rebecca Morgan taught the children in her one room country school without her usual enthusiasm. She had taught these same lessons over and over for more than fourteen years. Throughout those years, she had developed numerous ways of presenting the lessons to keep the children interested, but now she had other things on her mind. She hadn't slept well for almost a week. She was disturbed by Jotham's refusal to join her church so they could begin preparations for their marriage. She was afraid she had waited much too long for something that was not going to happen. Rebecca had made friends with other men over the years of her teaching in Eagle River, but only at school functions or town celebrations like the annual Fourth of July picnic. Her relationship with Jotham was the only one she had taken seriously. Now that was about to end and she didn't know if she should feel sad or relieved.

As soon as the school day was over, she planned to go see the priest at the Eagle River Catholic Church. She would prefer to go to her own priest in Wausau, but she only returned to her home on school vacations and that would be several weeks yet. Her thoughts were interrupted by the big clock on the wall chiming four o'clock. She anxiously dismissed the children and hurried to the Catholic Church only a few blocks from her school. Father Murphy saw her rushing down the path and was about to ask where she was off to in such a hurry when she abruptly turned toward the rectory where he stood in the yard.

"Well, Rebecca," he said with the trill in his r's that had always been his trade mark, "is it that you're in a hurry to get someplace else or is it this old country priest that you're so anxious to see?"

"It's you, Father. I need to talk to you," she said, then added, "It's a personal problem."

Father Francis Murphy could hear the agitation in her voice. "You sound troubled, my child. Come inside and tell me what the problem might be."

Rebecca hated it when the Father called her "my child," especially now when she had just passed thirty and was still unmarried. She realized, however, that to a man of Father Murphy's age, she was just a child and to a priest, one of his own. She tried not to let those feeling show as she followed him inside. Father Murphy motioned her to a chair while he slid in behind a large mahogany desk.

Rebecca told him about Jotham, about their going to the same school in Wausau and becoming close and planning, for all these years, on an eventual marriage. She told him how many years they waited while Jotham was in law school and, after that, a clerk for Justice Barnes in the state Supreme Court, "and now," she said, "I'm afraid it's all over."

"All over?" Father Murphy asked. "What happened? Did he find someone else?"

"No, nothing like that. "I could begin to understand that," she said. "It's worse than that. It's religion."

"Ah,' Father Murphy began, with a knowing look, "he's protestant. Oh my child, you must have known that could be trouble."

"We were children when we first became friends. We didn't even think of such things then. Even when we got older, I didn't worry about it. Jotham was raised by an aunt and uncle in Wausau. They attended the Episcopal Church and I never expected him to be that concerned about it."

"And he won't change? Usually young men will when they really love the girl," Father Murphy said. "He must have very strong feelings about his protestant religion."

"No, he doesn't," she said, "at least not the Episcopal Church. I didn't tell you the whole story."

"There's more?"

"Yes. When Jotham was little, he went to the logging camp near Lac Vieux Desert in the summer time."

"Oh, I knew some of the loggers in that area," Father Murphy said. "Which camp might that have been?"

"It was his father's. His name was Marichetti."

"Enrico's? I knew his father. A long time ago I was sent to Land o Lakes for a funeral. Marichetti's wife it was. The camps were far from our churches and travel in those days was slow and difficult and you didn't see them at mass, but they were still catholic. I'm surprised a Marichetti boy would not want to join our church."

"When Jotham went up there in the summers," Rebecca said, "he became friends with an old Indian Chief and his grandchildren. They taught him a lot about what the Chippewa believed. The old chief even gave him an Indian name. He won't consider our church now. He says he can't join a church whose beliefs about God are completely different from his own."

"There's no way, my child, no way you could marry him if he refuses to believe in Jesus, the Blessed Virgin and the Holy Fathers in Rome. No way."

"But if I believe," she protested.

"No, my child. You must try to convince him to change his sinful beliefs," Father Murphy said. "If you were to marry him without him confessing the faith and joining the church, you could not continue to be catholic either."

"But father . . ."

"I don't say this to you, Rebecca," Father Murphy concluded. "It's what the Holy Father says, it's what the church says, it is what God says."

Rebecca held herself together until she was well outside the rectory, then she burst into tears.

That night, she cried herself to sleep. She wanted to marry Jotham more than anything else, anything that is, but her belief in God and the doctrine of her church.

Jotham returned to Madison where he resigned his law clerk position and completed his enlistment in the United States Army. Because he was not only a practicing attorney, but a lawyer with experience in a State Supreme Court, he was sent to Fort McCoy, Wisconsin for a brief period of basic training, then on to Officers School. He was more convinced than ever that the United States would soon join the allied forces in Europe in the war against Germany. The president who had kept the country out of the war through the election in 1914, had changed his program calling for continued U.S. neutrality. His Press Secretary, George Creel, began to promote the slogans, "the war to end all wars" and "the war to make the world safe for democracy."

Jotham wrote to Rebecca but received no answer. He admitted to himself that he was holding back. His letters were not as personal nor as warm at they had been during his years working in the Supreme Court. If Rebecca had been that upset about delaying marriage because of his legal work in Madison, he could only imagine her reaction when he told her it would now have to wait until after the war. He talked about it to Cadet Ralph Robinson, a fellow officer candidate. The cadet was watching when Jotham came in from mail call and threw his letter from Dominic on the bed without opening it.

"Not going to open your mail, soldier?" Robinson asked in a voice that sounded more friendly and sympathetic than accusatory.

"I'll get to it later," Jotham answered. "It's just from my brother. It can wait."

"Oh, nothing from the girlfriend, huh?"

"I don't know if I have a girlfriend anymore. We had a little argument when I last saw her."

"A little argument?" Robinson asked with an inquisitory look. "You can patch that up, write to her again."

"Well, maybe it was a big argument. We've been talking about getting married, but with this war thing on the horizon, I told her we'd have to delay it a little longer."

"A little longer? How long has it been?"

"That depends." Jotham said, "for me just a few years, since I got out of law school. But for her it's more like fifteen . She went to Normal School right after we graduated from high school and it's been about that long since she started teaching."

"That might take more than a little sweet talk." Robinson mused.

"I'm not very good at that sweet talking stuff anyway," Jotham admitted. "I'm afraid none of my letters could be called romantic."

Robinson laughed. "That's because you're a lawyer, not a professional soldier."

"Sure," Jotham answered. "You professional soldiers are real romantics. You love your rifles, you love your cannons and you love your bayonets. You might even love a woman but only if she'll let you go before sunrise."

That ended the discussion with a good laugh but no fresh ideas on how Jotham might handle his problem with Rebecca. He decided it would be best to just wait until he completed cadet training. He would use his furlough before reporting to a unit for permanent duty to go up north again. He and Rebecca would work something out. He thought it strange that religion should come up at this point in their relationship. They had been good friends since sixth grade and they had never discussed religion. In fact, he couldn't remember even being aware of what Church Rebecca went to then. He knew his father was catholic, but there was no church close by so nobody seemed to be concerned about it, least of all Enrico Marichetti. Jotham grew up with a strong belief in God, but that came from a mixture of Indian and Christian traditions. He wasn't convinced either of them had it right, but then, what was right was a mystery he had long since given up trying to solve. His mind was occupied with other things. The only thing he did feel certain about was that he could not accept the doctrine of the Catholic Church.

After Germany started a campaign to have its submarines sink all ships found off the allied coast including ships of neutral nations, the war Jotham had been expecting broadened to include the United States. Such a naval campaign was a violation of international law and, at the request of President Woodrow Wilson, congress passed a declaration of war on April 6, 1917,

The mobilization began immediately. The army and navy had over one million volunteers within three months but that was less than a quarter of the governments estimated needs. In may of that same year the Selective Service Act authorizing conscription of young men suitable for induction into the military was passed. Johnny Bearheart, however did not wait to be drafted. As soon as recruitment centers were opened in Northern Wisconsin, he was one of the first to volunteer.

Johnny was sent to Fort Dodge, Iowa for training. While he continued to drink heavily, it was never enough to impair his ability to function as a soldier. He saw the war as a chance to prove himself. As a Chippewa he was not required to register for the draft, but there was nothing to prevent him from joining on his own volition. Military discipline came easy for him. As an Indian he saw himself as a naturally born fighter, but the dictates of his culture had always called for obedience to a higher authority. He learned to salute. He learned to say "yes Sir" at all the appropriate times and he learned to shoot like he had never shot before. He had hunted with a gun many times when he was still a member of the village at Lac Vieux Desert, but ammunition was always scarce and practice, when not in the woods hunting, was rarely allowed. He was adept at almost everything expected of a good soldier except punctuality. He could not get used to the idea of some event having an appointed time. Something started when it was supposed to start and somebody, usually a chief or a member of the mide told you when. It didn't start by the hands on a white man's clock. His notion of time and appointments was based on the powwow. The pow wow started when the chiefs said it should. There was no need for clocks. The bugle that called reveille in the morning made more sense, but he wished they could find a gentler way of making that announcement.

On the rifle range Johnny earned his expert rifleman's badge. A week later he demonstrated the same competence with a thirty caliber machine gun. But none of the exercises with weaponry were as great a demonstration of his skill as his capability as a runner. He could do one hundred yards in nine seconds flat and slowed only little on the second hundred. A soldier who was fast on his feet was a major asset in an army unit and Johnny's speed was duly recorded on his military records.

Jotham could tell his father was still worried about him being a soldier and the bright gold bar that he wore on his shoulder did little to comfort him. He kept telling his youngest son, "Officers get shot at, too." Dominic was more impressed by his sharp officers dress uniform. The draft was inducting men between the ages of eighteen and thirty-eight years, but Dominic was exempt. As the only remaining son of a man in a business considered critical to the war effort, the tentacles of the draft board could not reach him. The men in the logging community were also curious, many of them finding some excuse to stop by the Marichetti quarters to get a look at the new military officer. His being a lawyer had not been nearly so impressive to them as becoming a lieutenant in the United States Army. Rarely did someone who looked so important visit the far north logging camps

The last of the procession to arrive was Stanley Radzaczk. He, too, found The uniform impressive, but for him it was more a sense of pride for the man inside. Stanley had been Jotham's mentor when he was a young man learning the skills of the logging camp. Stanley took that role one step farther on those Sunday afternoons when they sat under a tree discussing items in the Sunday Paper.

The Beaver and the Bear

He felt that he had helped introduce Jotham to the outside world and now the boy he had helped to grow intellectually as well as physically stood before him as both a lawyer and an army officer.

"So, Lieutenant Marichetti . . ."

"It's Jotham, Stanley," the officer cut in.

"Jotham, Ahmeek, Esquire, Lieutenant. You've had a lot of names and titles," Stanley said. You've earned our respect. You're not the little boy I used to share my newspapers with anymore. Now your one of the men the new is about. You've made us all proud, Jotham."

"Thank's, Stanley," Jotham said, unable to hide his embarrassment. "I'm not there yet. You fellas in the logging camp are still my heroes, but I'll try to live up to it."

The four of them spent over an hour reminiscing, mostly about Jotham's childhood, how he brought the Sunday paper each week, how they used to call him Ahmeek because that was what the Indians called him, how the loggers teased him about Mourning Dove and how he had tried to settle the standoff between the loggers and the dam builders on the Lac Vieux Desert.

"That was your coupe de tat," Stanley laughed. While you were running back and forth between old Red's boys in the camp and the Wisconsin National Guard troops, both lined up waiting to see who would fire the first shot, your friends in the Indian village solved the problem for you. They blew that dam up and left both sides scurrying for higher ground."

Jotham joined in the laughter. "Stanley, that was the high point of my young life and I didn't accomplish one thing."

"Tell that to that Brooks fella from the dam company," Stanley said. "He was sure you were stalling for the Indians and wanted to skin you alive. That Major from the Militia thought so too, but he wanted to give you a medal for it."

"He wanted to prevent a fight as much as I did. It didn't change anything, though. A few years later the dam was built and the logging companies started to move out."

With that, Stanley excused himself with the same old comment. "Well guys, a hard day' startin' early tomorrow." The Marichetti's agreed and after he was gone turned in for the night.

The next morning Jotham took the Marichetti car and again followed the long trail to Eagle River. He wanted to see Rebecca Morgan and he didn't want to see Rebecca Morgan. He knew it was going to be a difficult visit, but he had no idea how difficult. It was early May. She would still be in Eagle River. In a few weeks, when the school term ended she would return to her home in Wausau and he wouldn't be able to see her at all on this trip. He shuddered to think of what a meeting would be like If it had to wait until the next time he could come north. No telling when that might be. His time belonged to the Army now.

Rebecca opened the door when he knocked and joined him outside. She had received the letter he wrote telling her when he would come but, like the other letters he had written, it remained on her dressing table unanswered. After they took their seats in Eagle River's only restaurant that didn't serve alcohol, she wasted no time getting to the serious matter under discussion.

"Jotham," she began, "you know I love you. You know I want to marry you, but you have to join the Catholic Church. There's no other choice."

"There's always another choice, Rebecca. Every problem has more than one possible solution."

"Don't talk like a lawyer," she admonished. "For this problem, there's only one solution. Why is that so hard for you to understand? I've given up years of my life waiting for you."

"I know. But when two people disagree about something, the solution is to find a compromise, some middle ground they can both agree to."

"We were looking for a compromise last time we met, Jotham. You said then you would think about it. I took that to mean you would look seriously into joining the Catholic Church, and I said I would discuss it with my Priest."

Jotham bristled a little. "That sounds like I'm supposed to look into joining your Church while you only looked into how I can do that."

"That's not what I said. Why do you say that?"

"Because that's really what it meant."

"No," she protested.

"No? What did you expect your priest to say?

"I don't know. I thought maybe he would give me some answers. Some way to work it out."

"Religion is a philosophy," Jotham answered. "It's a person's belief about the most important thing in the universe. There are many religions and there are a lot religious philosophies that don't agree with any of them. My beliefs aren't less important or easier to change just because they're not in total agreement with yours or any of the organized churches. What bothers me most about the Catholic Church, for that matter most any other organized religion, is that they are not nearly as concerned that I disagree with much of what they believe as they are that I really tend to agree with some of the beliefs of all of them."

"What do you mean by that?"

"Well, for example, I believe that one churches baptism is as good as any other baptism. I believe in the Ten Commandments, at least the essence of them. There's only one God, so I believe anybody who believes in a God has to believe in the same one. The golden rule is the most important commandment. I believe that. I can go on and on with things I believe in that are in complete agreement with what the Catholic Church believes and, for that matter, the Protestant Churches, too. What I don't believe in is the church politic. The need they seem to have to develop doctrine, even if it's false doctrine, that will allow them to claim they, and they alone, know the will and ways of God. When the churches got involved in politics, and it started with Moses, they lost most of the reason for their existence and that's why I'm very reluctant to become a member of any of them."

"And unless you can," Rebecca said with a small tear forming on her left cheek, "I can't marry you."

"Rebecca, that is the one thing I can't believe."

"It's true, Jotham. It's worse than that. Father Murphy says if I were to marry you, without you becoming catholic, I could no longer be a catholic myself. So I have no choice. I can't marry you"

"But you could, Rebecca. You could join any other church or join no church at all and still worship God. The whole world of people who are not Catholic, the Protestants, the Indians, Hindus or anything else can't all be doomed for eternity."

"No I can't, Jotham. I've never been anything but catholic. I can understand that what you believe can be different. Really I can, but I've been told what the right religion is all my life. I believe it. The Blessed Virgin, the Saints, and the Holy Father in Rome are all very real to me. I can't change that."

"Then this time, you will have to be the one to think about it. There are an infinite number of ways to find God, dozens of other Christian Churches. Think about it. Then we can talk some more." And with that Jotham paid for their meal and walked her back to her rooming house. They said goodbye, as warmly as they could manage under the circumstances. She went into the house.

Jotham cranked the ford, mounted the seat and drove back to the logging camp.

Chapter 4

Johnny Bearheart crouched behind a cluster of small trees in Belleau Woods. Except for the camouflage that covered his helmet and shoulders It reminded him of his first hunt with his grandfather, Chief Eagle Feather, in the woodland north of Lac Vieux Desert. This time, however, he wasn't hunting white tailed deer in Northern Wisconsin. Instead he was watching a troop of German soldiers advancing past his position. Johnny was a member of Company B of the 7th Infantry Battalion. Around him equally concealed by the forest were other members of the Third Brigade of the American Expeditionary Forces under the command of General John "Blackjack" Pershing.

Johnny had enlisted as soon as the news of America's entrance in the war reached the remote woods of his home in Northern Wisconsin. He knew little of what the war was all about. He only knew he wanted to be a part of it. An Indian, Johnny believed, found honor on the field of battle. The Chippewa had been a peaceful tribe for a long time, but, Johnny knew, they had not always been. He remembered the stories the tribal elders had told of the battles of their fathers and their father's fathers when the Sioux had tried to push them out of the Minnesota Territory. He remembered stories about the Leech Lake Chippewa waging their final battle with the United States Army forces against Colonel Hubert Eva and the troops of the Minnesota National Guard. That battle had occurred twenty five years ago, only a few years before Johnny was born. A war was what Johnny needed, for in his mind it was his only hope of regaining honor and position in his tribe.

The grown up Johnny Bearheart had taken to the Enfield Rifle as quickly as he had, in his boyhood, mastered the Bow and Arrow. In training camp he had the highest qualification scores of any soldier in his company. What he was doing in Belleau Woods, however, was nothing like basic training or hunting with Old Eagle Feather. The German soldiers passing in front of him as they advanced toward the Marine Second Division had rifles, too. Three of them particularly caught his attention. The first one carried the mount for a 50 caliber Maxim machine gun. A second German soldier, with the massive barrel and magazine perched on his shoulder followed and right behind him was a third struggling with the weight of two ammo boxes. How easy it would have been to eliminate that threat to the marine division right now, but Johnny didn't question his orders to remain motionless and let the enemy pass. His camouflage blended in with the tree under which he was standing and made him almost invisible to the passing enemy troops.

Other members of the Battalion, stationed in less dense forest, were dug deep in the earth with ground cover concealing everything but an occasional glint of gun barrel. The officers had reasoned that the most effective way for the brigade to assist the larger contingent of General Bundy's Second Division, U.S.

Marines was to let the Germans pass and engage them from the rear after the battle between them and the marines started.

It wasn't a long wait. As soon as the first 87th division of the German Army reached the meadow where the Marines waited in trenches, the sound of battle could be heard throughout the countryside. At signal from the Lieutenant in charge, his platoon moved out onto the trail behind the enemy. They could hear the whoops and yells from other units moving out on either side of them. Stealth was no longer important. They wanted the Germans to know that while they faced General Bundy and the Second Marine Division in front of them they also had to contend with General Pershing's Third Brigade at their rear.

The tactic worked. Several Battalions of the German Army disengaged the Marines and turned back to meet the attack of the Third Brigade. The American's began to retreat, but where? They were behind enemy lines when the battle started. To retreat from the frontal attack only took them father behind the lines and probably closer to troops coming to reinforce the German 87th. Terribly outnumbered, the retreat quickly turned into a rout with every soldier seeking cover in the woods, each hopelessly separated from his unit. Many of Johnny's comrades were killed or wounded. Those remaining were caught between the main division of Germans and the battalions that had started to reform behind them to counter attack the Americans at their rear. Having planned the maneuver as a pincer, other units of the Third Brigade had advanced too far ahead of the 7th to be of any help.

Jotham decided to take a break from the letter he was writing to Rebecca. The rolling sea and the less than comfortable quarters on the troop ship were beginning to get to him and he decided to go on deck for some fresh air. One trip across the Atlantic was enough to make him glad he had joined the Army instead of the Navy. Any thoughts that he would have been a good sailor had vanished. Besides that, he was running out of things to say. Perhaps he should wait a day or two, then he might at least describe the sights of Paris for her. They had started to write to each other again when Jotham finished training at Fort McCoy. Her letters were bland and Jotham couldn't help but believe she wrote only because they were at war now and it would be less than patriotic to refuse to write to a soldier.

The air over the North Atlantic was cold, but refreshing. Jotham walked leisurely along the deck watching the waves, hoping to see one of the whales that occasionally surfaced in that part of the Atlantic. That did not happen, but he saw something that didn't look exactly right. There was a flash that looked like a glint of sunlight reflecting off a distant wave, but as the ship drew closer he realized that it didn't come from a wave at all. It came from what looked like a pipe sticking straight out of the water. Before he had any thoughts about what it was, he heard the sailor on deck watch yell. "Torpedo!" Next he heard the deafening howl of the ships alarm and saw sailors running across the deck to their battle stations. When he looked back at the sea, the U-boat was gone. Instead a wake moved across the water directly toward the port bow of the ship. Jotham instinctively dove to the deck. He felt the ship list to Starboard, then jolt as the torpedo exploded on the port side. When he looked up, sailors were rushing to lower the life boats while infantrymen scurried into formations hurriedly called together by their noncommissioned officers. A sailor reached down and helped him to his feet.

"This way, Captain," The sailor pulled him toward the side of the listing ship where a lifeboat was waiting.

"No," Jotham said pointing to the soldiers on deck. "Those are the fighting men. They need to go first."

"Not in this man's navy, Sir. We load officers first. Naval officers, they can command the life boat. Army officers, well they just get their chance at the best seats before too many of us regular sailors get in."

Jotham looked, saw the man's grin, then, hurried with him to the rope netting that had been dropped over the side for men to climb into the boats. In minutes the life boats began to move away from the sinking troop carrier.

Jotham was impressed at the design of the lifeboat. It was much higher at both ends, which deflected most of the water from the heavy sea they encountered. The gunwales on both sides were curved inward at the top for several inches so that capsizing the craft was almost impossible. Brawny sailors manned oversized oars along both sides while a petty officer held firm on the tiller, the only appendage by which one could determine which was front and which was the back of the craft. Jotham was overcome by a feeling of helplessness. He was the highest ranking officer on board, yet he could do nothing but curl up on the Bottom of the boat and try not to think of the cold that was beginning penetrate to his bones. It was going to be a long night. A thought struck him. He laughed at himself for being so ridiculous at a time like this, but when he gets back to his letter to Rebecca, at least he will have something to tell her.

Johnny heard a whistle. He looked up to find a Sergeant from Company C motioning for the private to join him. He crawled carefully, bullets still splitting the trees above their heads, to the Sergeant's position.

"Looks like we're cut off, Soldier," the sergeant said.

"What do we do now?" Johnny asked. "I got separated from my platoon when they called for retreat. The German's came back at us so fast nobody even had a chance to tell us where to rendezvous."

"Same thing happened in our company," the Sergeant replied. "It wouldn't have helped if they had. This woods is crawling with enemy soldiers now. Trying to all relocate to any specific point would just let the Germans know where we are and open our lines to an attack. What do you think we should do, Soldier?"

"Fight," Johnny was quick to answer. "That's what we came for, isn't it?"

"You got it Private. This might be our last battle, but even if it's just two of us , we can raise a little hell with the Germans that drove us out. Those Marines need all the help they can get. They've been here for more than two weeks, trench war, the worst kind and I heard on their first day, they took more casualties than any time in their history."

Suddenly they heard an outburst of gun fire. Other members of the 7th Infantry had come to the same conclusion. To stay and fight was the only recourse. Johnny and the Sergeant moved carefully toward the sound. The Sergeant stopped abruptly. Both he and Johnny instinctively dropped to the ground. In the dark woods the muzzle flash from the German machine gun lashed out like the breath of a mythical dragon. When the dragon paused for another breath, a second 50 caliber began to put on a similar display on the far side of the clearing. In daylight that one would have been hidden by the forest, with only the sound reaching Johnny and the Sergeant, but in the darkness it was a beacon marking a fortification waiting to be breached.

"Was I right to peg you as an Indian, Private?" The sergeant whispered.

"You sure were," Johnny answered with a proud smile.

"I've heard Indians are good a slipping around in the woods at night without being seen. "How about I take this one while you slither over to the other side and knock that one out?"

"Okay. Give me about fifteen minutes."

Johnny moved quietly toward the German line. In a matter of minutes he was hidden from both the sergeant and the German soldiers by the woods and by darkness. He crawled on his belly until he was safely behind the German front line. Until then, the bullets flying over his head came from both directions. The German Mausers on his left and the British Enfield the American's carried on his right. He met only one German soldier as he traversed the battlefield. That one was dealt with quickly and quietly with the hunting knife Johnny always carried on his belt. He found the second Maxim emplacement on a knoll, dug unto the ground and well protected by sandbags on all sides. There were three soldiers in the pit whose hearing had been deadened by the ear splitting pom-pom of the 50 caliber bursts. At each burst, Johnny crept closer. When he was close enough, he lobbed a grenade into the pit and quickly rolled down the knoll as fragments flew through the air over his head. When he lifted his body to check the damage, he saw the German gunners lying outside the pit where they had tried to escape the grenade. The gun had been blown off its pedestal, but was otherwise not damaged. He lifted it back on its mount and began to turn it toward the German line. As he did he saw the flash of the other Maxim, also turned one hundred and eighty degrees from its former position. "He did it. The Sergeant got his, too," Johnny elatedly said to himself.

Johnny and the Sergeant kept firing until the Maxims were out of ammunition. Having their own guns turned against them drove the German battalion back enough for the small force from the brigade to move forward where they could join forces with the sergeant and Private Bearheart. There were only eleven left standing. Five from Company C, two from Johnny's Platoon and four from other units of the 7th Infantry.

"Any officers here?" the sergeant asked. No one answered. "Okay then, I guess I'm in command. Form up around me. Those Germans will be back as soon as they can regroup so we better be ready."

Twelve American soldiers, Johnny and the eleven that had joined him and the sergeant, did as they were told.

"Okay," the sergeant started, "There are only thirteen of us, but I want you to spread out along this line. Put about thirty feet between you. That way the thirteen of us will cover a front of almost four hundred feet. When the shooting starts, move around, a little to your left then a little to your right. When you stop fire a burst from you rifle, then move again. That'll do two things. First, you'll always be someplace else when they start shooting at your muzzle flash and second, it'll look like a hell of a lot more of us fighting them. They don't have all their troops either. I know I took out a dozen or more with their machine gun and I'm sure the Indian did the same thing on the other side. Wait 'til I fire the first shot, then give them hell. Got it?"

A chorus of "ayes" answered the sergeant and eleven soldiers scattered to the left and right, each re-energized because they were again going on the offensive, yet each believing deep down inside that they would not live to see daylight.

As expected the Germans advanced on the small contingent of Americans, thirteen soldiers of the 7th Infantry against more than one-hundred of the enemy. The battle lasted only minutes. A few enemy soldiers lay dead or wounded and their officers, unwilling to battle with such a large contingent without the fire power provided by their Maxims, raised the white flag. Only days later, the battle of Belleau Woods ended. It was the last major offensive of the German Army in the war. The sergeant who was credited with the capture of more than one-hundred enemy soldiers and the Private soon to be Corporal Bearheart both received the Bronze Star for their contribution in the defeat of the German 87th Division at Belleau Woods.

The lifeboat moved slowly through the choppy waters off the coast of France. A sudden squall swept over the small craft and Jotham was drenched before he could scramble into the oilcloth coat a seaman handed him. He lifted himself into an up-right position and immediately felt the sharp wind that seemed to drive the cold deep into his body. His eyes were drawn to the sailors fighting the waves with steady rhythmic movement of the oars. Jotham wished he could join them. The physical activity would ward off the cold a lot better than the oilcloth coat. He crawled over to the Naval Officer who was holding a light over a rain soaked navigation chart.

"Where are we?" He asked.

"I can't say exactly," the officer replied. "We have all the navigation equipment you can use in a boat like this, that would be a compass and a sextant, but we can't get an accurate compass reading in this chop and until the storm blows over the sextant is worthless. My best guess is that Cherbourg is still a good hundred and fifty knot. That's assuming we've been making some headway but I don't have much faith in that assumption."

"Is that where were going, Cherbourg?"

"It's where we were headed before the torpedo hit, but now I'm thinking it might be better to head north. The English coast is a little closer. Trouble is that will take us out of the shipping lanes. We really need to hope a ship spots us. If we don't get a break in the weather I doubt we could make it to either location on our own."

The officer turned to his chart and Jotham took that as a signal to break off the conversation. He settled back onto the floor of the boat. He tried to think of some warm place, hoping it would make the cold more bearable. After what seemed to him like a long time, he dozed off only to be awakened an hour later by a dream. The dream took him back to memories of playing outside with his brother Dominic during some of those cold Wisconsin winters when they were children. They would play in the snow for hours until their fingers and toes were numb from the cold. When they went in by the hot wood fire in the Marichetti house, warm blood returned to those appendages with a resulting pain far worse than any cold they had felt. He lifted his head over the gunwale and peered out, but all he could see was a wall of darkness. There were perhaps twenty on board, but it was a very lonely feeling. He fell asleep again. This time, a sound sleep that would last until daylight.

Jotham and the other officers from the life boat were helped onto the deck of the battleship shortly after dawn. They were taken to the ship's doctor who treated them for hyperthermia. Each was given a warm blanket and a place to sleep. Two days later at Cherbourg they were met by Army trucks that took them to their new assignment. For Jotham that meant Paris and the headquarters of General Pershing. The war was now going well for the Allied Forces of England, France, Italy and the United States. After their losses at Belleau Woods the German army was heavily outnumbered and Jotham was sure the war was almost over, but when hostilities between Germany and Russia ended in March of 1918 with the treaty of Brest Litovsk, that changed. The Germans repositioned troops from the Russian front to launch a counter offensive. It was Germany's final effort and became known as the second battle of the Marne, but the commander of the allied forces, French Marshal Ferdinand Foch ordered a counter attack that pushed the Germans back.

Jotham took a brief break from the stack of papers on his desk to enjoy the autumn view of Paris outside his office window when he heard footsteps entering the room.

"Captain Marichetti!," It was the voice of Colonel Williams from General Pershing's staff.

"Yes Sir," Jotham answered.

"We've got a job for you Captain. Blackjack Pershing wants a staff of lawyers to accompany the officers that are supposed to be negotiating the end of this war."

"The what?"

"The armistice, the peace agreement. Seems old Von Hindenburg has contacted Supreme Allied Command and asked for a meeting."

"What do I know about negotiating a peace?" Jotham asked. "That's not the kind of thing we did in law school or in JAG training for that matter."

"You don't need to worry about the details. Just sit with the other JAG's and make sure all the I's are dotted and all the T's are crossed. It seems our President, Mr. Wilson, has already been talking to the commander. It started back in October. They've been at it for about two weeks now and have it pretty well worked out."

"But how? The President hasn't been in France, has he?"

"Radio," the colonel answered. "This is the twentieth century, Captain. Wilson talked by radio from some station in New Jersey."

"I've heard about President Wilson's fourteen points, but . . ."

'He says he's going to come over to meet with the top brass later to work out a complete treaty. For now it's just something official to stop all this damn shooting that's been going on. But like I said, you're just an observer. Better get to packing, Son. Your train leaves at 5 A.M. tomorrow." Colonel Williams opened the door to the Captains Quarters. They exchanged salutes and the colonel left. Jotham packed his briefcase for the trip, then sat down to finish his letter to Rebecca.

The next Morning, November 11, 1918, he was aboard the train headed for Compiegne. The train stopped on a siding where they were met by the German delegation. The Allies were represented by Marshall Foch, the French Supreme Commander, Admiral Rosslyn Wemyss, of the Brittish Navy and Foch's chief of staff, General Weygand. Jotham sat with a group of lower ranking officers and the press corps. Only minor changes were made in the document, based on Wilson's fourteen points. Jotham noted that they were primarily to correct errors of fact such as the requirement that Germany dismantle more submarines than remained in their fleet.

Johnny Bearheart and his buddies were enjoying a bottle of French wine in Leuze, a small town that was used by the allied headquarters, when they heard the bugle call. At first they thought it was a call to return to quarters. Troops began to pour out into the streets from hotels and bars throughout the town. Then a trumpeter sounded the 'stand fast' and a parade of soldiers and gun carriages proceeded down the street. Johnny heard the voices of the soldiers yelling for all to hear, "The War is over." Next a band played *God Save the King*. The crowd began to cheer on the final note but they were silenced by the band continuing with the *Marseillaise* and finally *The Star Spangled Banner*. Johnny, who never shed a tear in battle, choked back a large lump in his throat. The war was over. He was a hero. Now, he thought, he could go back to Lac Vieux Desert and be given his rightful place in the tribe.

When Jotham returned to his quarters on the afternoon of November 11, he found a letter from Rebecca. She had regularly answered Jotham's letters while he was in France with the AEF but while the letters were friendly they were anything but warm. He opened it quickly, anxious to see what she had written. His letter to her would not have been delivered yet. Rebecca's letter started as most of her letters did with noncommittal remarks about mundane things on the home front. She said nothing about their earlier plans and nothing about her religious beliefs that, as far as Jotham could tell, had scrapped those plans. Eventually, he read the final short paragraph. It hit him like a punch in the gut when he read about her upcoming marriage.

Chapter 5

It was almost two years after the signing of the armistice before Jotham saw the lush woodland he had called home for most of his life, a life so bucolic and serine. What had happened? It now seemed to be flitting away without direction or purpose. He was anxious to get on with it. When he had accepted his army commission he committed himself to an extra two years of service. Most of that time had been spent in Europe with no opportunity to return to Wisconsin even for a short visit. He was now stationed at Fort Sheridan, Illinois, but he had resigned his commission and was only awaiting the papers that released him from active military service. As he traveled north he thought about those early years. He wondered about Johnny Bearheart and Mourning Dove. Johnny was discharged from the Army two years earlier. Jotham wondered if he had been able to give up whiskey and return to the Lac Vieux Desert village or was he still frequenting any saloons in Hurley or Ashland that ignored the law against selling liquor to Indians. He had seen Johnny in

France when the First Division, AEF commander brought him to the Headquarters Company of to receive the Bronze Star. It was given for acts of bravery in the Battle of Belleau Woods in June of 1918. He returned in September of the same year to receive an Oak Leaf Cluster. That was the equivalent of a second Bronze Star for acts of bravery during the American offensive in the Argonne Forest.

Dominic quickly transferred Jotham's duffle from the baggage car to his Model T ford. He was anxious to start the drive home and to hear all the stories about France and his younger brother's army experience. It was about twenty-five miles to the camp and that would give them a little more than an hour to talk. He knew that Jotham had been promoted to Captain before he left the service but it surprised him to find the two silver bars on each shoulder, much more eye catching than the single gold bar he had worn when he was home the last time. He found it difficult to follow the narrow road because he kept glancing at those bars and the colorful ribbons that adorned his brother's chest.

"Gee, Jotham, you must have been some kind of hero to get those medals and all them colored cloth things on your uniform."

"Ribbon's," Jotham prompted. "The big medal is for hitting the target with an Enfield rifle. You taught me how to do that with your 30.30 Winchester. The little one was for something they called exemplary service. I'm not sure just what that means. The ribbons are the American Expeditionary Forces ribbon, the European Theater Ribbon and the Good Conduct Ribbon. The first two mean I was there and the last one means I didn't get into trouble when I was. The closest I came to being a hero was to send more paper and ink to the armies in Europe than anybody had ever seen. By my calculation, I probably used enough pulp wood to cover the cost of your earnings for at least two years."

"Then my little brother wasn't a hero?" Dominic feigned sadness.

"No, but I did the things at Division Headquarters that made it possible for the real heroes out there to do what they did."

"I don't getcha."

"I mean I did the paper work that made sure they had the guns and ammunition, as well as food for their battle rations. You know, lawyer work. That also included the papers that sent what was left of those that didn't live through it to their families in America or to a suitable resting place in France."

"I read about all the battle casualties," Dominic said. "Thousands of them. That must've been rough."

"There were a lot of them. A lot of good American boys were lost," Jotham agreed, "but nothing compared to what happened to the British, French and Italians. In one battle at a place called Ypres the British troops had almost a quarter of a million men killed or wounded. The newspapers over hear make it sound like we went over and saved all of Europe from the Germans, but they did most of the fighting before we even got involved. Those people were the real heroes."

"You know, Jotham, Papa was real troubled when you joined the army. I mean on one side he was proud of you as anything, specially when you came home in that officer's uniform, but on the other side, he kept talking about Gino dying at San Juan and how much he was afraid of havin' another boy die in some foreign place. No matter what I said, he kept thinkin' about Gino."

"So did I Dominic. That's why I had to join."

They drove on without talking for a few minutes while Dominic thought about what Jotham had said. "Then you didn't see any of the war, I mean you weren't in on any of the fighting."

"No, not really. I did see it, but not close up. The only danger I had to be concerned about was when a stray artillery shell exploded near the headquarters building or when a plane went over, dropping bombs that rarely hit their target. But that's enough talk about my war experiences. What about you? Talk about facing danger. I'm sorry I missed your wedding. I was in Chateau-Thierry when I got your letter."

"Well it was scary at the time, but it's turned out okay, Jotham."

"What happened? I thought you were way past marrying time long before I went to France."

"When we got the car, Papa asked me to take the cook into town to get a supply of fresh vegetables an' when the cook was at the vegetable market, I went over to the drug store to have a soda. Well, I got to talkin' to this young woman that was fixin' the soda for me. She was talkin' about the town picnic that was comin' up that weekend and ask if I was gonna be there. Well, I went and we got to talkin' some more an' I ask her if she'd like to go to and see a movie with me. You know the camp's close to a bigger city now. Woodruff's got a movie house. We saw a movie called *Hell's Hinges*, starring William S. Hart. He's one of the best actors there is. He played a mean cowboy that met a woman he liked and she really turned him around. I guess I saw a little bit of myself in Hart. After that I started goin' to town more often just to see her and finally we decided to get married."

"Good for you, Dominic. You old coot, I thought you'd be a bachelor for life. I can't wait to meet her."

When Enrico Marichetti saw Jotham this time, he made no attempt to conceal his pride. His son not only returned safely from the war, but returned as an army Captain. His father's reaction was not that his rank was more impressive than the last time he was home as a lieutenant. This time, his father had no need for concern that he could lose another son in a foreign war. Jotham opened his duffle and dug in until he found the two bottles of Italian wine he had been saving for the occasion.

"What you do now?" His father asked. "You stay in the army?"

"No, Papa," he replied. "I don't want to be an army lawyer. I want to come back here and start a regular civilian law practice."

"Here? Nobody needs a lawyer here. Lumberjacks, they get drunk, they fight, they go to jail, they stay in jail a few days then come back again." Marichetti laughed.

"I wasn't thinking of the logging camp, but somewhere up north. I thought I might try to start a law office in Hurley. There's a lot going on there that might call for a lawyer now and then."

"Oh, yeah. You might be safer in army, even in a war, than you be a lawyer in Hurley." At that all three of them broke into laughter, and before Jotham could answer, the door to the kitchen opened and an attractive woman with blond hair and blue eyes came into the room carrying a pot of coffee and a stack of china saucers.

"Lillian," Dominic called. "Come on over here. I wantcha to meet my brother, Jotham."

"Hi Jotham," she said, "be right back." Lillian disappeared into the kitchen, then quickly reappeared with cups to go with the saucers.

"Now I can give you a real greeting," Lillian said. Jotham stood up and was mildly shocked when Lillian threw her arms around him. "Nice to meet you, Jotham." She said releasing her grip, "I've been looking forward to it. Dominic talks about you all the time."

Jotham smiled, a bashful smile, then took a good look at his new sister-in-law. *Her hair was not just blond*, he thought, *it's the color of a full moon in October.* It hung down to her shoulders with just a bit of natural curl at the ends. She stood five feet four inches tall. She looked like she might be several years younger than Dominic. *Mid-thirties,* he guessed. Her face was very light to match the hair. *Finnish,* Jotham thought. She wore a simple, but attractive, house dress. The dress was loose fitting and even Jotham could tell he not only had a new sister-in-law, but there soon would be a new niece or nephew as well. He had a fleeting thought that this could have been him and Rebecca, but he dismissed it as fast as it came.

"Jotham," she said as she filled three cups and passed one to each of the men. "I hear you're a lawyer."

"I finished law school and passed the bar," Jotham answered, "But I'm not a lawyer yet, just a law clerk."

"For a judge in the Supreme Court, Dominic says," Lillian said. "That's pretty important. Excuse me. I'll be back in a little while." Again she exited to the kitchen.

Jotham waited for the door to close behind her. "Congratulations, Brother. You married a very attractive woman." Then he asked, "do I see the beginnings of a new family member there?"

Dominic grinned with a little embarrassment, then answered, "It didn't look like you were going to keep the Marichetti name in America going so I figured I'd have to."

"Well, she looks like a good addition to the family to me," Jotham said. "Even got you and papa drinking your coffee out of something other than a tin cup and eating from real plates."

"It's good," Enrico Marichetti said as he lifted his china cup. "Coffee taste better this way." He turned to Jotham, "What happened with you and the girl from Wausau, Jotham?" We thought you come back married too."

"Just didn't work out. When I joined the army, she decided it was going to be too long to wait. She married somebody else when I was in France." Jotham decided not to go into the real reasons he and Rebecca parted. His father and Dominic never could understand his strong feelings about the Catholic Church any more than Rebecca could.

"Is too bad. What you gonna do now?" His father asked.

"Hard to tell. It all depends on how the law practice goes," Jotham said, "but that's enough about me. How's the logging business going, Papa?"

"Is okay," Marichetti answered. "Not as good as during the war, but is okay."

"You have trouble moving the wood from Boulder Junction without the Wisconsin river nearby?"

"River's not so good for movin' pulpwood anyway," Dominic answered. "We're plannin' on gettin' a truck next year or the year after. Trucks are the way of the future. They can take a whole cord of wood in one load and with the federal road act we expect to have regular macadam roads up here by then. Would have had 'em now, Stanley says, but the government needed the money for the war so they had to back off on road buildin' for a few years."

Jotham was glad to see Lillian come back into the room. He was concerned the conversation might come back around to his relationship with Rebecca Morgan. That was the last thing he wanted to talk about. Lillian carried a cake, with one candle buried in thick chocolate frosting, in one hand and four small plates in the other. "This celebration needs more than coffee," she said. "Happy birthday, Jotham."

Jotham looked puzzled, then broke into a smile. "Well, I'll be darned. You won't believe this, but I've been alone so much on my birthday that I didn't even remember."

After cake and more conversation, Dominic helped his wife clear the dishes, then left her in the kitchen while he returned to the men. It was getting late and Enrico Marichetti excused himself and retired to his bedroom. Jotham thought his father looked tired and made a mental note to talk to Dominic about it before he left. Dominic was anxious to talk to his brother about all the new developments since the last time they were together.

"Jotham," he began. "You remember how we used to read the newspaper to papa when we were growing up? Let me show a somethin' I got durin' the war."

He led his brother to a corner of the living room and pointed to a contraption that, to Jotham, was a complete mystery. It consisted of a little peace of silvery colored metal and a big coil of wire around an oatmeal box.

"Well, that looks interesting, Dominic, but what is it?"

"It's a radio."

"Come on now." Jotham look down at the contraption on the table and squinted.

"I saw an ad for this in the back of a magazine Stanley had. It told how to make a radio with a bunch of wire, a small galena crystal and an oatmeal box. I sent for the parts and Stanley helped me put it together. On a good day we can get KDKA in Pittsburgh. Can you believe it. We could listen to the news about the war from some fella talkin' mor'n a thousand miles away. There's another station in Detroit, but that don't come in as good most of the time. Stanley says, 'this little machine's gonna to change the world'."

"I've seen radios," Jotham said. "We had them in the army and I know a lot of people out east have them in their homes already. But they're a lot bigger and they run on batteries."

"Yeah, I've heard about them, too, but there real expensive. Can't see as that makes a lot of sense when KDKA, Pittsburgh's about the only station you can get most the time. Stanley says some day there's going to be radio stations across the whole country. He said he heard the Johnson brothers, up in Michigan, just a little way up from Hurley, are already plannin' to build one."

Of course radio had been around for a long time, but it was new to Northern Wisconsin. Jotham had read about Frank Conrad broadcasting music for entertainment from a transmitter in his garage in 1916, but he avoided contributing a lot of information. It was his brother's chance to show that he was keeping up with the world events, too, and he wasn't about to spoil it for him.

The next morning when Dominic was helping him load his duffle into the car for the trip to Hurley, Jotham asked about his father's appearance the night before.

"He looks tired and kind of pale compared to when I was home a few years ago. Is he okay?"

"Yeah, I've noticed it too," Dominic answered, "but I never hear him complain or anything. You gotta figure, Jotham, he's more'n seventy years old now. Gotta expect him to slow down some. As for his color, he spends a lot more time in the house now, not so much out in the woods with the men."

Jotham took his seat beside Dominic and they headed for the train station. Some how, he had never been able to think of his father as old, but Dominic was probably right. When they arrived at the station, he thanked his brother for the ride, then boarded the train for his return to Fort Sheridan.

Upon release from the army at Fort Sheridan, Jotham took a bus back to Madison where he had stored all his worldly possessions with a friend before his departure for Europe. He packed them in two Steamer Trunks and sent them by Railroad Express to Hurley. He knew the Express office there would hold them until he found suitable quarters and was ready to retrieve them.

Two days later he was staying at the local hotel while he looked for a room to rent and a place to open an office, if possible in the same building. Hurley was a bustling town, a center somewhat larger than Eagle River that provided for the logging industry and mining in a rich vein of hematite that ran deep under ground a few short miles to the southwest. North Silver Street, hurt by passage of eighteenth amendment the previous January, looked strangely quiet. That amendment outlawed the sale of alcoholic beverages in the United States.

The signs that once advertised everything from Old Crow whiskey to Pabst Blue Ribbon beer on the front of buildings along the main street were gone, as were most of the marquee beckoning hard working miners and loggers to come in for the city's unique entertainment offerings. Many of the old saloons looked like they had been closed. Others displayed signs offering food. Jotham thought this was not the Hurley he had heard about from the loggers when he was a young boy.

When he chanced to enter one of the establishments for breakfast one morning, he wondered, with prohibition the law of the land, how did so many men get so drunk at such an early hour. He purchased a copy of the daily paper and sat down to his breakfast of bacon, eggs and coffee. He heard a voice behind him and turned to see who it was.

"Hi," the voice said. "Don't I know you from someplace? You look familiar."

"I don't think so, " Jotham said. "I just got into town yesterday."

"Then let me officially welcome you. I'm Sheriff Dan Vigonallo. In my job I'm always watching for new people in town, but I was serious, you do look familiar."

"I don't know where that could be. I've never been in Hurley before."

"You from the area?" Vigonallo asked.

"Originally from over by Land O Lakes, but I've been out of the area for a long time," Jotham said. "You might have run into my brother. The name's Marichetti."

"Marichetti! Your folks ran a logging camp, down by Lac Vieux Desert, I think it was." Vigonallo smiled. "Did you ever finish your schoolin' to be a lawyer?"

"What? How did you know about that?"

Vigonallo laughed. "I'm the sheriff. Sheriffs know everything." He laughed again. "I was just a kid when I was there, not much older than you were. I was in the State Militia, the Bayfield Rifles, as a Corporal at the time. We hauled over all the way from Ashland to try to quiet some ruckus at the lake. I remember seeing you running from one side to the other trying to keep them damn fools from killing each other."

"Really. You were one of the soldiers there?"

"Yep, but you wouldn't have noticed me. I was just ducking behind a wagon waiting for someone to tell me whether to shoot or run for cover. I was scared as hell. I tried to re-enlist when they started to fight in Europe, but they wouldn't take me. Said I was too old. I thought you looked a little Italian. Tell you the truth I'm relieved to hear your name is Marichetti, not Capone or Genovese. What brings you to our fair city?"

"To answer your earlier question, yes I did become a lawyer," Jotham said. "Then I worked for a judge in Madison for a few years, then four years in the Army. I just got out a few days ago. I'm here looking for a place to start a law office and a place to live while I'm doing it."

"Well, Mr. Marichetti, I can help you with that. There's a place down in the south end of town, the quiet end. It was a small working man's saloon. No connections with the wrong people, if you know what I mean. They had to pull out last January when the country went dry."

That solved Jotham's first two problems at the same time. The sheriff drove him to the home of the owner of the former saloon. They agreed on a monthly rent Jotham thought he could afford and sealed the deal. The saloon building had a small apartment in the back that provided perfect living quarters. The bar and all the accouterments of a saloon had already been removed and sold. Jotham retrieved his Steamer Trunks from Railroad Express and moved in. He bought a bed at the local hardware and a small desk for the office. That was enough for a start. He planned to watch the newspaper and buy other furnishings as people advertised them for sale. The next morning he returned to the hardware for a bucket of paint and a paint brush. Then the final touch. He painted a sign on the front window. It said; *JOTHAM MARICHETTI ESQUIRE, ATTORNEY AT LAW.*

Chapter 6

Jotham's law practice in Hurley was not an instant success. Most cases that went to trial in that city were competing interests in the thriving gambling, bootlegging and prostitution businesses and the defendants all had their own out of town lawyers. While there he became very much aware of the activities of the crime syndicate. Prostitution was an accepted fact and a primary activity of the Mob. Most of the operators in Hurley were minor figures in the underworld. The prostitution ring was controlled by the Memphis operation and it seemed almost everybody was, in one way or another, connected with the production and distribution of illicit alcohol. Moonshine. Obviously those were federal cases and no one was interested in a small town lawyer getting involved.

Hurley was a uniquely interesting place to have a law office. He heard about all the gang activity, both, rumors and fact, the former attracting the greater attention and newspaper coverage. As a lawyer, Jotham was provided with information, cases and legal activities, not available to the general public. As entertaining as that was, none of it added a single penny to his bank balance. If he was to continue to eat and pay the rent on his modest living and working accommodations, he had to spend most of his time on the mundane tasks in which lawyers are frequently engaged. His day was filled with legal documents, writing wills, developing or reading contracts or papers involving a bankruptcy. Frequently he represented one side or the other in a property dispute and rarely, a divorce. There were also cases involving shoplifting and petty theft but those almost always ended in a guilty plea without the aid of legal counsel.

Jotham put the contract he was drafting in his desk drawer and tried to decide which eating establishment he should choose for lunch. He looked up in time to see the door open and the lean and lanky form of Sheriff Dan Vigonallo.

"Jotham, Want to join me for lunch? I might have a client for you."

"Somebody you're holding in the jail?"

"Nope. Held him last night for a while, but we let him go home and sleep it off."

"What's he charged with, Dan?"

"Well, we haven't filed any charges," the Sheriff said, "He says it was and accident and he asked who he might get for a lawyer. Course you were the first person that came to mind."

"I don't get it," Jotham said. "Why haven't they charged him with anything?"

'The county attorney says he doesn't know what to charge him with," the sheriff said. "We can't find a case where anything like this has ever happened before. If it did, we have no idea what the charges would have been. I suppose it might have gone before a civil court judge. I don't know."

The Beaver and the Bear

"Dan, will you just quit beating around the bush and tell me what happened."

"Well, okay Jotham." "Seems Waino Mattila's car hit old farmer McCafferty's cow. Happened on the town road up by Kimball. McCafferty says, he want's Mattila to pay for it. Mattila says McCafferty should've kept his cow off the road."

"Thanks, Dan," Jotham said with a wry smile. "A big case like that ought to just about cover the cost of our lunch."

"Might do that, Jotham. But that's only if you can get either one of them to pay you."

Jotham opened the door and motioned for Vigonallo to accompany him. They walked together up the main street to the town's only café that wasn't also a saloon. They took a table in a corner of the room. Sheriff Vigonallo was a fan of Will Bill Hickock in that he always looked for a chair where he could sit with his back against the wall. He knew that Hickock had been shot the one night he ignored that practice. Soon the waitress came. She asked what they wanted to order. The menu was posted on a sign, scratched out with black paint over white boards, hanging on the wall behind the counter. The Sheriff ordered the beef stew, suggesting to Jotham that it was the best in town. Jotham did the same and each ordered a cup of coffee.

"I've been meaning to ask you, Dan," Jotham said. "When I was having breakfast that morning I met you, there were a lot of fellas coming into the restaurant obviously a little drunk. How do you suppose that can be?"

"You mean you don't know?"

"Well, I wanted to hear what you thought about it."

"Are you sure they were drunk?"

"I'm sure," Jotham answered.

"Then I'd say it was probably whiskey." The sheriff laughed. "Can't quite figure where they got it, though, with prohibition and everything."

"Whiskey!" Jotham's lips curled into a knowing smile. "You don't suppose it's the home made kind the boys down south call Moonshine?"

"Seems the boys up north have learned that word, too. They must be sellin' it someplace in there, but they won't let me into those back rooms, so I've got no way of knowing. You're a lawyer. You tell me what you think about it."

"Have you though about getting a warrant and taking a look?" Jotham was sparring with the sheriff. He knew what the sheriff's answer would be.

"Well, Jotham. Let me teach you some country boy lawyering. Assuming I was fool enough to want to get my head blown off, you have to get a judge to sign a warrant. Now as a city trained attorney, you know that, but what you don't know is how much trouble that's going to be. First, it's not going to be easy to find a judge here that wants to destroy the only thriving business the town ever had and second, it's a federal law. Seems to me the only sensible thing to do is to leave it up to the federal government to enforce it."

"I see your point, Dan, but if the federal government comes in, they'll take it to the federal courts, the defendants will all get big lawyers out of Chicago or someplace and then how does a little country lawyer like me make a living?"

"Jotham, I want you to be able to make a living, but I want to live to see it happen. I'd suggest you do some legal research and see whose fault it is when a car runs into a cow."

If it wouldn't be too much trouble, Sheriff, would you quit milking that joke?"

Jotham did settle the dispute between the farmer and the Ford, however, even if only out of boredom. One afternoon when he had caught up with all his paperwork, struck the final key on his new Remington type writer to complete a working agreement he had been trying to avoid for days he decided it might be an interesting diversion.. Jotham had used the typewriter for only a few weeks and was already getting adept at finding the right key at the right time. He had not intended to learn to type. He bought it looking to the future when his law practice might bring in enough money to hire a secretary. Jotham had researched the various kinds of machines available for transcribing the written word into print and decided on the Remington. He was familiar with Remington rifles and respected their product almost as much a Winchester. Christopher Sholes had invented the machine more than fifty years earlier, but refused to put it on the market until he had developed a model that allowed someone to type faster than a person could write. When Jotham read that, he was impressed. When he heard that Remington Arms Company was the manufacturer, he was sold.

He rented a horse from the local livery and asked for directions to the McCafferty farm and the Waino Mattila home, which he found out was also in Kimball, a ride of about six miles from Hurley. He also discovered they were next door neighbors with a long history of fighting over the property line that ran between their two farms. He found the McCafferty farm first. Jotham pretended to be lost and struck up a conversation with McCafferty who was working on an outbuilding near his barn. "Hi," Jotham said, "suppose you could tell me how to get to the Mattila place?"

"I could do that," McCafferty admitted briskly. "What would you be wanting to see him for?"

"Maybe I don't," Jotham said with a hesitant voice. "Tone of your words sounds like you don't think much of him."

"I don't. Trouble ever since he moved in next to my pace. Damn Finlander. Couple of weeks back, he got drunk and killed one of my cows."

"How'did that happen?" Jotham asked.

"Drunk, I said. Ran into it with his car, he did?"

"Think I might have heard about that in town. I'm pretty much a city boy myself," Jotham lied. "What happened to the cow? I suppose you just have to bury it, huh?"

"Guess you are from the city," McCafferty said. "We butchered it."

"Really? The meat still good after being hit like that?"

"Course the meat was good. She was a healthy three year old, damn good cow," McCafferty said. "Course she'd be a damn site better if she was alive," he added.

"Well, Mr. McCafferty, I'm a lawyer," Jotham admitted, "and somebody said you were thinking of suing Mattila for your loss."

"Yer just the man I want to see then. Save me the trouble of going into your office. When can we get this law suit started?"

"'I was thinking of representing you, but now I'm not so sure you'd want me to do that."

"Why not?' The farmer's voice was rising in anger.

"Look at this way, Mr McCafferty." Jotham began. "The way the law works, if you take the value of all that meat and subtract it from the value of the cow when she was alive, you probably won't get more than fifty or sixty dollars left. Out of that your going have to pay my fee which is going to be at least five dollars an hour for both the paper work and appearing in court with you. Even if the case goes well you'll end up with thirty dollars at the most. Then there's another problem."

"What's that," McCafferty asked, looking a little confused by all the figures.

"Well, Mattila's got a car to fix and that could cost a lot of money, that is, if it can be fixed at all. I hear he's thinking of suing you for the cost of repairs. Automobiles are expensive. As I see it, he stands to get a lot more money than you will."

"But the damned fool was drunk,"

"Probably," Jotham admitted, "but there's no way to prove it. Especially now, with prohibition, you won't find anybody that's willing to admit selling anything to him. If he had been drinking you won't even be able to find out where he got the stuff. Besides that, the automobile is pretty new for common folks like you and Mattila. There aren't any cases on the books yet to back up a claim that drunk makes a difference in a situation like this. You could try it, but I think you got a lot more to lose than you could win."

"Well, I'll be damned," McCafferty said. "I hadn't thought of all that. Then you don't think we should sue him?"

"No I don't," Jotham said, "but Ill tell you what I can do. I can go over and see Waino Mattila and try to talk him out of filing a suit against you."

Jotham then rode to the neighboring Mattila farm and said essentially the same thing, except this time the loss of the cow would probably exceed the cost of repairing the car. Mattila agreed not to sue if McCafferty didn't. Since it was very likely neither of them would talk to the other until the next fight broke out, Jotham was sure the case was settled out of court. It was his first pro bono work in Iron County. He didn't make a cent, in fact it cost him the rent of a horse and saddle for a day, but he could now tell the sheriff he took the cow versus car case and it was all settled. It was well worth it.

Jotham continued to work in his law office in Hurley and watch the months turn into years. He visited his father and his brother in Boulder Junction as often as he could, distance being more of a deterrent than time. On those visits he became the favorite uncle to Gino, Dominic's son, named for the brother they both lost in the Spanish American war. As the boy grew, Jotham wished he could be there enough to teach little Gino the things Old Eagle Feather had taught him, but he knew that would not be possible. From this time on he would always have an office to run.

While Jotham's legal work lacked excitement, the same could not be said of the town in which he practiced. During the first years of prohibition, It seemed like the whole Chicago mob had moved to Hurley. Out of the mainstream, Hurley was not frequently visited by federal marshals. When they did come, the town looked quiet and serene. As soon as they left, the bustling business of the speakeasies and gambling halls erupted like Vesuvius. Moonshine came overland from the deep woods of Wisconsin's north country and by sea across Lake Superior from Canada.

The small hand on the clock on Jotham's desk was almost pointing straight up when he heard the knock on the front door to his office. "Come in" he called out, assuming it was Dan Vigonallo. He and the sheriff still shared a table for lunch whenever Dan was in town for the day. The door opened Dominic entered the room.

"We've got to talk," Dominic said.

"What is it Dominic?" Jotham asked. "Is something wrong? Are Lillian and Little Gino alright?"

"They're fine. It's papa. He's real sick. Lillian said I needed to come to get you."

"I knew the last time I was over to see you he seemed to be losing ground," Jotham said. "I've been kind of expecting to hear from you anytime. Give me a few minutes to close the office and pack a bag."

Dominic followed Jotham into the living quarters as they continued to talk. Enrico Marichetti had been feeling sick for a long time, but insisted it was just advancing age and that he'd be okay. When he and Dominic had been in town loading supplies for the camp onto the truck, he had complained of being very weak and dizzy. Dominic insisted that they go to the doctor's office to be sure nothing more serious was wrong. At that time the doctor said the elder Marichetti had a "heart flutter." He said it was an indication of heart disease but not necessarily life threatening. Dominic said that two weeks earlier his father had fallen and, since that time, has been in bed or in his favorite easy chair listening to the radio most of the time. "He has little apatite and has lost a lot of weight," Dominic said. Lillian has tried preparing the dishes he's always liked, Italian style spaghetti, of course, and also a variety of fish he had been fond of, but it hadn't helped. They had sent for the doctor from Woodruff who came out to the camp. He told them his father's condition was worsening. The flutter had become more consistent and the doctor no longer saw a chance of recovery.

Jotham locked the safe in his office and placed a sign on the door that said "closed." He joined Dominic in the Marichetti car, a Buick that had replaced the Tin Lizzie, and returned with his brother to the logging camp. Jotham could not help but compare the car to the one he drove. He confided that his Hurley law office brought in only enough money for him to buy a Ford Roadster that cost two-hundred and fifty dollars. As they drove the sixty two miles to the logging camp, less than three hours with the new Buick, Jotham engaged Dominic in other subjects of conversation. He thought it might help free his brother's mind from his father's illness. He was worried, too, but knew nothing would change during their three hour drive to the camp. He told Dominic about Hurley and the problems the government had trying to control the inflow of alcohol.

"I don't think prohibition's going to last anyway," Dominic said. "Stanley said he read that a grand jury in Philadelphia said they wouldn't send any more liquor cases to the courts. The judge sent 'em home, but they're not dealin' with liquor cases any more."

"I'm not surprised," Jotham said. "The temperance union got congress to pass the prohibition Amendment and the states ratified it but the people weren't ready for it. Prohibition probably wouldn't have passed if the people had to vote on amendments to the constitution."

"You mean they don't?" Dominic asked.

"The constitution says amendments have to be ratified by three fourths of the states, but it doesn't say the people vote on them. It leaves ratification in the hands of the state legislatures. In most cases they're the only ones who get to vote on amendments."

"Well, it wouldn't have passed if the guys in the logging camps got to vote on it," Dominic quipped. "What's gonna happen in Wisconsin now that Bob LaFollette's dead?"

"Don't know, Dominic. I only hope the Progressive party died with him."

"Me too," Dominic said, "but they can monkey around with the rivers all they want to now. We move our logs with the truck."

They went on to talk about other recent news events, Benny Leonard's retirement from boxing and Babe Ruth being sent home from a ball game in St. Louis when Miller Huggins, the Yankees manager, suspended him for misconduct. Time passed quickly and Dominic soon pulled the Buick up to the Marichetti house.

When Jotham saw his father he knew Dominic's concern was justified. His skin was grey and his voice almost too weak to greet his youngest son. Jotham knew he could do little for his father other than provide comfort and companionship for whatever time was left. He, Dominic, Lillian and, most of all, little Gino would also need comfort. Only one thing appeared to be certain. This was a time for the family to all be together.

"You'll need help, Dominic," Jotham said. "You can't take care of Papa and run the camp, too. I'm going back and close my office. Then I'll come back and help you."

"You can't do that, Jotham. I mean you're just getting started. We'll make it okay."

"I haven't got enough work in the law office anyway," Jotham said. "This is a good reason to close it. After . . . " He stopped, unable to say what was on his mind. "I mean when I'm no longer needed here, I can start the office again someplace where there's more work for a lawyer. I might even be able to work in some office that's already started and has plenty of work to do."

"Are you sure, Jotham?"

"I'm sure. I've been thinking about moving anyway. I'll go back to Hurley long enough to say good bye to a few friends there, Sheriff Dan Vigonallo, and a couple of others. Then I'll close the office and come back."

Jotham was adamant. He planned to stay as long as he was necessary to help Dominic with the camp and comfort his father until comfort was no longer needed.

Chapter 7

Johnny Bearheart came out of the General Mercantile in Manitowish Waters carrying the two rolls of sausage and a loaf of bread he had just purchased. Stanley Rodzaczyk, seated on a park bench across the street called to him. It took a few minutes, but after a long look, Johnny recognized the logger he had worked with in the Lac Vieux Desert camp the Marichetti's had when he was still a young man. Stanley waited patiently for a sign of recognition, then waved for Jotham's Indian friend to join him. Johnny hadn't liked all the people in the logging camp and almost none in the nearby, town of Eagle River, but he had especially liked Stanley. It never seemed to matter to Stanley that he was an Indian. Johnny nodded assent, crossed the street and joined Stanley on the bench. .

"Been a long time, Johnny, Stanley said. "How're ya doing?"

"Okay, Stanley. Okay. I get a little work now and then, enough to keep me in meat and tobacco. How about yourself? Still with Marichetti?"

"Yep."

"I haven't seen the Marichettis for a long time," Johnny said. "What ever happened to the boy I skidded logs with, Enrico's son. My grandfather called him *Ahmeek*, the beaver, I don't even remember what his white man's name was."

"You mean Jotham. He never used that name in the logging camp back then. It was always Ahmeek. He finished school and moved to Hurley to be a lawyer. He's back in the camp now, though, over by Boulder Junction."

"Hey, that's good," Johnny said. "Maybe I'll get a chance to see him."

"He'd like that, Johnny. He always asks if I've seen you."

"You been with them a long time," Johnny said, "Ever think of doin' something else?"

"Na. What else would I do? I tried farming down by Steven's Point when I first came to this country. Didn't like that and I'm just not made for working indoors."

Johnny paused a long time. "But you're smart, Stanley. You could do almost anything."

"Wouldn't say I'm smart, Johnny. I'm self educated and that's not enough for most jobs in these modern times. Besides, I like working in the woods. What have you been up to since I last saw you?"

"For the last year or so I been working in the logging camps off and on," Johnny answered without revealing that the "off" part was usually spent in his shack sobering up. "Before that," he continued, "I was in the army."

"No kidding," Stanley said, feeling sorry he had sounded so surprised. "Good for you, Johnny. I tried to join myself but they said I was too old. Were you in Europe?"

"Sure." Johnny's pride showed in his subdued smile. "I was at Belleau Woods Argonne and Paris. Fought the German's at the first two. Paris was just for fun after the Germans were chased out. Got two medals for the first two."

"Two medals?"

"Yep, but it was really just one medal, a Bronze Star for the first one. The second one was an Oak Leaf Cluster," Johnny said. " The first was for sneakin' up on a machine gun nest that had our whole platoon pinned down and takin' it out, second was for throwin' a potato masher back to the German that threw it at us. Made a big boom. They said I'd saved a whole bunch of our guys lives and that made me a hero and they said cuz I already had one Bronze Star they couldn't give me another one. They gave me the cluster so people would know I'd earned it anyway."

"Johnny," Stanley said, "I'm proud of you."

"Thank's Stanley. I believe you are, but you know what?" Stanley didn't respond so Johnny went on. "If I'm a war hero, why can't I go into a saloon and buy a drink of Whiskey?"

"It's called prohibition, Johnny," Stanley said. "Nobody's allowed to go into a saloon and buy whiskey these days."

"I know that, but I couldn't do it after I came home from the army, almost two years before that law was passed. And that was just cause I'm an Indian."

"I know, Stanley consoled, "but now it's not just you. It's all of us."

"It is, and it isn't," Johnny said. "It's against the law, but all the men at the camp have a bottle hid away someplace. They're buyin' it, but they won't tell me where and nobody will sell whiskey to me. Could you get me a bottle, Stanley, I know they'll give it to you."

"I can't do that Johnny. They'd throw me in jail."

"Stanley, Please."

"I can't, Johnny," Stanley protested, "but I'll tell you what I'm gonna do. I've got some left in a small bottle one of the guys gave me last night. It's rot gut, but it's all I've got. I can give you one drink, No more." He produced the bottle from his coat pocket, a pint only about half full of a pale yellow alcoholic fluid that had never seen the inside of a charred oak barrel.

Stanley knew that Johnny would not want to settle for just one drink. He had played this same game with a logger named Frank that he roomed with in the Lac Vieux Camp a number of years before. Of course then it had been Old Crow, a whiskey with a healthier color but an equally vile taste. He knew he had to stick to his guns. If he did, Johnny would eventually settle for the single drink. He'd make sure it was a lot more than a sip, but if it was all he thought he could get, he'd settle for it and go on his way. It worked.

Jotham and his brother took turns sitting with his father. Enrico had always liked a good conversation. He liked a good argument even more, but they tried to avoid that for fear it would upset him and make his condition worse. When Enrico slept, which was most of the evening, Dominic and Jotham had a chance to visit with each other. During the day, they went to the logging area to check on the workers and their progress. Lillian stayed with their father on the days when Dominic had logs to haul to the loading docks. The docks, built up so trucks could park level with the gondola cars for ease in transferring pulpwood logs, were located on a spur line in Manitowish Waters. With Jotham to help load and unload the logs, that job required much less of Dominic's time and also gave him an extra chance to visit with the brother he hadn't seen much in recent years.

Dominic wanted to talk to him about all the things he heard on his radio. He tossed his crystal set out and bought a real radio the previous year. It was an odd looking contraption built into a big box with a circular "speaker" about eighteen inches in diameter that usually sat on top of the box. On the floor next to it was a series of batteries. Dominic said it ran on one "A battery" and three "B batteries." That meant nothing to Jotham, whose only experience with radio had been in the army. Most of what his brother was saying was totally foreign to him. The army radios were a crude device that could communicate from one headquarters to another, but they were cumbersome and required specially trained technicians to operate them. The more sophisticated set in the Marichetti home was a *Silvertone,* Sold by the Sears and Roebuck Company. It had five knobs on the front. There was one to turn it off, another to control the volume, Dominic said, "to make it louder or quieter," and three, above those, with complicated dials that, through some mysterious manipulation, picked the station the listener wanted to hear. As Dominic turned the three dials alternately for what seemed like an eternity to bring in WGN, Chicago, Jotham watched in awed amazement. Dominic said WGN had broadcast the political convention in 1922 but, he hadn't bought the radio yet. He had tried to listen on his crystal set but the reception wasn't good enough to follow. That's when he decided the Marichettis needed a real radio.

Dominic's other interest was the music. It was the flapper era and the music on radio was a drastic digression from his father's Gramophone. The technical quality wasn't any better, but his fathers collection of clay discs featured almost nothing beyond the Italian tenor Enrico Caruso and Fritz Kreisler, the Austrian violin virtuoso. Dominic's musical taste tended toward performers like Louis Armstrong who had just set his clarinet aside in favor of the trumpet. He also liked the novelty tunes like Barney Google. Jotham listened to the lyrics: *Barney Google, with his goo goo googly eyes. Barney Google had a wife ten times his size. She sued Barney*

The Beaver and the Bear

for divorce. Now he's living with his horse. Barney Google, with his goo goo googly eyes.

Dominic laughed. "That sounds like a lawyer's song. He's livin' with his horse while the lawyer gets the house for his wife."

"She didn't have a very good lawyer," Jotham said. "I would have gotten her both the house and the horse."

Dominic laughed again. "While we're talking about the law," he said, "what do your think of that big trial down in Tennessee a while back. You know the one about the guy teachin' that man sprang from monkeys."

"If he did," Jotham said, "I don't think he sprang far enough. Seems there are a lot of places where the monkeys are still way ahead."

Such friendly banter went on night after night while Jotham and Dominic waited, knowing what the eventual outcome of their father's illness would be, but avoiding any direct comments on that subject. Finally, one evening, Lillian interrupted their verbal antics to tell them she was worried about their father. When she went in to check on him, he was awake and tried to talk to her, but she couldn't understand what he said. They ran into his room. Enrico tried to say something, but he spoke very fast and Jotham found it unintelligible.

"He's trying to talk to us, Dominic, but I can't understand him. He's having a hard time forming the words. It sounds almost like a foreign language."

Dominic moved closer and listened. "It is a foreign language, Jotham. He's not having trouble with the words. He's talkin' Italian. I can't follow most of it either. His voice is real weak. Papa always insisted that Gino and me talk English. He'd talk Italian with some of guys in the camp that came from Italy, but we never learned how."

"I'll drive over to Hurley," Jotham said. "Almost everybody there speaks Italian. In fact, I think one of my closest friends there might understand enough to find out what Papa wants to tell us."

Dominic and his wife stayed in the room trying to comfort the elder Marichetti until he fell asleep. They took turns sleeping throughout the night. Shortly before dawn they heard Jotham's Model T Roadster along with another car that did not sound familiar. Dominic saw the word Sheriff painted on the side and the figure of a uniformed officer with a star on his chest. His first thought was that Jotham had been chased all the way into their driveway, but when Jotham and Dan Vigonallo walking side by side to the door, he knew that was not the case.

After introductions, the four of them went into their father's room. Enrico was just beginning to stir. He looked at Jotham, then became agitated and began to speak rapidly in Italian. Vigonallo moved closer and listened.

"What's he saying?" Jotham asked. "Can you make out the words?"

Vigonallo held up his hand gesturing Jotham to wait. Then he spoke very slowly and quietly in Italian. Marichetti settled back and lay quiet in his bed.

"He says he knows he doesn't have much time left," Vigonallo said. "He wants you to write a will, Jotham."

For the next half hour Marichetti gave instructions in Italian to Dan Vigonallo who passed them on to Jotham and Dominic. He wanted everything, all his personal possessions and the logging business divided equally between his two sons. When Jotham had Dan tell his father that he would be happy to have some of his father's personal things, but the logging camp should belong to Dominic, his father tried to object. Jotham persisted and his father's weak smile signaled his assent. It would be all right for Dominic to get the logging camp.

The rest of the week found Jotham and Dominic close to their father, taking turns to be sure one of them was there whenever he was awake. He continued to talk in his native language, but did not appear to be directing the comments to either of them. When the elder Marichetti slept, Jotham and Dominic went about other chores and Lillian went in to, occasionally, check on him. It was late in the evening when she came out to tell them he had stopped talking and didn't respond when she called his name, both sons left their other duties and spent the rest of the night sitting with him. Early the next morning, Enrico Marichetti's breathing stopped.

Chapter 8

Father Murphy drove from Eagle River to conduct a Low Mass funeral for Enrico Marichetti. It seemed that loggers from every camp in Northern Wisconsin attended. Rebecca and her new husband were there, but departed early with little more than the necessary words of sympathy. Jotham thought that she would have liked to say more but was not comfortable with her husband present. The bitterness he observed in their last meeting was no longer there. He kept his comments friendly, but subdued. At the cemetery Jotham saw Jimmy Little Wind, with his wife, Mourning Dove. They lingered until the loggers were all gone before they approached Jotham and Dominic.

"Ahmeek," Jimmy Little Wind said, "Mourning Dove wants to talk to you about her brother."

Mourning Dove was less direct. She began as others did with her expression of sympathy. "You came to my Grandfather's burial," She said. "We were all very sad, but we were happy that you came. Now I am here for your father. I did not know your father, but we are very sad for you and for your brother."

"Thank you Mourning Dove," Jotham answered. "I am very sad, too, but I am also happy that you and Jimmy are here." Jotham continued. "Your husband says you wish to talk to me about your brother. Is he not well? What has happened to him? I saw him when we were in the Army, in France. He was a hero and was awarded medals, but I have not seen him since we came back. I had to stay in the army a little longer."

"The army and the medals did not make him better," Mourning Dove said. "All he can think about is the whiskey. When we see him in town sometimes, he does not even talk to us. Then he goes away from our family and from our people where he grew up and moves to another people at the Bad River."

"I don't understand what happened to him," Jotham said. "Sure, he drank a little when I saw him in Europe. Almost all of the soldiers did. Is that where it started?"

"No," Mourning dove protested. "I do not blame the army. He started to drink before the army, when he found out . . . " She hesitated.

"Found out what?" Jotham pressed.

Mourning Dove began slowly and deliberately, choosing her words with great care. She told Jotham how Johnny thought he would be selected to be the new chief when Eagle Feather died, but could not be because he was half white and his mother had been ostracized by the tribe for failing to follow the mourning custom, how she had gone to work for the white senator and, as a result, Johnny was born. She told how Johnny had found the senator's home and had become bitter not to have been raised by a wealthy father. That was before the army, she said, and that was when he started to drink and to treat his family badly. "Now that he is a war hero," Mourning Dove said, "he thinks it is his right to have whiskey like a white man."

"Nobody has a right to drink whiskey now," Jotham said. "The United States government made it against the law."

"I know that," she said, "but Johnny gets it anyway. He works only long enough to get money to buy more whiskey. I know you cannot make him stop. Nobody can make him stop, but maybe you can help him, keep him from trouble."

"I don't know if I can, Mourning Dove, "but I'll try. I promise, I'll try."

She said no more, but thanked him with a shy smile. Then, Mourning Dove and Jimmy Little Wind left. Jotham wondered if he would ever see them again.

Johnny Bearheart had left the logging camps and accepted an invitation from a cousin to join his family on what had formerly been the Bad River Reservation near Ashland. Like the Lac Vieux Desert, the Bad River Indians had retained their communal structure with few opting to divide the reservation under the Allotment Act of 1887. Johnny was accepted as a war hero by the Bad River Band of the Chippewa and, for a time, avoided alcohol and tried to be a contributing member of the community. He was honored at Powwow and awarded an Eagle Feather for his acts of bravery in the army. To Johnny, the awarding of an Eagle Feather was more meaningful than the Bronze Star he received as a member of the military. Such an award was an age old custom of the Chippewa and Johnny was sure somewhere in the land of the dead his grandfather was proud of him. At last he was getting the recognition that the Lac Vieux Desert had not been willing to give.

The village was located near the place where the Bad River and the White River joined only a few miles from Lake Superior, known to the Chippewa of an earlier day as *Gitche Gumee*. It was a land of wild game and fish with two of Wisconsin's richest beds of wild rice on the Kakogon and Bad River Sloughs. It provided Johnny with the life he had always dreamed of, the life or a real Indian. He spent his days through the summer hunting and fishing. When the band went to the slough in August to gather rice, Johnny did more than his share. He liked living with the Bad River Band and they liked him.

When the winter winds began and ice formed on the rivers and in the slough, Johnny went out with his cousin to trap muskrat. Selling the hides of the small furry rodent was one of the few ways the Indians of the band could obtain cash needed to survive the cold winter months. Each day, Johnny and his cousin traveled a long pathway through the slough stopping and setting a trap wherever they found one of the dome shaped houses the animals constructed from mud and cattails or other under water vegetation. The traps had to be staked to prevent the animal escaping and to hold them under water. Johnny's cousin told him a muskrat that was not drowned in a short time after the trap snapped would chew its foot off to escape the steel jaws that held it. Trapping was new to Johnny, but he quickly learned how to open the springs and set the trap. Always adept with his knife he could skin an animal and mount the pelt on a board for drying faster than any of the others. Soon, however, the daily trip along the trap line to collect animals and reset the traps became an unpleasant chore. It was cold work without the thrill of catching the big walleye from Lake Superior or killing deer in the forest. When the lakes and pond froze over and the ice became too thick for trapping Johnny became bored with life in the Bad River village. He missed his forays into town.

When Johnny heard some of the younger men planning a trip into Ashland it lifted his spirits. Of course they would have no objection to him going along with them. As they undertook the ten mile walk from their village, he asked the others what they planned to do.

"I've never been to Ashland," he said. "It was too far from the camps at Eagle River. What is there to do there?"

One of the men, who had been given the name Round Tree by a Chippewa namer answered, "I know of a place where many white people come to dance and sing and counsel in the evenings. They also have strong drink there. It is called a speakeasy."

"They will sell strong drink to an Indian?" Johnny asked.

"Now they will," another man in the group called Little Fox answered. "In the summer there are many sailors from the big ships that carry iron ore to the east, but now, the ships cannot come in through the ice so they are as happy to take Indian man's money as white man's money."

When they reached Ashland, they walked down the main street looking at items in the store windows. Frequently one of them would break into a laugh and comment to the others about the useless things white people spend their money for, particularly women's hats. They found nothing in the store windows they were interested in buying except tobacco which they stocked up on. They then followed Round Tree to a house on the west end of town a few blocks south of Main Street.

"Stay back in the shadows," Round Tree said, "while I speak to the man at the door. They won't let anybody in unless they know them."

Round Tree and the doorman exchanged a few words with the doorman glancing over at the others from time to time and it seemed to Johnny that they were not all going to be allowed inside. Finally Round Tree raised his hand to signal them to follow and

The Beaver and the Bear

they were ushered in. Beyond a small foyer, they were led through a room that looked like the sitting room of any large home.

"What did you say?" Johnny asked Round Tree. "I thought he would not let us in."

"I told him you were a hero in the big war and the three of us wanted to come in so we could buy you a drink."

Johnny smiled. There was no bar, only a few small tables around a small dance floor. Music was provided by an electric phonograph which had been developed about three years earlier and played music from a ten inch shellac disc that revolved at seventy-eight revolutions per minute. Soon a young woman came to their table with a tray of drinks. Round Tree placed two one dollar bills on the tray and retrieved one glass for each of them along with the sixty cents change the woman handed him. A variety of mixed drinks might be available in similar establishments in New York or Chicago, but in this one you had one, a shot of whiskey in a small glass along with of glass of water for those who might want it. Johnny and his friends declined the water.

After their second drink, a patron at an adjoining table stopped the doorman as he returned from escorting a young man and woman to their table.

"You servin' Indians now?" the man asked. He was a large muscular man wearing bib overalls over a red and black checkered shirt. He had the rugged look of the outdoors and a lip that curled back like a snarling bobcat whenever he glanced toward Johnny and his friends. Either a logger or a farmer, Johnny thought.

"It's winter," the doorman replied. "We serve whoever can pay. Gotta make a living, you know."

"Okay if it's one or two, but four of them together is always trouble," the big man said.

"They'll be all right. They said they just wanted to buy a drink for the one in the middle," the doorman said, indicating Johnny.

"They said he was a war hero. You know, he doesn't even look that much like an Indian."

"Half breed," the man in the bib overalls said. "They're the worst kind."

Johnny bristled. Little Fox reached over and touched Johnny's arm. "Don't pay any attention to him, Johnny," he said in a soft voice. "There's always going to be some damned fool lookin' for trouble in a place like this. Don't let him get us kicked out of here. We got as much right to be here as he has."

"Bastard," Johnny said. "I'd like to show him my medals. No, I don't mean that. What I'd really like to show him is how I got 'em."

"We're about finished here anyway," Round Tree said.

Johnny Bearheart pulled two dollar bills out of his pocket. "I want another drink," he said. glaring at the man in overalls.

"Not tonight, Johnny," Round Tree said. "We don't want trouble. We'll come back another time," then, with a stern look at the man in the overalls, "when the people here are a little more friendly."

Johnny was reluctant to go, but he did not want to cause trouble for his three new friends. They stopped on the sidewalk outside the house to light a cigarette. While they were in the speakeasy, the sun had slid behind the grove of pine trees that bordered Ashland on the west. They had just started their long walk home when they heard footsteps in the darkness behind them.

"You boys don't belong here, you know," came the gruff voice from the bib overalls. "I think you'd be better off if you stayed in your own village."

"We're free people," Johnny answered. He looked up at the big farmer whose head stood at last a foot above his own. "We belong here just as much as you do."

"So you're a war hero," the big man said. "What was that, the French and Indian war?" The word Indian slipped out over snarling teeth. "Now you get out of here if you know what's good for you." He took a step toward Johnny with his finger extended ready to tap him on the chest.

Johnny treated the finger like a bayonet attack. His right hand came down on the farmer's right arm causing him to bend the elbow upward. Johnny's left hand grasped the farmer's wrist and with a flash his right hand slipped behind the big man's upper arm and gripped his own left wrist to make a shoulder wrenching arm lock. Before the man could recover, Johnny's right heel caught his leg behind the knee and dropped him to the sidewalk with Johnny's own knee on the man's chest. Johnny got up. The farmer sat on the sidewalk rubbing his right shoulder.

"I learned that in the army," Johnny said, then turned and walked toward the main street with his three awe struck friends.

Chapter 9

After his father's funeral, Jotham drove to Hurley where he met with his old friend Dan Vigonallo. Jotham hadn't seen Dan since his trip to the logging camp to translate his father's last instructions for his two remaining sons, and the division of what little property he owned. Dan had not been able to attend Enrico's funeral but Jotham took no offence. He knew Dan was busy with his work in Hurley and he hadn't really known Jotham's father. Dan hadn't known Jotham long enough for his presence to be expected. The Sheriff looked up from the stack of papers on his desk.

"Sorry about your dad, Jotham, I wanted to get over for the funeral, but with the federal agents dropping in on us so much of the time the locals wanted me to stay close."

"You keeping those guys in line for them, Dan?"

Dan gave a hearty laugh. "Nobody keeps those guys in line, Jotham. Did you hear about the big Silver Street Bust?"

"Sorry. I didn't. I haven't kept up much with the Hurley happenings in the last month or so. Tell me about it."

"Well," Dan said, "they came in about nine o'clock in the morning. I thought there were only a couple of them when they stopped in my office. They said they wanted local law enforcement on the scene so nobody could complain and local law was going to be me, no deputy or town constable. I think they just wanted to have someone to blame in case they screwed up. Turned out there were a lot more than the two of them. Most of the agents came out of Chicago. Federal Marshals, probably a few or the treasury agents from Ness's bunch, I don't know."

"Sounds like a big operation."

"It was big all right. About a dozen squad cars came screaming down Silver Street, sirens blaring. They hit every club in the north end of town at the same time."

"Who were they after?" Jotham asked.

"It wasn't who it was what" the sheriff answered. "They broke up crap tables and any gambling equipment. Hauled the slot machines out into the street, then went back and got what liquor they could find at nine in the morning which wasn't much. The marshals left the prostitutes alone but you can bet they weren't getting much sleep."

"That sounds like a lot of man power for raid on a brothel or gambling place," Jotham said.

"They didn't stop there. They went through every room from the basement to the third floor in each place. They confiscated maybe a dozen or so Tommy Guns and I don't know how many revolvers. Loaded the whole bunch into a truck and took it someplace over on the Michigan side and dumped them in the Montreal River."

"Seems the Hurley folks could have just gone out the next day and fished them out again."

"Benny Benito tried. He claimed they even took his deer rifle, but the federals must have scouted that river out good. Found some place where the water was really deep with a bottom of pure muck. Nobody that went looking found much of anything. But that's enough of my exciting life." Dan laughed. What are your plans? Going to open up your law office again? You might find some new business after that raid"

"I didn't hear you say anybody was arrested."

"Well, I guess I didn't, did I, Jotham? Truth of it is nobody was. They just took the guns and what little liquor they could find and left."

"Not much work for a lawyer after a raid where no one was arrested."

"There'll be more. With Ness turning up the heat in Chicago I'd say we will be seeing a lot of petty crooks moving north. You could find plenty to do here, Jotham."

"No, Dan. That cow versus car case you got me into demonstrated that running a law office like this in Hurley is a good way to starve. I thought I'd look for a job in an office with two or three other lawyers, someplace where there's a little more for a country lawyer to do than there is here."

"Sorry to hear that," Dan said. "I don't have a lot of friends in this town. I'm not fond of losing one."

"I won't be going far, Dan. I have no desire to move back to a big city. I'll look for something up north, maybe in Wausau or Eagle River."

"Hey, I got it, Jotham. I heard there's a law office in Ashland looking for a lawyer. Old fella that ran the place is getting' ready to retire. They want to replace him with somebody new, a younger person."

"Thanks, I'll look into it. That's only about thirty miles from here. We can still get together for breakfast once in a while."

Jotham's first weeks at the law office of Witherspoon and Stewart were quiet. He had no cases assigned to him and felt more like a law clerk than a lawyer. Marcus Witherspoon, senior member of the office, had been impressed by Jotham's work with a Supreme Court Justice as prominent as John Barns, then being selected to accompany the allied officers that worked out the Treaty of Versailles. He made it clear to his junior partner that he wanted Jotham to be on his team. Jotham chuckled when that thought struck him. He felt that he was more like the water boy than a member of any team. He had written a few wills, rental agreements, contracts for business ventures and loans, but through the long summer months had still not appeared in court. By the time the first snowfall of winter began, Jotham thought briefly he might have been wrong not to have taken Dan's advice and reopened his office in Hurley.

By Christmas, there were plenty of clients for Witherspoon and Stewart and even a few left over for Marichetti. They were not big cases, but they kept Jotham busy. The boats were in the harbor and that meant that the sailors were in town. The Ashland County docket was filled with saloon owners looking for compensation for damage to their establishments where, of course, they never sold a bit of liquor. Automobiles were becoming commonplace on Ashland streets and, when ice covered the roads, so were accidents.

The court was not in session for most of the Christmas week so the law office was shut down for a brief holiday. Jotham spent it with his brother Dominic and his family. He had visited with more regularity after moving back to the North Country. He enjoyed seeing his brother's children on each visit and being somewhat of a doting uncle to them. Little Gino was no longer so little. He was six years old and anxious to start school the following fall. His sister Maria was four and, and as near as Jotham could tell, had no big plans as yet for her future. He had stopped in the Ashland five and dime and bought a doll house for Maria. He had wanted to buy a doll that caught his eye. It was the biggest doll he had ever seen so he thought better of it. He decided it would not be appropriate for him to bring a big present like that. An uncle's gift should not be so ostentatious that it overshadows what the child's parents might choose. Of course Maria could be convinced it came from Santa, but that would not make Dominic and Lillian feel any better. For Gino he rejected a big red fire truck for the same reason and instead brought a set of tin soldiers. Within the first half hour of Christmas morning it became obvious that what he gave the children made little difference. It was Christmas and they were happy with everything.

For dinner Lillian prepared roast turkey, even more delicious because it was wild turkey that Dominic had bagged only the day before. After dinner they reminisced about the good old days in the logging camp, good times with their father and fascination with all the new and wonderful things the future held. It seemed every day there was news of some new invention to make life easier. Telephones had been around for a long time, but only in the cities. Now even Boulder Junction was getting telephone lines and soon the Marichetti's would be able to communicate with brother Jotham right from their living room.

When it appeared that every subject they might imagine had been exhausted, Jotham excused himself and packed his belongings, including his presents, one from Dominic and Lillian and one from each of the children into his car for the trip home. Dominic protested that it was still early in the afternoon, but Ashland was more then an hour the other side of Hurley and with winter roads it would take close to five hours of travel. Jotham wanted to get home early enough for a good night's sleep. He planned to go to the Bad River Reservation and try to find Johnny Bearheart the next day.

Jotham had not expected a warm welcome from the people of the Bad River Village and was surprised when they greeted him as they would an old friend. He introduced himself to one of the tribal elders as Jotham Marichetti and asked where he might find Johnny Bearheart.

"Marichetti, yes!" the older man acknowledged with a big smile. "You are the lawyer, right? You are Ahmeek."

Jotham returned the smile. It was obvious Johnny Bearheart remembered him and had made his name well known among the Bad River Band. "Yes, I am a lawyer." Jotham said, and I was given the name Ahmeek by Chief Eagle Feather of the Lac Vieux Desert. But I am not here as a lawyer today. I am only looking for an old friend."

"One who will be happy to see you, I'm sure," the old Chippewa said. "Come. I will show you where he stays."

Jotham followed along the narrow path with steep snow banks on either side. The building Johnny lived in was a low log cabin with clay chinked walls. It was no larger than the two man shack Frank and Stanley had lived in the Marichetti logging camp, but it was the home of Johnny Bearheart's uncle, aunt and three cousins. Smoke was drifting from the stove pipe that extended from a barrel stove through the roof of the cabin.

"Ahmeek," Johnny roared. He turned to his three cousins. "Look, it is Ahmeek, my friend from those happy days when we were children."

Jotham returned the compliment. "Johnny Bearheart, Grandson of my name giver, Eagle Feather, how happy I am to see you again. The last time I saw you, was in Paris, where they gave you the Bronze Star for bravery in battle." Jotham turned to Johnny's cousins who were listening intently to their conversation. ""Johnny was a hero in the battle of Belleau Woods," he said. "He knocked out a German machine gun nest all by himself and saved the lives of hundreds of American soldiers and marines, maybe more."

"Yes, we know," Johnny's cousin Round Tree answered. "Our band gave him the eagle feather at last summers powwow."

"Ahmeek was a captain, and a lawyer for Black Jack Perching," Johnny said.

It was as if the two of them would not run out of complements for each other. They talked about Paris and the good times, and their experiences in the army in general. Finally, Jotham changed the subject.

"Johnny," he said, "Mourning Dove asked me to stop and see you. She is very worried about you." The cousins looked down and drifted back into one corner of the room. Jotham saw that, while they had faded into the background, they quickly glanced back at them, then down at the floor again, apprehensive about the conversation they knew was to come. "Come outside and walk with me," he said quietly.

Johnny looked at his friend for a long time, then turned and opened the door. It was much colder outside but neither of them noticed. They walked a short distance away from the lodge. Jotham stopped and turned toward Johnny who immediately looked away.

"Mourning Dove is very worried about you," he said.

Johnny, still avoiding eye contact, said nothing. Jotham waited several minutes until Johnny looked up at him.

"Your mother is worried, too, Johnny," he continued. "It's about your drinking."

Johnny looked down again, then after a log pause he took as deep breath and said, "It is always my drinking, But I do not drink now, Ahmeek. "No one drinks now. I go with my people. I hunt and fish. I gather the *manomin*, the wild rice. I trap the muskrat. I do not drink very much. Tell my sister and my mother I am happy with my new family."

"Johnny, I heard about the big farmer you met in the saloon."

Johnny smiled. It was a proud smile. "That was a long time ago, Ahmeek. I have not gone back since."

"It was more like a few weeks ago," Jotham said with a comforting tone in his voice.

Johnny smiled, too, this time a smile of resignation and comradeship, as if to say: yes, it was just a short while before Christmas. Perhaps I fibbed a little, but that is nothing between friends. "You remember Paris, Ahmeek?" Johnny asked, still smiling. "We drank together, you and me. Remember the wine, the beer the ladies. Those were the good times."

"And the war, Johnny. Perhaps that is why we drank all that wine. But now the war is over. The ladies of France are no longer with us. Instead we have our families, our old friends. The drinking does not help us now. It is no good for you, Johnny. It is not good for me either and the government has made it illegal."

"What you say is true, Ahmeek. Tell my mother and my sister I am well and I will come back to see them sometime."

"I will tell them that, Johnny, but do go back to your people, the people at Lac Vieux Desert, at least for a visit. You should make it a long visit."

They parted and Jotham drove back to Ashland. He had kept his promise, but he knew it was unlikely Johnny would keep his.

Chapter 10

Of all the seasons Jotham liked spring best. As Jotham started to drive back from a brief visit with Dominic and his family, he remembered his early childhood when he went from his aunt's house in Wausau to his father's logging camp at Lac Vieux Desert for Easter vacation. It was on one of those early spring trips when he was only eight years old that he met Eagle Feather and formed a relationship with, not only the old chief, but his grandchildren, Johnny Bearheart and Mourning Dove, that would last until the present day. He saw that he had plenty of time so instead of turning onto the road that would have taken him back to Ashland he took the old logging road that led to Lac Vieux Desert. He drove past the logging camp, then, followed the trail to the old Lac Vieux Desert Village. As he crossed the bridge over the Wisconsin River, not much more than a creek so close to the lake where it started, he looked at the dam. It was new, but not much different than the one he remembered. He stopped the car and walked out to the lake. Jotham could not help but chuckle as he remembered his vain efforts to make peace between the loggers and the dam builders as the men in his father's camp faced off with the militia only to see the dam blown up by a Johnny Bearheart and a bunch of young Indians.

When he reached the tribal village, much smaller than he remembered it from his childhood, he stopped, hoping to find Mourning Dove or her mother to tell them about his visit with Johnny. Instead, he saw Jimmy Little Wind crossing the ceremonial grounds to him. Jimmy has seen him drive up and wanted to intercept him before he saw Mourning Dove.

"Good morning, my friend," Jimmy said. "I have been hoping you would come."

"Good morning to you, Jimmy. I came from my brother's place in Boulder Junction hoping to see Mourning Dove or her mother. I've been wanting to tell them about my visit with Johnny Bearheart."

"She will be happy to hear from you, but I will have to hear your words and take them to her. She cannot join us today."

"Is there some trouble?" Jotham asked. "Is she sick?"

Jimmy Little Wind smiled. It was a proud smile. "No, no, Ahmeek, she is well. After her grandfather's funeral, Mourning Dove joined the *Midewiwin*. Her training is almost finished. She is ready to pass the fourth degree and has completed her instruction in the matters of the spirit and knows now how to give many drinks and medicines made from the plants. She is not to have visitors until her training is finished. She came to your father's funeral because it was the right thing for a Mide to do. She did not know your father, but she said you were her friend when you were children. Because you were friends, and because her grandfather treated you as he did his own grand children, she had to respect you father as if he was her father. She said this is what a Mide does."

'Then tell her that I thank her for her respect for my father, and tell her that I have seen Johnny Bearheart."

"Tell me about Johnny. Tell me the words I can take to her," Jimmy Little Wind said.

"That he is well and living with his cousins in the Odanah village, near Ashland, tell her. Tell her that he is highly respected by the Odanah. They have honored him as a great warrior for what he did in the army."

"And he does not drink the alcohol anymore?" Jimmy asked hopefully.

"I wish I could tell you that," Jotham said. "I said that Mourning Dove and his mother wanted him to stop, but I cannot promise that it will happen, but you can tell them, Jimmy, that he promised to try."

"Thank you, Ahmeek. It is not all that we hoped for, but it is enough. You can do no more. I will tell Mourning Dove and her mother what you have said."

"And thank you, Jimmy Little Wind, and tell Mourning Dove that as an old friend of her grandfather I am proud of her work in the *Midewiwan*."

Jotham returned to his car and started the long drive home. His days at the law office had been busy, but uneventful between Christmas and Easter and, while he wanted some meaningful legal work, perhaps even trial work, he looked forward to some time off to enjoy the North Country he had been away from for so long. That was not to be.

Jotham pulled his new Nash Roadster next to the sheriff's office in Hurley. With the new car that boasted a sixty-nine horse power engines he was able to make the trip from Boulder Junction

The Beaver and the Bear

in time to catch his friend and have supper at one of the local restaurants. Jotham knocked on the door to the sheriff's office. There was no answer but Jotham heard sounds of voices inside. He knocked again. Just as he was about to turn away, assuming Dan was busy with and should not be bothered, he heard the loud "Come in." He opened the door quietly and slipped inside,

Dan Vigonallo was sitting at his desk with one hand holding the telephone receiver to his ear and the other twisting the knob of his new radio. He leaned over his desk to speak into the mouthpiece.

"Yeah, it could be, but if it was, you're going to play hell finding out who did it." Pause. "Okay, Milo, I'll keep a lookout for anyone who looks suspicious." He hung up the phone. "Hi Jotham," came Dan's quick greeting. "Be with you in a minute. I want to tune in the old cowboy here. Ah, there he is; at least that's the station."

Jotham heard the sound coming from the speaker which was much clearer than his memory of his brother's crystal set. "No Jokes tonight," the voice was saying, "a brave aviator from Minnesota is out over the ocean on his way to Paris."

That was a surprise to Jotham. He had read about Lindbergh's preparation for his attempted transatlantic flight, but the news of his departure from a small airfield in Massachusetts would not reach Northern Wisconsin's by Newspaper for at least another two days. Jotham sat with Dan and laughed at the jokes Will Rogers had said he wouldn't tell for the next half hour. They stared at the radio while their minds created a picture of the body and facial features of the cowboy they could not see. When the show was over, Dan clicked the radio off and turned to his friend.

"That was your county sheriff over in Ashland on the phone when you came in," Dan said. "Seems he has a big case to solve."

"In Ashland? I thought all the big cases were in Hurley."

"Not this time, my friend. This one might be that court trial you've been aching for."

"Maybe, if it's something big enough for more than one of us. If it's work for only one lawyer, Steward will probably handle it himself. He's the one with trial experience in that office. What kind of case is it? What was the crime?"

"Robbery. Took some kind of jewelry off an old lady."

"Where did it happen, Dan? Was it out on the street some place or was it a burglary?"

"Neither, Jotham. It was Mrs. Bancroft, old Doctor Bancroft's widow."

"What is this, Dan? Another joke on the new lawyer. You trying to set me up like you did with that farmer up in Kimball?"

"No, Jotham. This time I'm serious."

"Sure you're serious, Dan." Jotham said with a slight chuckle. "Mrs. Bancroft died last January. I remember reading it in the newspaper."

"Read about that myself," Dan said. "But the ground was frozen for a solid six feet in January. They did the burial rites just a few days ago. If they find the robbers, my guess is old Witherspoon will turn the case over to you. Any lawyer defending whoever it was isn't going to be too popular in Ashland for a while."

When Jotham returned to Ashland he found the town buzzing. Not only was a grave opened, but it had happened on Easter weekend. He was not surprised that a number of citizens jumped to the conclusion that it must have been someone from the Odanah village at Bad River. Jotham tried to tell them that would be very unlikely. He said the Chippewa had a great respect for the dead, but no one would listen.

The next day at the law office the topic of conversation was the same, but the mood was more somber. Instead of the excitement, the curiosity, the speculation of the street talk, the comments carried an air of apprehension. Witherspoon suggested that none of them should draw any conclusions. It would be a difficult case for both prosecution and defense. Newspapers as far away as Superior and Duluth were carrying the story. By nine o'clock, the office staff had settled into the routine work that made one day like any other.

Only a few days went by before an arrest in the grave robber case and on Thursday of that same week that news swept over the Ashland grape vine faster than any newspaper could report it. Almost as soon as it reached the offices of Witherspoon, Stewart and Marichetti, Annabel Hansen, their legal secretary saw two men standing in front of her desk asking to see a lawyer. Jotham heard one of them say that their sons had gotten into some trouble and they thought they needed some legal advice. For a moment nothing moved. It seemed that even the hands on the big pendulum clock stood still as Annabel ushered the men into the office of Marcus Witherspoon, Esquire. When she returned several minutes later, she stopped at Jotham's desk. He thought his heart had stopped beating, then he heard her say, "Mr. Witherspoon would like you to join them in his office."

"Jotham," Witherspoon began as soon as he entered the room, "this is Mr. Klastenberg and Mr. Wanstein. They would like you to represent their sons. It seems the county prosecutor's office has charged them with . . ." he stopped in mid sentence. "Well, I'll let them explain the details." He opened the door leading to a small room next to his office. "You can discuss the case in there where you can speak privately. I'll be out of the office with another client for a while."

Witherspoon quickly left. Too quickly, Jotham thought.

Jotham shook hands with the two men then, gestured toward the open door. "Come into the conference room where we won't be disturbed," he said. The room had a small table and several comfortable leather chairs. Jotham indicated a chair away from the table for each of the fathers and pulled a third one up to face them for himself.

"All right, gentlemen," he said. "Who would like to start?"

"It's our boys," Klastenberg began, "there in a lot of trouble. The sheriff says . . ."

"They're good boys," Wanstein cut in. "They get good marks in school and never give the teacher any trouble. My boy Lester, he always goes to church on Sunday. He could never do a thing like that. The sheriff's got it all wrong."

"Herman is right," Klastenberg affirmed. Neither of the boys could do a thing like that,"

Wanstein and Kastenberg both turned and looked at Jotham, obviously waiting for him to agree with them. They continued to stare for so long that Jotham had to stifle a laugh. Of course Jotham was sure he knew what the boys were accused of, but he could not be the one to say it.

"Perhaps you could tell me what it is the boys are accused of," Jotham said very calmly.

The two fathers looked at each other then, turned in unison to Jotham with mouths open but emitting no sound.

Finally Herman Wanstein spoke, a slight crack in his voice. "Y-y-you tell him, Otto."

"No, Herman. You're a better talker than me. You tell 'em."

"Well," Wanstein began with slow and deliberate words, "The county attorney, he says they dug up a grave." He dropped his head breaking eye contact with Jotham.

"But it couldn't have been them," Klastenberg quickly added.

"Would that have been Mrs. Bancroft's grave," Jotham asked?

Kastenberg and Wanstein both nodded.

"Did the county attorney tell you what the boys are charged with?"

Both fathers whispered a faint "yes."

"And what was the charge?"

They looked at the floor and remained mute.

"Were they charged with robbing a grave?"

Silence again. Then Wanstein heaved a sigh and replied, "yes, grave robbing, but they couldn't have. At least Lester couldn't have. I know that."

"And I know my Mort would never do such a thing," Klastenberg added. Can you get them out of the jail. I don't want my Mort to have to spend the night in jail."

Jotham told the two fathers he would see the county prosecutor and that he was sure he could have their sons home before nightfall. He then led the men out of the conference room and asked them to give Annabel their names and addresses so he could contact them as soon as he found out anything.

It was the first time Jotham had met the Ashland County Attorney, Bob Norton, but he found him congenial and ready to be of any help. He said he would release the boys to their father's recognizance. Judge Thompson agreed. Norton was confident Otto Klastenberg and Herman Wanstein would make sure they showed up in the unlikely event that charges would be filed against someone that young or if the judge wanted to see them. He provided Jotham with a list of the evidence and a narrative written by Sheriff Emile Johanson on the circumstances of their arrest. It read:

I received a call from Anderson's Drug Store at four-twenty Wednesday afternoon. He said there were two boys who stopped in on their way home from school bragging to some of their friends that they had taken some items from a grave in the cemetery just south of town. He said one of them was Otto Klastenberg's son Mortimer; the other one was Lester Wanstein. They were both gone by the time I got there so I went to the school Thursday morning and ask them to come down to the office with me. Deputy Williamson questioned them, one at a time, about their comments at the soda fountain. Both said they were just jokin' with the guys. They said they hadn't been anywhere near the cemetery. We scraped some of the dried mud from the soles of their boots. It was similar to the ground at the grave yard. They told different stories about where they had been on Easter Sunday. Wanstein said he had been at home with his parents all day, Klastenberg said they had been in church in the morning and after Sunday dinner, they met at the pool hall. We checked with the owner of the pool hall but he said he hadn't seen them at all that day. When we took them home, we asked the parents of each boy if we could look around. They agreed and we found a spade in Klastenberg's garden shed that had the same brown clay caked on it that was embedded in the boy's boots. We also took a dirt sample from Klastenberg's yard and another from his garden. They were both good, black dirt, not the clay loam that we found three feet down at the grave site where we also took dirt samples. We looked around both the Klastenberg house and the Wanstein home. Both families gave us permission to do that, but we found nothing that was on the list of missing items from the grave that the Bancrofts had provided. Deputy Williamson made some sketches of the foot prints at the Bancroft grave but with the number of people that were there on Sunday, it's hard to tell which might belong to the robbers and which to the people that came and found the grave open.

The narrative included a list of the things the family had said were buried with Mrs. Bancroft. The only item on the list that might be valuable was a string of pearls. While pearls had been prized throughout history they had been so popularized during the roaring twenties that only the most exceptional pearls would be worth a substantial amount of money. Jotham knew such an item would have been important to the family but of only moderate monetary value. The problem was moral outrage and political pressure. There was desecration of a grave on Easter Sunday and the good people of Ashland wanted someone to be punished. He knew neither the judge nor the county prosecutor would see the two boys as criminals. If Lester and Mortimer were guilty of disturbing the grave he was sure he could prevent criminal charges from being filed, but if they were not guilty he would still need evidence to satisfy the family and other residents of the city.

Jotham went back to the office to study the notes he had made while reading Emile Johanson's report then, made arrangements to talk to the two boys. He drove first to Klastenberg's home. He wanted to talk to each boy separately. He had prepared questions, much the same as those asked by the sheriff. When he went to see the Wanstein boy he asked the same questions of him. The sheriff's report had said they had each given different answers to some of the questions, particularly those relating to what they had done on Easter Sunday, the day the grave had been disturbed. This time, however, the answers they gave were remarkably similar. A little too similar, Jotham thought.

Back at his office that evening, Jotham went over his notes again and again. He still did not know if he was to provide a defense for two boys falsely accused of a crime or advise their fathers to convince the boys to admit the offence and, because of their age, throw themselves on the mercy of the court. Their stories sounded too much alike, obviously rehearsed. He had little doubt that the boys had gotten together after the sheriff had questioned them and ironed out the differences. When he asked about the mud on their shoes they said it was from the park on the east side of town, more than a mile from the cemetery. It would be easy to believe it was all fiction, yet, something bothered him. He didn't quite know what it was. Then it struck him. It was a little thing that could prove neither guilt nor innocence, but it might be enough for him to decide which approach he would use handling the case. He had asked Mortimer Klastenberg why he told the deputy he and Lester had met at the pool hall while the owner of that establishment said they hadn't been there at all on Sunday. Mort had said, "I don't know. I think it was Jimmy Ledbetter I met at the pool hall. The three of us hang out together sometimes and I guess I got it mixed up. I meant to say the soda fountain with Jimmy." When Jotham asked Lester about Mort lying to the sheriff, Lester said, "I dunno. I guess he was just scared. You know, with the sheriff and his deputy askin' all them questions like they thought we was the ones that robbed that old ladies's grave. Geez, I'd be so scared I wouldn't know what to say."

Jotham read it again. . . . *askin' all them questions like they thought we was the ones that robbed that old ladies grave.* That didn't sound rehearsed and it didn't sound like a pat answer. It sounded like a sixteen year old boy who had really been given a scare. Jotham picked up the phone and asked the operator to connect him with a number in Madison.

It was more than a week before Jotham received the letter he had been expecting from Madison. He anxiously read it, then carefully composed a letter to an old friend from his days as a law clerk for Judge John Barns of the state supreme court. Another week went by. Jotham began to think it was all a waste of time. No reason to believe a Supreme Court justice would respond favorably to his request, but when Annabel Hanson put the letter on his desk he almost screamed for joy. First he showed the contents of the letter to Mr. Witherspoon and Mr. Stewart.

With their approval, he placed all his papers on the Klastenberg/Wanstein affair neatly in a file and asked Annabel to arrange an appointment with Bob Norton and Judge Thompson.

Jotham handed the file to Judge Thompson and began to explain what it contained. The top page was an Amicus Curiae brief. The signature read: Robert P. McIntire, Legal Assistant to Chief Justice Marvin B. Rosenberry, WI Supreme Court.

Judge Thompson put the papers on his desk. "Well, Mr. Marichetti, you seem to have some pretty powerful friends."

"I knew McIntire when I was a clerk for Justice Barnes," Jotham said. "That was a long time ago."

"Well, you've done your homework." What is this other material from, the judge adjusted his spectacles and held the paper out in front of him. It was from a Professor Burns at the University of Wisconsin.

"Results of soil tests," Jotham said. "The sheriff had taken some soil samples from the grave site and matched them with scrapings from the boy's boots. The boys told me the mud on their boots came from the park. The samples looked alike, but they were much different. The soil in the cemetery is more acid with a PH value of only three while the soil at the park has a PH of nine. He said that was due to tannic acid that leached into the ground from the hemlock that grew in the cemetery. Also there were traces of copper in the cemetery soil and none in the samples taken from the boots. I knew if I was going to ask McIntire for the brief I needed to give him a reason to doubt that the boys had been at the grave site."

"A good job," the judge said. "Of course we would have let the boys go with a good talking to anyway, but this might help with the citizens of our fair city." He turned to Norton. "See that this gets a good write up in the newspaper."

Jotham accepted the gratitude of the relieved parents and the congratulations of his colleagues. He knew boys of that age would never have actually been tried in court, but he felt satisfied with the result. That satisfaction would soon end.

Chapter 11

Jotham sat at his desk thinking about the grave robber incident. Not much to celebrate about in this, demonstrating that the boys were not guilty in front of a judge that was going to release them anyway. There was neither money nor satisfaction when there was no trial, and the accused were so young, children in the minds of most people. Everyone who was a part of the legal system knew the outcome even before he met their fathers. No one could build a law practice on cases like that. Still, something about the whole affair didn't seem right, but he just couldn't put his finger on it. When Jotham looked up, he was mesmerized for a moment by the pendulum of the big clock on the far wall of the law office swinging back and forth. It was several seconds before he noticed the hands approaching twelve noon. He left the office and headed down to Main Street to Ruby's Café for lunch.

He sat at the counter and had just passed his order for the Blue Plate Special and a cup of coffee on to Ruby when he felt the presence of a very large man taking the seat next to him.

"You're the lawyer that represented those two boys they thought robbed the Bancroft grave, aren't you?" The big man asked. "Good trick, getting that soil sample. Of course you know Bob Norton would never have filed charges anyway, but I can't help but wonder what happened to the jewelry."

"Not too much to that," Jotham answered. "The only thing on the list that Norton gave me was as string of pearls. Not much value in those. I'll leave that up to Sheriff Johanson to work on, that is if he thinks it's worth the trouble."

"Only a string of pearls? That old lady was buried with a lot more than that."

"What?" Jotham turned toward the man.

"I'm sorry Mr. Marichetti. I should have introduced myself. I'm John Doakes. Folks in Ashland all call me Big John. I'm the local undertaker. I prepared her body for interment and I can tell you she was wearing a lot more than that. My helper and I wondered why they would have buried her with all that jewelry, but maybe money doesn't mean a whole lot to people who have so much of it."

"What do you mean by 'all that jewelry,' Mr. Doakes?"

"You can drop the mister, or better yet just call me John. Just so you don't call me Digger. I hate that. Now, regarding the jewelry, she had a diamond broach that would have cost more than my salary for a year and a couple of rings, ruby one of them looked like. Where did you get the idea she only had a pearl necklace Mr. Marichetti?"

"You can drop the mister, too, John. Just call me Jotham. I never liked it, but it's my name so I've decided to go along with it. The pearls were the only thing listed in the sheriff's report."

"I wonder where he got that," Big John mused. "He didn't contact me about it. It must have come from the family."

"I wonder, too. Who all was there at the funeral? Big family?" Jotham asked, "and, if you remember I'd like to know who was at the burial, too."

"Well, at the funeral, just about everybody of any importance in Ashland and quite a few out of town big wigs with business connections to the family. The ones you'd be interested in are the Bancroft Children. There were seven of them in all. I can get their names for you. Two of the men and all four women live a good distance from Ashland now. Two in Minneapolis, a couple in Chicago and I think one of the boys lives in Detroit and one other one but I don't know where she is. There's only one left in Ashland, that's Jack Bancroft. There were three of them that came back for the interment, Michael and Ruth, both from Minneapolis, Elaine, she's one of the two from Chicago, and of course Jack, right here in town."

"Any of them stay for Easter?" Jotham asked.

"Only Jack," Big John replied. "The other's high tailed it back to their business ventures or medical practices or husbands as soon as the grave was covered. Didn't look like a friendly family gathering. Each was just paying respect for their mother as was their duty. You know, rich folks, I never could understand them."

"What does Jack do?" Jotham asked. "I hadn't heard of him. He's not a doctor, is he?"

"Jack was the youngest. All the others were a lot older, sort of a child of Mrs. Bancroft's later years. He joined the Army during the big war, got in some kind of trouble and was kicked out. Went out west someplace where he tried working on a ranch. Work didn't agree with him so a few years ago, when Doctor Bancroft died, he came back and made a career out of spending his parents money. He couldn't even finish that job. When she died, the will left the house to Jack but most of the money was divided up equally between his siblings.

Well," Jotham said, "I guess that's for Norton and the sheriff to sort out."

He thanked the undertaker and returned to his office. There was something really strange about all this, but he didn't quite know what. He had just decided it was no longer his problem when the phone rang. It was his old friend Dan Vigonallo, the Iron County Sheriff.

"Jotham, I heard about your big case with the kids who didn't, or maybe did, rob the Bancroft grave."

"What do you mean, 'or maybe did,' Dan?"

"I just got a call from the owner of a Hurley pawn shop. I've been leaning on him a little because I've heard he sometimes takes in stolen property so He's trying to be careful now. He said one of your boys came in to pawn a string of pearls. He told the boy, I think his name was Mort something or other that he had just locked the safe and was going to lunch. He said he should come back at one o'clock. Then he picked up the phone and called me. I was there at one to meet the kid."

"What happened then, Dan? Are you holding him?"

"Nope. That will be up to Emile Johanson. I just went down and ask him what he was doing with the Bancroft necklace. At first he said it wasn't the Bancroft Necklace, then he said he found it. I suggested he found it in the old ladies grave. He stammered a while, then admitted it was hers, but said you had already proved to the judge that he wasn't the one who dug it up. I asked who dug it up, but he said he didn't know and then went back to the 'I found it' story. I took the necklace, put him on a bus back to Ashland then called Emile. He's coming over to get the necklace, but I thought you'd like to know about it so I called you."

"Thank's Dan, I appreciate that. I don't know if they can do anything about the kid, but it helps me sort some of this out."

"Any time, Jotham, If I can be of any more help just let me know."

"You can do one thing, Dan. I don't know if anything will come from it, but ask your pawn shop friend to be on the lookout for a diamond broach and a couple of rings. At least one has a big ruby in it."

Jotham went back to the office of Witherspoon, Stewart and Marichetti and asked Annabel if Mr. Witherspoon could spare him a few minutes. She went in to the senior partner's office and immediately returned to say that Marcus would see him. He told Witherspoon about his call from Dan and his chance meeting with the undertaker. The older man cautioned him about "playing detective," but agreed that, since it involved a client Jotham could do whatever he thought necessary. This time, because stolen property was involved, Bob Norton could decide to file charges without considering Mortimer Klastenberg's age. If that happened," Witherspoon said, "your client relationship with the accused will still be a factor."

Taking that as an approval, Jotham told Annabel he would be out of the office for the rest of the afternoon. What he would do if Norton arrested Mort was not what Jotham was concerned about. That was for tomorrow and only an if. Today, things were beginning to fall together. Bits of information that made no sense floated through his mind until a pattern began to emerge. There was still one piece missing, but Jotham hoped he could get Mortimer Klastenberg to provide that. He reached the house a short time before Mort arrived. Otto met him at the door and asked him to come in.

"Mr. Klastenberg," Jotham began. "I'm very sorry to have to tell you this, but Mortimer still might be in a little trouble concerning the Bancroft case."

"Trouble? How? You proved that Mort didn't rob that grave didn't you."

"No. I'm afraid not. The law doesn't work that way. All I did was to show Judge Thompson that the sheriff's evidence didn't prove he did. But now something else has come up. I'd like to talk to your son about it when he gets here. Where is he by the way?"

"He's in school, in school all day." Otto Klastenberg looked intently at Jotham, then asked. "No? Not in school. You are going to tell me he was not in school?"

"I'm afraid so. I got a call from the Iron County Sheriff. Mort was in Hurley."

"In Hurley? How could my son get to Hurley? Why would he go there?"

"He took the bus," Jotham answered. "If he had a spare quarter it was enough to cover his bus ticket. He went because Hurley has a pawn shop and he tried to pawn a pearl necklace. It was the same one that was taken from Widow Bancroft's grave."

Otto Klastenberg looked at the floor and spoke quietly, as though trying to convince himself. "My son, my Mortimer was not in school? He went instead to Hurley?" He raised his voice as his eyes again met Jotham's "Yes, you talk to him." He clinched his fist. "Then I talk to him."

Jotham got into his car planning to return to the office. His interview with Mortimer answered a lot of questions, but how much of it was true? He thought Otto's talk with his son might have yielded more information, but his tools were more persuasive, probably a razor strap. Jotham did not wait around for that.

Even if everything Mort told his father was true, could he use it to convince a judge? Probably, and that's all it would take to keep his former client out of trouble, but that wasn't what he was thinking about as he started the engine and pulled away from the Klastenberg house. The right outcome of all this should be justice, not just keeping somebody out of trouble. Justice, that's what he was really concerned about. No longer was Mort Klastenberg a school boy falsely accused based on flimsy evidence. With Jotham's feigned concern that the new evidence would make it difficult to keep him out of jail this time, Mort had admitted he had opened Mrs. Bancroft's grave and helped lift her coffin out. Otto Klastenberg, remembering bits and pieces of what he had learned to obtain citizenship, asked how he could be tried a second time. Jotham again reminded them that Mort had not been tried. All he did was convince them not to file charges. Even if there had been a trial, trying to sell stolen property would be a new charge and not covered by double jeopardy. "But I didn't steal it," Mortimer had said, "that guy gave it to me." The words rung in Jotham's ears. He made a U-turn in the middle of Main Street and set a new course to the Sheriff's Office.

The sheriff greeted Jotham with a smile that said, okay smart ass lawyer, what do you want this time? He said, "Well Marichetti, it seems that your boy did it, didn't he?"

"He did dig the grave up," Jotham admitted. "You had that part right."

"And he took the jewels, too, the pearl necklace, right?"

"Well," Jotham said, "that's what we have to talk about."

"You gonna say he didn't?"

"Whether he did or didn't isn't important, Emile, where did you get that list of things missing from the grave?"

"You may say it's not important," the sheriff responded, "but it makes big difference from this side of the law."

"Sheriff, that necklace was pin money, fifteen, twenty dollars at the most. Hardly what you could call grand theft, but add diamonds, ruby's and maybe other jewelry, that's the real theft."

"You mean the kid had more?"

"Not the Klastenberg boy," Jotham said, "but somebody. Those things weren't on the list you gave Bob Norton. Where did you get that list?"

"I got it from, wait a minute, you said diamonds, rubies, maybe some other stuff?"

"Right! A diamond broach, a ruby ring, another ring, but I don't know what kind of stone it had."

"It was an emerald, all big rocks too," the sheriff added, "but she could not have been buried with 'em. They were all stolen along with some other stuff in a burglary close to a year ago."

"What? Who gave you the list from the grave robbing, Sheriff? This is a lot bigger than Klastenberg and the pearls."

Emile Johanson broke into a big smile, a friendly smile this time, not the one that greeted Jotham when he entered the office. "I got that list from the same person that filed the report on the burglary and the other jewels he said had been stolen. It was Jack Bancroft."

"I'm not surprised," Jotham said. "Mort Klastenberg told me somebody else had him dig the coffin up, but he said he didn't know who he was. He said the man he talked to told him about the necklace and said he could have it for opening the grave. I don't know if I believe him or not, but I guess that doesn't make much difference now."

"Only when it comes time for him to testify in court and identify the real crook. But I think you and me have to work together on this one, Marichetti. We'll need a lot more evidence. I'll get some help and call you when we're ready to move on it."

Jotham returned to the law office. He didn't tell his partners about discovering another suspect in the grave robbing case. He was sure now it would become a case, but knowing who the defendant would be was information he preferred to keep to himself. Already Stewart was lecturing him on the job of a defense attorney. "We don't care if they're guilty or not," the other lawyer had said. "Our job is to defend them. Get them off when we can and if we can't, work to get them the lightest sentence possible." Jotham had no problem with that. He had served the Klastenberg family well. The county had not filed charges and with the new information already discovered, much less that which he was sure would come out of Sheriff Johanson's investigation, they would still not file any against Mort Klastenberg. He had no doubt, however, that they would threaten charges to make sure Mort would testify.

Chapter 12

Jotham found the mundane tasks he had been working on for the past three weeks almost unbearable. His concentration was not on making out wills and going over purchase agreements looking for errors that might cost his clients a penny or two. Instead, his mind conjured up scenes of Jack Bancroft sitting in a cell trying to convince his defense attorney that he was innocent. He had met Jack Bancroft when he became an associate of Witherspoon and Stewart. That was troubling because Bancroft was one of Marcus Witherspoon's best clients. He was always coming in with some scheme for making a lot of money in a hurry, seeking information on how to make a potentially shady deal look legitimate on paper. More often he would be trying to find some loophole in a contract that would allow him avoid paying for some service rendered.

Jotham went over his conversation with Emile Johanson again. He was sure he had not committed any breach of ethics. It was Emile who provided the information that made Bancroft a suspect. Marcus Witherspoon, however, might not see it that way.

Jotham still found one thing puzzling. It was obvious that Jack Bancroft had been the one to talk to Mort Klastenberg, and it was equally obvious that he had removed the jewels from the grave. Either that or Mort took them from the grave and gave them to him with the exception of the pearls. Mort kept those as payment for a job well done. It was also obvious that Bancroft filed the false insurance claim and a safe assumption that he intended to sell the jewels, but why the extra step of burying the jewels with the body and then finding a boy who, for the promise of a pearl necklace, would open the grave for him? His thoughts were interrupted by Annabel's voice. "Mr. Marichetti. It's for you. It's Sheriff Johanson."

Jotham waited a moment for Annabel to pull the cable from its place on the switchboard and plug it into the Jack that would send the call to his phone, then lifted the instrument from his desk, removed the receiver and placed it over his ear. "Hello Emile," he said, raising his voice to override the line noise. "Have you found anything?"

"Sure have," came the muffled sound from the Sheriff's Office some six blocks away, "Quite a bit. Why don't you come over here and I'll bring you up to date."

When he arrived at the sheriff's office, Jotham was surprised to find that Emile was not alone. The Sheriff began with introductions.

"Jotham, this is William Waller," he began. "He's an insurance fraud investigator from Wausau. His company insured the Bancroft jewelry."

"Just call me Bill," Waller said.

"The fella to his left," the sheriff continued, " is Martin Schuller. He's a detective with the Milwaukee Police Department. Of course you know our County Prosecutor, Bob Norton."

The four men exchanged greetings.

"I hear you're a defense attorney," Schuller said. "It isn't often we get help from defense lawyers."

"I am an attorney," Jotham replied, "and the law office I'm associated with works primarily on defense, but I look at myself as an officer of the court, and that means that my definition of a win is seeing that justice is served."

"You think like that," Schuller said, "you aren't going to make it as a defense attorney."

Jotham laughed. "You know, Detective Schuller, you just might be right."

"Does that mean you don't expect to represent the accused in this one?" Bob Norton asked.

"Not if this assemblage of distinguished citizens means what I think it does," Jotham answered. "That will more likely be Marcus Witherspoon's problem. That means, Bob, that I'm out of it altogether. I have no desire to risk a conflict of interest charge. Which brings me to the salient question, what am I here for?"

"Well Jotham," Emile began, "we thought you'd be interested in knowing what we turned up, since you made the discovery that put us on the right track." The Sheriff nodded toward the insurance investigator.

"You see, Mr. Marichetti, " Bill Waller added, "the information you got from the undertaker opened up the case for the insurance company. I alerted every pawn shop and known jewelry fence on my list, and believe me I've got a pretty good list. If they know we're well underway with an investigation they'd rather not handle the stuff. They can make enough from things that either were not worth insuring or that somebody was too naive and too cheap to bother insuring. You'd be surprised how much of that there is. Anyway, one of my contacts in Milwaukee came through when a man tried to fence off jewels that matched those reported stolen by Bancroft. Detective Schuller picked him up for us and Sheriff Johanson has a deputy on the way down there to bring him back to Ashland."

"And of course, that was Jack Bancroft," the sheriff added.

"Pretty much what I expected," Jotham said, "but there are still few things I don't understand. If Bancroft reported those things stolen last fall, why would he keep them for so long before he tried to sell them?"

"We wondered about that, too," Waller said. "Sheriff Johanson cleared that question up for us." He nodded toward the sheriff.

"I contacted the out of town members of the Bancroft family," Johanson began. "Jack never bothered to tell them about the burglary. It seems, as the faithful son that lived with her at home, he took care of that for his mother. He stashed the jewels somewhere planning to fence them on a trip he had planned right after the first of the year. His mother died before the trip and he was stuck with a funeral where his sisters would not only know which pieces of jewelry she would want to be buried with, but might ask a lot of other questions about the rest of the stuff that was missing. The way Bill and I have it figured, Jack saw that as an opportunity. Bury it all with his mother, tell the family it was her wish, and none of them would be concerned about it not being part of the estate. Dig it up and fence it later and he not only gets paid for the jewels twice, once from insurance and again from the fence, but he doesn't have to share it with his seven brothers and sisters either time."

Jotham smiled and shook his head. "Nice guy," he said. "I'm glad you fellas got it all figured out. I can see the headlines; Ashland County Sheriff gets his man."

"Just like the Mounties," the sheriff chuckled.

"And those headlines won't identify a local citizen that provided the first tip," Bob Norton interjected, right Emile."

"Right Bob," the sheriff responded, "but you know how the word gets around the law enforcement community on something like this."

"That's alright as long as the word doesn't move too fast," Jotham said. "I'm revising my plans for the future anyway."

During the trial that lasted for almost three months, Jotham's part in solving the crime did not once come up. A jury found Jack Bancroft guilty on all counts: robbing a grave, defrauding an insurance company, and attempting to sell stolen property. Witherspoon had tried to argue that, since the jewelry had not left the Bancroft family, it was not really stolen property and he could not be found guilty on that charge, but the jury would hear none of it. Bancroft was sentenced to seven years in state prison.

The rest of 1927 passed slowly for Jotham. Business was booming under the hands off policy of President Calvin Coolidge and that meant more money for the office of Witherspoon, Stewart and Marichetti, but nothing more interesting in work assignments. There had been a few minor law suits that gave Jotham a chance to appear in court arguing a case for his client, but most of his work was shuffling papers. He visited his brother on weekends and on each occasion stopped in Hurley to visit his old friend Dan Vigonallo. He confided with Dan that he did not find his work with the Witherspoon law office very satisfying. He had plenty of work and was making more money than he ever thought possible, but helping one wealthy person take money away from another wealthy person was not his dream when he had decided to become a lawyer. He had referred two criminal cases to Stewart, partly because they were petty crimes and partly because he was not convinced of the client's innocence. The possibility of winning freedom for a guilty person in a criminal case had haunted him since the Klastenberg affair. He had found his part in putting the guilty man behind bars more satisfying than anything he had done in the name of Witherspoon, Stewart and Marichetti. Of course Dan could see only one side of the issue. As a lawman, he had no time for defense lawyers, Jotham possibly being the one exception.

New Year's Eve had been uplifting compared to the months that had preceded it. Jotham referred to it in his journal as his "year of discontent." The past year had been filled with a series of mundane legal tasks. The only exception was helping the sheriff solve the grave robber case, and he had to make sure no one knew about his involvement in that. The village dance to celebrate the New Year helped. All the young women from Ashland in attendance brought two thoughts to his mind. First, not one of them compared to either the Rebecca Morgan or the Morning Dove he knew when they were that young and second, the realization that he was getting old. He was no longer the young man that might be attractive to a potential wife, a mother of the children he would like to have had. When his unspoken engagement with Rebecca Morgan had ended, Jotham was already thirty four years old. In the ten years that followed he had been too busy for any of the young women he met to become the *affaire de coeur* that might have led to marriage. He chuckled to himself at the thought that his short stay in Paris during the war should bring that term back after so many years. When he had heard the phrase in France, no one was thinking about a long term relationship.

The next morning Jotham looked in the mirror for a longer time than usual. He noticed the tufts of grey hair that now adorned his temples and the small wrinkles that had began to form around his eyes. *I must have toasted the new year one time too many last night*, he thought. *Sure, I'm forty-three years old, but I'm healthy and strange as it might seem, I still have a good job. Emile must have been wrong about the grape vine in the law community I got through the whole year without hearing a word on the street about my part in the Bancroft case.* He got dressed, feeling a lot better about himself than he had the night before. The clock said nine-thirty and he looked forward to a relaxing day off, a breakfast at Ruby's, then maybe a good book and some music from the radio. "I need to get caught up on what the young people are listening to," he joked out loud to himself. Then he heard knock on the door. When he opened it, he saw a tall man with thin gray hair and a matching short cropped beard. He was probably twenty years or more Jotham's senior. He wore a sheepskin jacket with dark flannel trousers, but he held an expensive homburg in his hand.

"Good morning Mr. Marichetti," he said. "I am sorry to come calling so early on your day off, but I didn't want to contact you in your office. I'm Joe Flynn, District attorney over in Washburn, Bayfield County, and I'd like to talk to you about a case you were involved in."

"Well, come in and sit down." Jotham gestured to an easy chair as he spoke. "What case would that be."

"We've heard a lot about you over in Bayfield County. The people I work with were pretty impressed in the way you handled that grave robbing affair,"

"That wasn't much of a legal case," Jotham protested." Bob Norton would never have filed charges against those kids anyway."

"I wasn't talking about those two boys, Flynn said, "though getting that brief from the law clerk of the chief justice of the Supreme Court was a clever move. I am more interested in your work on our side, the prosecutor's side of the law, the Jack Bancroft case."

"I didn't handle the Bancroft case," Jotham cut in a little too quickly, "That was Marcus Witherspoon's case."

"Of course, of course. I know Marcus served as Bancroft's defense lawyer, but that is the case I want to talk about."

Chapter 13

Jotham discovered just how far the information exchange among the law enforcement people Sheriff Johanson had alluded to extended. Not only was Joe Flynn completely aware of Jotham's part in the ultimate conviction of Jack Bancroft, he was also aware of the doubts Jotham had expressed to Dan Vigonallo about continuing to work as a defense lawyer. Jotham had briefly thought Joe Flynn had come to question his ethics in the Bancroft case. Instead he presented Jotham a proposition. Flynn had served Bayfield County as District Attorney for more than thirty years. He was preparing for retirement and, along with the county board, had decided Jotham would make a suitable replacement. He suggested that Jotham come to work in Washburn as Assistant Prosecutor during his last two years in office. At the end of that time, he assured Jotham, he would easily win election as his successor. When Jotham hesitated, concerned that he was not sufficiently experienced for such a position, Flynn told him he had no need to worry about that. Even without experience as a prosecutor, his work as a clerk in the state supreme court and his selection to be one of the officers at the signing of the Armistice would make him a shoe in. They shook hands and Jotham promised to be in Washburn and ready to start in two weeks.

By the end of January, Jotham had settled into his new job in the Washburn County Court House. Most of the work was as mundane as it had been in the Witherspoon and Stewart law office, but he found processing arrest warrants more interesting than processing wills even when the offence was minor. He also liked the fact that he met far more citizens in the prosecutor's office than he ever would have in his former position. He felt like he was serving the public, not just a few people wealthy enough to hire a lawyer. Most of his visitors came with a request for information. It was only on rare occasions that the request resulted in a formal complaint. His explanation of existing law more frequently resulted in the aggrieved party deciding they would have to tolerate whatever minor inconvenience their neighbor, the school board, town official, or some other person had subjected them to. On a rare occasion a complaint resulted in an investigation into something or someone and, as assistant prosecutor, Jotham was asked "to look into it." When there was a criminal matter involved, he had the sheriff or one of his deputies accompany him. In situations where there was no danger, nor the possibility of an arrest, he went alone. Jotham's first year passed with no major incident.

For the few years that Jotham had worked in Ashland, his compensation had been far more than his quiet lifestyle required and he had considered investing in the market. He had listened to the political rhetoric during the 1928 presidential campaign and heard Herbert Hoover's promise of a chicken in every pot and two cars in every garage. "Ladies and gentlemen," Hoover had said in a radio address, "the business of America is business." Jotham had invested a modest sum, most of it in automobile manufacturing companies. He thought the "two cars in every garage" was an unbelievable expectation, but he was sure the future of travel in America was the automobile so he bought some stock in the Studebaker Company and a few shares of Ford. Other than that, he stayed out of the market. Because his father, Enrico Marichetti, had never trusted banks, he also kept most his money in a safe he had installed in his Washburn home. That bias inherited from his father plus being one of the lucky ones with a good paying county job saved him from the market crash in 1929.

When the paper mills stopped buying pulp Dominic and his family moved to Washburn to live with his brother. Jotham also helped Jimmy Little Wind and Mourning Dove move from the tribal village at Lac Vieux Desert to Red Cliff, just north of Bayfield. Jotham had not expected the depression to have an effect on the Lac Vieux Desert Indian band, but after the passage of the Allotment Act in 1887, which took away much of the ceded land that provided for Chippewa sustenance, they had become more and more dependent on the white man's economy. Their grandfathers had sold hides to the white merchants so they might buy back some of the lands lost to white settlers in the allotment program, but their success was limited.

Too many members of the Lac Vieux Desert had moved to L'Anse, far into the Upper Peninsula of Michigan because the size of their tribal holdings was no longer enough to provide for the band that had accepted the treaties which, thirty years earlier, created a vast reservation. Loggers had clear cut so much of the forests that hunting became unproductive. Deer, which the Chippewa had always counted on for their winter's meat, had become elusive. Work in the logging camps that for a time compensated for the wild game loss, disappeared with the forests. At least the Red Cliff people had an abundant supply of fish to keep them alive until jobs became available again.

"Jotham," Dominic said, "it sure is nice of you to help us out like this. I never thought the logging business would ever fail us. I remember the big depression back in '93. It was tough and we didn't have a lot of money but we got through. I don't know how I can ever thank you."

"You already have, Dominic. This is chance, my chance to repay you for all of those times I stayed with you at the logging camp before I found a job."

"That was different. You were part of the logging camp when we were growing up, just like I was. I was living with my wife in Dad's old house and besides, you were family."

"That family thing goes two ways, Dominic. I couldn't let little Gino and Maria go without a place to live and good healthy meals. I couldn't figure out how to take care of them without letting you and Lillian come along, too."

"Sure, Jotham. I don't know how you do it. You keep your spirits up and keep makin' jokes like that. I mean, I know you work for the county, but the counties don't have a lot of money now days either."

"Well, Dominic," Jotham said, "I didn't go wild in the market like a lot of city people did and, so far, the county hasn't run out. Even if they do, I think I can hold out until things pick up. I was too young to remember much of the depression of '93, but I don't recall going hungry."

"Yeah, but there are four of us. We've got to be a big drain on your budget."

"Don't worry, Dominic. Sure, I bought a few shares of stock but I haven't lost anything yet. I will just hang on to them and maybe they'll be worth something again some day. But when so many people were buying into a bunch of fly by night companies, I invested in real estate. I bought some prime land in the Bayfield, actually a couple of old farms. Now some of the people that lost their town jobs are working the farms for me and giving me most of the food I need in exchange. They keep trying to give me cash, but I'm not taking it until things get better for them. I also own part of the general store and hotel in Washburn and I get a few dollars a month from them. We'll do just fine" Jotham didn't tell Dominic that his job as Assistant County Prosecutor was only going to last for two years. Then, he will have to stand for election to replace Joe Flynn as District Attorney. He thought Dominic might not be as convinced as Flynn was that Jotham would win.

The next morning Jotham sat in his office reading the morning newspaper. It was the first of May. The snow had all melted and the ice had disappeared from Chequamegon bay on Lake Superior, but there was little sign of a thaw in the economic situation. President Hoover opened the new Empire State Building in New York City. The article said it was more than 1,240 feet tall and had 102 stories. Jotham's first thought was to wonder where with a world wide depression people could find the money to build such a structure. His second thought was to wonder why they would want to. A headline for another article said the *Star Spangled Banner* had been named the national anthem but he had heard that on the radio several days before so he skipped that one.

A brief item on page two said that Ralph Capone, a brother of Al Capone had purchased a summer home in Mercer. Jotham made a mental note to call his friend Sheriff Dan Vigonallo in Hurley about that. Mercer is a short distance south of Hurley and he might suggest that it is Dan's responsibility to roll out the welcome mat for new residents in Iron County. He was about to reach for the phone and start the long process of placing a long distance call when the door to his office opened.

The short, slightly balding man entered and asked for a few minutes of his time. Jotham noticed how the man was dressed. He wore a black suit, double breasted and a white shirt with a neatly starched collar. He held the hat that he took off as he entered in his hand. It was also black. His collar was unbuttoned, and his oxford style, black shoes were polished to a high gloss. This was not the usual visitor to the District Attorney's office. Jotham directed him to a seat and asked what he needed.

"My needs are humble, Mr. Marichetti. I am the pastor of the Lutheran Church in Iron River, over on the west side of the county. Now, I don't want to be the one to complain, but some of my parishioners are concerned."

"Concerned about what, Pastor?"

"Oh, I'm sorry. I should have told you my name. It's Eric, Pastor Eric Norquist. It's about a fellow who moved into the area from Chicago. He has been here for some time, but no one in my congregation seems to know just how long. Anyway he owns some kind of establishment down in the southern part of the county." The Pastor wrung his hands nervously as he spoke. "He receives a lot of material by rail. Boxes and boxes, the depot agent says. Nobody knows what it's all about, but with the element that has drifted into the North Country since they have been cracking down on criminals in Chicago, well, the people in my congregation are just, you know, worried."

'Is there any evidence of anything illegal?" Jotham asked. "Anything you want to file a complaint about?"

"Well, no. But we were wondering if you could look into it, check and see if there is any danger. It is a small community, Mr.

Marichetti. People are not accustomed to, well you know, odd behavior."

Jotham smiled. "I suppose I could look into it, but it does not sound like any cause for alarm. Can you tell me where this person is located?"

"I don't know exactly. They said it's on Wilderness Lake, but I have no idea where that is. That whole area is really out in the woods, very primitive."

"I can look it up," Jotham said. "Can you give me the man's name?"

"Oh, yes," Pastor Norquist replied. "I can do that, assuming of course that it is his real name. It's Chauncey Bottum. He calls himself Chauncey the Bear Hunter."

In the southwest corner of Bayfield County a man with one eye on the nail he has just driven into a fresh piece of lumber and the other on the bass breaking water in the lake less than one hundred yards to his right stepped down from a wooden ladder. Dressed in his Oshkosh Bib Overalls, donated for the project by no less than the Owner of Oshkosh, Chauncey Bottum looked unimpressive, a Northern Wisconsin woodsman with no connection to the outside world of big business and industry or organized crime. He was large, but in no way obese. His shoulders were broad and his facial features generally attractive. He also failed to convey the impression of anyone who might pose a problem for the good people of Reverend Norquist's congregation. Any assumption, however, about his isolation from big industry would be misplaced.

The Bear Hunter migrated to the north woods years before the Capones or Dillingers found it. In 1926, Chauncey left his engineering job in Chicago to find a new life. He said he wanted to find the "wildest place in the country" and The Wildernest Lodge, in Southeastern Bayfield County was to become that place for him.

He told the Indian who had been helping with the building project to take the rest of the day off. He was going fishing. As Chauncey started for the shed where he kept his fishing equipment, the best the Pflueger Corporation could provide for him, he heard a car approaching. He turned to meet whoever it might be that had the audacity to intrude on his solitude.

"You're a hard man to find," Jotham said as he stepped out of his car. "If I hadn't seen the sign for Wildernest Lodge I don't know where I might have ended up. My name is Jotham Marichetti, assistant to the District Attorney for Bayfield County, and I assume you are Chauncey the Bear Hunter."

"I am," Chauncey affirmed. "Chauncey Bottum is my real name, but if you came out here on business from the county attorney's office I'm sure you already know that. I haven't done anything to attract the interests of the DA's office, have I?"

Jotham laughed. "I doubt it, but some of the good folks in Iron River ask me to find out. I told them I'd drive out and have a look."

"Yeah. Some of those same good folks asked me what all the stuff I was getting at the rail yard was for. I told them I had to build a few guest rooms onto my cabin. I knew that might scare them. I know a lot of people loosely connected with the gangs in Chicago have moved into the North Country since the G-men have been putting the heat on, but I never was tied in with that crowd."

Jotham looked at the lodge building. It was obvious that it started as a relatively modest cabin and, over a few years, had several rooms added on. It had become a large structure capable of housing two or three dozen guests and even more when the rooms

Chauncey was working on are completed. The walls were all made of logs, but the windows, doors, awnings and other features were manufactured elsewhere and shipped in. This was not the typical cabin in the woods.

"Then do you mind telling me what all that stuff was for?" Jotham asked.

"Course not. It was building material for guest rooms, like I said. Now before you ask me who the guests are, why don't we go inside? I brew some coffee and tell you my life story, at least the more interesting parts."

"I didn't mean to cause you any trouble, Mr. Bottum," Jotham protested, "I'm just doing what some people asked me to do."

"No trouble," Chauncey said. "I like company. Tell you the truth, I like having someone around to talk to. The guests I'm expecting won't be coming until the weather warms up. I have my wife, of course, but she spends most of the day schooling our daughter. We live too far from the cities to have her enrolled in a regular school." He turned toward the cabin. "Come on in."

They went into the main section of the lodge. It was rustic, but at the same time, modern. The building was equipped with a thirty-three volt DC electrical system that Chauncey said was powered by a bank of batteries and a gasoline generator in the shed. Jotham followed Chauncey into the kitchen and watched as he added a few sticks of wood to the range and filled an aluminum coffee pot with water from a small pump mounted on the counter top. He added some ground coffee and placed it on the back lid of the stove.

"Take a while to get it boiling," Chauncey said. "Have a seat Mr. Marichetti." He directed Jotham to the great room and followed him in. "Now what is it you'd like to ask me about?" He gestured toward a very comfortable looking leather covered easy chair and took an identical one for himself.

The Beaver and the Bear

"Your life story, like you said," Jotham answered as he settled into the chair, "but first tell me about the bear hunter thing. That is what they call you isn't it? Chauncey the Bear Hunter? Tell me, how many bear have you bagged?"

"None. Get deer now and then, but no bear. I just thought it went with the surroundings. Has a nice ring to it, don't you think? If people call me Chauncey the Bear Hunter they won't make jokes about Chauncey Bottum. You know Chauncey bare Bottum, stuff like that. Got any idea what I had to go through when I was a kid in school. Besides, it's good for business. You ever have a nickname when you were a kid?"

"Matter of fact I did," Jotham answered. "An old Indian that lived near my father's logging camp gave it to me. It was Ahmeek."

"Ahmeek. What kind of a name is that?"

"It's the Chippewa word for beaver. I liked it when I was in grade school, but it doesn't go well in the courtroom so I dropped it in favor of my real name, Jotham."

"Jotham. Yeah," Chauncey mused, "King Jotham and the cedars of Lebanon. It's from the Bible. But I like Ahmeek better. Tell you what. When you're at my place, you call me Bear Hunter, I'll call you Ahmeek."

"Sounds good to me," Jotham agreed. "Ahmeek was okay when I was a kid. Sort of miss it now. The only people who still call me Ahmeek are my older brother and a couple of my friends from the old Chippewa village."

Chauncey got up and returned to the kitchen. "So, what's your next question, Ahmeek?" He called back just before he came back with two cups and matching saucers. Jotham thought they looked like the might be bone china, not the kind of dishes one would expect in a wilderness cabin. Without waiting for an answer, Chauncey returned to the kitchen, removed the aluminum pot from the stove, sprinkled some cold water from the pump into it, then, after a brief pause poured the contents into the china pot that matched the cups. He returned and poured coffee, first for Jotham, then for himself. "What's your next question?" He repeated.

"Well, this doesn't look much like a typical country cabin. This furniture looks more like it belongs in a palace. That is Dresden China, isn't it?"

"It is and this isn't your typical country cabin. It's the Wildernest Lodge. I am expecting some very important guests."

"I'm guessing that's what the folks in town were worried about, but we can talk about them later. What I'm curious about now is where do you get the money for all this?"

"What money?" Chauncey asked. "I don't have any money. I gave up on money when I moved out of Chicago back in '26, don't need it."

"Then, if you'll pardon my asking, how do you get all this."

"Ahmeek, listen carefully to this. Chauncey the Bear Hunter lives by a very simple philosophy. If you see something you like, ask for it. You'd be surprised how many people will just give it to you. All that you see here at Wildernest Lodge, the building materials, the furnishings, were all given to me by the top man in whatever corporation or company manufactured it."

"That's a little hard to believe, Bear Hunter."

"You're tellin' me. I found it more than a little hard to believe myself when I started, but it works. I just go right to the top and ask for what I want. Most of the time, I get a response a few days later telling me when it will arrive."

"Are you telling me that all this, the land and everything . . ."

"Not the land. I had to buy that. It was owned by Bayfield County when I came here. Bayfield County doesn't have the same generous nature the corporations have. Up until I moved up here, I worked for a living like anybody else. I was born into a family with some money so I didn't learn to value it like most people. I attended some of the best private schools in the Chicago area, went to college and studied engineering. After I graduated I went to work. I worked in an office in Chicago, sat at a desk all day long and hated it so I decided to move to a place where I could work outside, still as an engineer, of course. I got a job in South America, got tired of it. It was as boring as my Chicago job. When I got home I heard about an article submitted to the *Post*. It was about the people who owned all the big companies in the country. The writer said they were all a bunch of skinflints with no heart. I knew the editor of the *Saturday Evening Post*. Nice guy, his name was George Horace Lorimer. We were talking about the article and he suggested I test that idea. So I did. I wrote letters to the top man in fifty of the big companies, told them what this guy wrote and ask if they wanted to prove he was wrong by sending me a case of whatever it was they manufactured. Believe it or not forty-eight of the fifty sent me a box of their stuff."

"What did you offer them in return?" Jotham asked.

"Not a damned thing. That might be what made it work. One guy sent a letter along with his product saying how refreshing it was to have someone be so straightforward and just ask with out some angle that made the request look like a big con." The Bear Hunter walked across the room to his big mahogany desk and returned with a stack of papers. "Here," he said, "read a few of these. That one on top is from Tony Mansfield. His company just sent me the roofing material for the addition I'm building."

Jotham looked at the letters and read a few sentences of several of them. He stood up, smiling as he moved toward the door. "You've convinced me, Mr. Bear Hunter. I don't see anything that my office would be interested in. I'm not sure my story will satisfy the people that asked me to come out here, but that will wait for another day."

"Don't wait 'til somebody complains to come back," Chauncey said. "You know all about me now. I'd like to know more about you, your life up here in the north woods and how you grew up in such a place and ended up as an Assistant DA. You're welcome at Wildernest Lodge any time. I don't have too many people to talk to out here, particularly men and especially in the winter time."

"I'd like to come back sometime. Thanks. Now I have to get back to Washburn while I still have a job as Assistant to the DA."

Chauncey opened the door for Jotham. "I'm serious Ahmeek. When you get down into this part of the county, drop in."

Chapter 14

The following summer was a busy one for Jotham. People displaced from the cities, where manufacturing remained at a standstill for more than two years, sought any kind of work a rural setting could provide. Residents who had a dairy herd or worked the fields found farm hands willing to work for nothing but their meals and a place to sleep. In the summer, daily meals and even a tent in the yard was sufficient payment for their labor. This self-imposed slavery was of little concern to the county prosecutor's office, but those who could find no place that would take them in or had no skills for agricultural work, resorted to petty theft or a variety of confidence schemes to get the few dollars others might have saved. While theaters closed for lack of an audience, free movies made a regular outdoor appearance in the small town parks. As people waited for the movie to begin, pitch men offered a chance to win a set of dishes or some other item beyond people's means if they could still come up with twenty-five cents for a lottery ticket.

Of less concern to the prosecutor's office was the plethora of migrants from Chicago who moved north to escape the crackdown on organized crime. They brought their money with them and, except for what Jotham thought was an unreasoned fear of their Chicago mob aura, imposed no real threat for the local population. Few of them had ever been involved in any illegal activity and even those who had limited their crimes to prohibition and prostitution. They might have been a problem for Dan Vigonallo and Emile Johanson but only when federal officers requested their help. Jotham more frequently found himself trying to explain that, unlike lawmen in the western movies, Mike Flannigan, the Bayfield County Sheriff could not just "run them out of town."

When October's night time temperatures began to drop below freezing, many of the transients, who had worked all summer for nothing but food and lodging, hopped the freight trains to warmer climates. Others, who had moved to the North Country to avoid Chicago's crackdown on crime and corruption, remained. Jotham was called upon to check on some of the complaints from locals who thought they had been taken advantage of in one way or another, but he rarely found a violation of the law. More often he found a new friend. One of them was Don McCain. A farmer had complained that McCain had overcharged him for overhauling his tractor. Don's charges were not excessive for an auto mechanic in Chicago, but perhaps a bit out of line for a rural economy more than four hundred miles north, in Washburn Wisconsin.

Jotham found the McCain repair shop in an old dilapidated building that, at an earlier time, housed a blacksmith shop. McCain was a burley man with broad shoulders and rapidly receding light brown hair. He wore thick glasses, but his huge hands looked like they could take an engine apart without the aid of tools. Jotham's first thought was a latent memory of Longfellow. He almost glanced up to look for a chestnut tree.

The smith, a mighty man is he, with large and sinewy hands.

"Now don't tell me you're having trouble with that car," McCain called out as Jotham opened the door of his Studebaker.

"Nope," Jotham responded. "I'm looking for a man named Don McCain. That you?'

"Depends on. What are you looking for McCain for?"

Jotham laughed. It was not an unusual response from one of the newcomers from Chicago. "Nothing serious, Mr. McCain. One of your customers asked me to check on your business. It seems he feels you overcharged him."

"Really! I sure didn't mean to."

"I'm from the County Attorney's office, but let's not think of this as an official visit. I'm sure you haven't broken any laws. My name is Jotham Marichetti."

"And, since you're not with the feds, I am Don McCain. You can call me Don. If you don't have trouble with your car, and I haven't broken any laws, what can I do for you?"

"And you came to our small city from Chicago?" Jotham asked, ignoring McCain's question. "What did you do there?"

"Same thing I'm doing here. I was a mechanic." Jotham didn't respond, just looked at McCain as though he expected more. "Okay, not quite the same. In Chicago I worked on a fleet of cars for one owner."

"And the fact that you came up here tells me that one owner wasn't the cab company was it? Why did you decide to move out of the city?"

"The cars belonged to Capone, Al Capone. When the G-men started to break up the Capone empire, they played as loose with the law as the Capones ever did. They didn't differentiate between their legitimate employees and gang members. If you cooked or cleaned house for Al, you were suspected of something. Al went to prison. Ralph kept talking about moving north. I decided maybe I should move north."

"You have any contact with Ralph?"

"No, but I'd fix his car if he asked me to. That is what I'm here for honest work."

"I don't doubt that at all, Don, and if you do the job, you can charge whatever you want to, but folks up here don't make the kind of money they do in Chicago. That was true even before the depression. It would make my job easier if you cut them a little better deal now and then."

"I hadn't thought about that, but I guess you're right. I'm not here to make enemies. Who was this fella that complained? I'll Give him a bill for a few dollars less. It'll be good for my business, too. Maybe then he'll pay it."

A week later the farmer came to Jotham's office to thank him. His repair bill had been cut in half. He maintained a file of such complaints and the result of his contact with both the one who complained and the target of the complaint. The McCain file clearly indicated that the county prosecutor's office found no wrongdoing. The record served two purposes; to provide a background for any future problems should they come up and to justify that portion of the county budget that paid his salary. He knew the depression continued to put pressure on county funds and only the respect the County Board had for Joe Flynn permitted the Assistant Prosecutor's job to continue. The file will also serve another important purpose when the time comes for Jotham to run for District Attorney. Flynn had told him to always leave the impression he was working for the individual citizen not the state or the county.

Another recent migrant from Chicago had ruffled the feathers of a farmer in Orienta Township a few miles south of Oulu. The farmer had been unable to pay the taxes on his eighty acre farm for five years and was concerned that the county would file a tax lien foreclosure on his property. Unable to borrow money from the banks he had gone to Dan Koepp for a loan. The loan papers were drawn up and, since the farmer could not read, explained to him. The interest charge was clearly stated, but when it came time to pay, the farmer thought it was too high.

Finding Oulu was Jotham's first challenge. He started in the county clerk's Office. Oulu did not appear on the crude road maps that were available free from any gas station. It was a community, but not recognized as a town. County land records indicated the Koepp property location by Range, Section and a legal description of the forty acre tract, but no indication of what road or trail might take him there. The clerk said it had to be very close to the western edge of the county several miles north of Federal Highway 2, but her best advice was to go to Iron River, or maybe even across the line into Douglas County to Brule, then ask someone. Jotham remembered his first trip to Chauncey the Bear Hunter's lodge. That had been easy. Almost everyone in Iron River was able to give him directions that were clear even if they were all based on the recognition of landmarks. "When you get to the big pine tree with the top blown off by the windstorm two years ago," they had said, "take the left fork in the road." Apparently there were no big pine trees on the way to Oulu.

Once he reached Oulu, however, Dan Koepp's place was easy to find. It was small for someone rich enough to be in the loan business in the third year of a major depression. He lived in a one room house located behind the town hall. It was heated by a wood stove. Dan lived a simple life with no luxuries, a sharp contrast of the comparative opulence of Chauncey the Bear Hunter. At the same time, Dan Koepp was no recluse. He mixed well with the local people, not only in Oulu, but also Iron River and wrote the Oulu News column for the weekly paper.

Dan had been a tax consultant from Chicago. He moved to the North Country at the end of the twenties and soon became the rich uncle for a number of victims of the depression in Bayfield County. He had somehow amassed a small fortune in his city job and was generous about making loans to people in need. Jotham told him about the farmer and Dan brought out the papers for the loan. They were all in order. It was obvious that Dan was familiar with all usury laws in the state of Wisconsin and had been careful not to break them. Jotham agreed that no law had been broken, then, to satisfy his own curiosity, he asked Dan why he had left the city.

"You know, Marichetti, I didn't do anything against the law, but in Chicago it got so they were investigating everybody who made money. I had been doing taxes for some big corporations and a few wealthy people. I'd show them where they could save a few thousand dollars on their taxes. Some time later they'd send me a gift, you know, a few dollars in appreciation. I didn't break any laws. I just followed the tax code the way congress wrote it."

"I'm not sure I understand," Jotham said. "If you didn't violate any of the tax laws, I would think any qualified lawyer could keep you out of trouble Anything extra they gave you could have been justified as a bonus for doing a good job."

"Not quite that simple," Dan answered. "I never worked directly for the mob, but some of the people I did work for were, let's say connected. After they convicted Ralph Capone for fudging on his taxes, that was in April of 1930, the feds started a campaign to go after anybody loosely tied to Big Al."

"But your's was really a loose connection. I doubt they could have ever gotten a conviction."

"Oh, I covered my tracks as best anyone could." Dan said. "I was a good tax man, but Elliot Ness was good at what he did, too. Bottles, that's Ralph Capone, became a test case for him. He was really after Alfonse. I thought about fighting the IRS in court, but that would have been risky. Even being questioned outside of court by any of Ness' people could have made me a target for guys like Jake Guzik and Frank Nitti. Al and Ralph were business men. Those guys were real thugs."

They continued to talk for an hour and Jotham left with the thought that Dan would ease up on some of the locals who were really in financial trouble.

Early in July, Joe Flynn had announced his retirement and endorsed Jotham for his replacement. As soon as the news was published, Jotham filed papers for the fall election. Campaigning was a new experience for Jotham, but Flynn gave him plenty of assistance and advice. By the end of September there were signs posted throughout the county. Flynn helped write a news release that emphasized Jotham's experience as a clerk in the state Supreme Court as well as his involvement in the signing of the armistice that ended the fighting in World War I. Franklin Roosevelt looked like he would easily beat Hoover and it began to look like Flynn had been right and Jotham was a shoe-in for Bayfield County Attorney. He was sitting at his desk rehearsing the speech he was scheduled to give in Bayfield the next day, when, the telephone rang. It was his friend Bob Norton from the County Attorney's Office in Ashland.

"I need a little help," Norton said.

"Sure Bob," Jotham answered. "What can I do for you."

"We've got a fugitive from a fight down at Kelly's place on West Main street. The city police brought him in and locked him in a cell. He was totally unresponsive last night. This morning when we told him what happened, he remembered being in a fight, but other than that had no idea what happened. He said he knows you."

Jotham paused and took a breath. He was afraid to ask, afraid he knew the answer he was going to get. "If I know him, I'm sure willing to try to help. Who is he, Bob?"

"Indian fella. Been hanging around here for three or four years now. Quite a scrapper. He's spent a few nights in our jail. We always let him go as soon as he sobered up, but this time we can't do that."

Why is that, Bob? Saloon fights around here are weekly entertainment, always have been. You're not starting to file charges on Saloon fights are you? Who did you say he was?"

"I didn't say. He said his name is Johnny Bearheart, but this time it's not just a saloon fight. The guy he was fighting was killed. When the Indian knocked him down, his head hit the front bumper of a parked Model A Ford. Dead before the doctor could get there, and the doctor was at Kelly's, too."

The next morning, Jotham got up early and drove to the Jail in Ashland. Bob Norton was there and told the jailer to open the cell and let him in to see Johnny.

"Johnny," Jotham said trying to sound calm and reassuring. "I hear you're in a little trouble."

"It's more than a little, Ahmeek. The police said I killed somebody, but I don't remember that. I know I hit him, but that's all. We got in a fight after he said he didn't believe I ever served in the army. I showed him my medals and he just asks me where I got 'em and said I probably stole 'em.."

"Then did he hit you or grab onto you or something?"

"No he just started cussin' and saying all kinds of bad things about Indians. Said we were all a bunch of robbers. He said they never would have allowed us in the army 'cause we weren't good enough to be American soldiers. He said we weren't the real Americans we were just a bunch of savages that couldn't even take care of ourselves 'til the white men came along. I told him we were the real Americans 'cause Indians were here before the white man and I said I was just as much an American as anyone. Besides I said I was half white and a decorated war veteran. He just laughed at me and said I was a damned fool to go fight a war to save Europe. Then He gave me a shove. That's when I grabbed his arm and spun around like how they showed us in the army and when he went down he just lay there like he couldn't get up again."

"Then what did you do, Johnny?"

"I just took off runnin'. I was scared, Jotham, scared I might have hurt him real bad. The next thing I remember three cops in their car caught up with me in the east end of town. I didn't try to fight with them. They knew me. Besides, there were three of them and they'd picked me up before a couple of times. I always had to spend a night in the jail and they'd let me go again in the morning. They were okay guys, those cops."

"Did anybody see you throw the guy down, Johnny?"

"Lot's a people saw it. Most of them were white." Johnny looked away, breaking eye contact. "I don't guess any of them will stand up for an Indian. My cousins from Odanah were there and saw the whole thing, too, but who's gonna believe them. They're just Indians. Gosh, Ahmeek, I wish I could be like you, a hero in the big war."

"I wasn't the hero, Johnny, you were. I didn't even get into a battle during the war. You fought like a tiger, no, even better. You fought like an Indian."

Johnny smiled, a sad smile. "Thanks Ahmeek, but you were the hero in the war. All I did was get a bunch of medals."

"It sounds to me like the man's death was an accident," Jotham said. "I'll talk to Bob Norton, he's the Ashland County District Attorney, and maybe I can get him to reduce the charge."

"I want you to be my lawyer, Ahmeek"

"I can't do that, Johnny. I work for Bayfield County now, but I promise I'll get the best lawyer I can find to take your case. I don't think they'll let you go altogether, but maybe we can fix it so you won't have to spend too much time in jail."

"Try hard, Ahmeek," Johnny pleaded. "Try real hard. I can't live like an animal in a cage. Try real hard."

Jotham left the jail and drove directly to the county building. Bob Norton wasted no time letting him in. He told Norton what Johnny had said and asked if he could drop or reduce the charges.

"Bob, you know I'm running for the Bayfield County Attorney's office. Officially I can't represent him, but as a friend," Jotham said, "I'm asking you to consider something less than a murder charge. I might be able to get Bearheart to agree to plead guilty if it wouldn't give him too much jail time."

"I'd like to do that," Norton answered, "but that would be a hard sell to the people of Ashland."

"It's an Indian versus a white man, Bob. We both know you can't get an unbiased jury."

"I agree with you that everybody deserves a fair trial, but the townspeople want blood. It was all I could do to keep them from lynching the Indian."

"The United States government granted citizenship to Indians eight years ago, Bob."

"I know it isn't fair, Jotham, but people won't listen to reasons or extenuating circumstances when the man who died was white and the assailant was an Indian."

"That is why this case can't go to a jury, Bob."

"I'll try, Jotham, but there will be other people involved in that decision. That's all I can promise. I'll try."

"And that's all I can ask. Thanks for calling me, and thanks for listening."

Jotham understood Bob Norton's reluctance. Norton had to stand for election, too, and the past few months taught him that was no easy job. He knew how difficult he would find it if the decision were his. Even in Bayfield County, he knew his prior friendship with Johnny Bearheart might impact his own election prospects.

Chapter 15

Jotham knew if word got around that he was a friend of Johnny Bearheart it would complicate his election campaign. He also knew there was no way to prevent that from happening. More importantly, no matter what he had become, Johnny was a friend and friends mattered more than elections. He decided not wait for his opponent to use his association with the Chippewa against him. He rewrote a part of his speech to tell people about Johnny. He worded the revision carefully.

That afternoon in Bayfield a large crowd had gathered to hear the former Supreme Court clerk who wanted their vote for District Attorney. Jotham started with the usual background information about himself. He took time to praise the people of Bayfield County, to flatter them actually, for their patriotism and their tradition of support for the American soldier. He told them about his experience with the Bayfield Rifle Company of the Wisconsin National Guard when they had come to his father's logging camp to bring a peaceful settlement between the loggers and the power company workers. He knew some former members of that company would be in his audience. Then he went on to his own experience in the Army including his role in the signing of the Armistice. At that point, his voice broke slightly and, as though it was not a part of his written speech he said, "I can not go on with my story as though I were a hero in the war. I was just a soldier who was fortunate enough to be in places where important and vital events in our country's history were taking place. I have to tell you instead about one of the real heroes in that war."

He tried to sound like he was speaking spontaneously, from the heart, he told the Bayfield audience about Johnny Bearheart. He told them how he and Johnny met, how they had served together in France and how Johnny had earned not one, but two Bronze Stars. He included the details about how Johnny and the Sergeant together had taken out two machine gun nests and stopped the movement of a whole German battalion. Then he told them about Johnny's arrest and his visit to the Ashland jail. "He asked me to be his lawyer, Jotham said, "and it almost broke my heart to have to tell him I couldn't do that because I was a candidate for District Attorney of Bayfield County." He paused for several seconds then told them what had happened at Kelly's Saloon. First only the story that Bob Norton had told him, then the same story as Johnny related it. He said he could not take a side in Johnny's case, but whatever happened he hoped it would be considerate of all, Johnny, the family of the deceased and most of all the cause of Justice.

A thunderous round of applause followed Jotham's speech. Members of the audience crowed the platform to talk to him. As soon as the crowd thinned and he was able to escape, Jotham took the road north to the Red Cliff Chippewa village. He wanted to tell Mourning Dove and Jimmy Little Wind about Johnny's arrest.

He found Mourning Dove with her two grandchildren in the lodge where he had taken her and Jimmy Little Wind three years earlier. She was wearing plain Indian clothes with no ornaments and rocking back and forth in her crouched position, her hands locked together around her knees. Jotham noticed that her hair, once worn in braids down to the middle of her back had been cut short. He at first thought that the news of Johnny's arrest had preceded his arrival, but then he realized the Chippewa Mourning ritual was not for the living, but for the dead. She looked at him, but with a blank expression. He knew this was not the time. Outside the lodge he looked again for any sign of Jimmy Little Wind, then asked one of the tribal elders what had happened. Who had died?

"Six of our strongest brothers," the old man said. "They were fishing by the island we call Manitou when a strong wind came up. So strong it turned the long boat over. All six, good swimmers. Nobody can swim in Gitche Gume in the moon of first frost. Jimmy Little Wind, husband of Mourning Dove, was with them, also oldest son, David Walking Boy, four others you do not know, all gone. All joined so many before them in the big waters."

Jotham thanked the old man, told him how sorry he was for the loss of so many good men then, went to his car and left the village. Mourning Dove would learn soon enough about Johnny Bearheart's trouble and no matter how much he wanted to comfort her, that was not permitted during the time of mourning. He knew he would not see her for a full year. If it had been just her son, the father of those two beautiful young children who shared her suffering, it would be sooner, but Jimmy Little Wind was her husband. It would be a year.

On the way back to Washburn Jotham couldn't get his mind off Mourning Dove. He had seen her very infrequently over the past thirty years, only when there had been an occasion, Eagle Feather's funeral, his father's funeral and the few times he was asked to come to her mother's home to discuss some problem with Johnny Bearheart. He remembered Smiley Bartle, the logger in his father's camp when he was a child. "They're pretty when they're young," he had said. Jotham didn't remember exactly what the rest of it was but it was not complementary. *Well,* he thought, *Smiley Bartle was wrong. Mourning Dove looks older, but she is still an attractive Indian woman at . . . how old now?* Late forties, he was sure, but he could not remember. Was she his age, or was she a year older? He knew about her two sons and her grandchildren, but had never met them. She was married to Jimmy Little Wind, and a visit from any other man, Indian or white, without the invitation of her husband was against Chippewa custom.

He stopped to visit his brother Dominic and his family before going home. Dominic had moved to the farm Jotham owned when his tenant found another job in the same city he had come from three years before. He had left one cow as a final payment for Jotham. He and Lillian took over the large garden in mid summer and were happy to no longer be totally dependent on Jotham's generosity. It seemed that little Gino and Maria had grown over night.

"What do you think about the election?" Dominic, who was always ready to talk politics, asked.

"I think Roosevelt's going to win," Jotham answered. "He says he's got ideas to pull the country out of the depression and that's going to appeal to the voters whether it's true or not. At times like this voters will go for the candidate that's the most optimistic."

"Not that election," Jotham, "Your election. How did the speech go?"

"Pretty good, I think. I can't be sure until people start telling us what they've been hearing on the street. Flynn will let me know about that. He's in touch with folks whose specific job in the campaign is to listen for comments."

"And if it's all good, you can start to relax, right?"

"I won't be able to relax until the election is over. From now until November, I have to be on the stump every Saturday and Sunday."

"On the stump? That sounds more like logger talk. What's that mean, on the stump?"

"That's just the way campaigners talk, Dominic. It means out giving speeches. I suppose it goes back to the days of Davy Crockett when there weren't any big towns and they actually had to get people together in the woods. The only place for them to stand where a crowd of people could all see them was standing on a big, tall stump."

"So you gotta keep givin' speeches," Dominic said.

"Next Saturday I talk to the people at Port Wing in the morning, then to the folks in Iron River that afternoon. Sunday I'm back in Washburn. Then the following Saturday it's Grandview and Drummond. Then, if there's time, I'll stop in some of the smaller towns."

"That sounds like a lot of work to me, but I suppose you can keep usen' the same speech over and over, can't you?"

"Not a chance. I have to change the speech for every town. Dominic, I'm beginning to believe getting elected is a lot more work than the job you get elected to."

Jotham stayed for dinner with Dominic and Lillian, spent a happy hour in play time with the children then, went home for a good night's rest.

Jotham had a light work schedule the following week. He spent most of his time revising his Bayfield speech to make it relate to each of the towns on his schedule. Port Wing was a fishing village so he worked in references to the fishing industry and the stalwart men who engaged in commercial fishing. He told them about Jimmy Little Wind and his son, along with four other Red Cliff Chippewa who, died in the tragic accident off Manitou Island. He believed that the emotional attachment of men who fought the vagaries of Lake Superior winds and weather would outweigh the prejudice most commercial fishermen had against the Indians. In Grandview he talked about the quarry industry and complimented the town for it's contribution to population expansion by providing high quality marble for building material. Each town was unique and he was careful to talk about its attributes.

When not working on the speeches, he turned his attention to Johnny Bearheart. With help from Dan Vigonallo, he found a lawyer who was willing to represent Johnny pro bono. Oliver T. Burnside was a judge from Detroit who had moved to Ironwood, Michigan for his retirement. He was recipient of a good stipend courtesy of the tax payers in the Great Lakes State and enjoyed revisiting his earlier occupation now and then. Jotham had heard that Bob Norton was going for an indictment of second degree murder. He hoped the judge would be an imposing enough figure to change Bob's mind. Jotham continued to lobby for a plea bargain, involuntary manslaughter with jail time of no more than a year, but Norton was sure that would make him unpopular with Ashland County Residents.

After his speech in Drummond, Jotham decided to take the long way home and stop to see Chauncey again. Most of the people in Iron River had accepted his statement, after his earlier visit that Chauncey was not engaged in anything illegal. A few enjoyed the touch of notoriety that the Bear Hunter brought to their small community. One tavern owner quipped, "he's a bear hunter all right. He hunts the bears of Wall Street and he's made fools of the lot of them."

Jotham noticed that the road leading from Drummond west had been graveled and graded as had the road that headed north toward Iron River. There were indications that what had been a trail continuing east to Wilderness lake had also seen some improvement, but it was still far from smooth. When he made the left turn from that road toward Chauncey's Wildernest lodge, however, he followed the single set of tire tracks through the plush pine forest he had driven through earlier in the summer.

"What happened?" Jotham asked his burley friend who came out of the lodge to meet him. Your benefactors run out of money before the road work was all done?"

"What?"

"Your road, it's graded like a federal highway all the way from Iron River. The last half mile into your place looks more like the trails I used to skid logs on when I was a kid."

"Didn't want 'em to do anything with it. My patrons like it rustic and secluded. You know, Ahmeek," ," Chauncey added with a laugh, "all those criminals the town folks think I'm harboring up here don't want it to be too easy for you DA's to come wandering in and surprise them."

"I see your point," Jotham answered obviously looking up at the structure centered at the top of the lodge roof, "But I'm not the DA yet. The voters will decide that on Tuesday. By the way what is that structure on the top of your lodge for?" The structure was similar to a cupola, but square, just large enough for one person, and open on all four sides.

"I'm the bear hunter, Ahmeek. Let's say it's for hunting bear. Bear come by, I don't have to leave the lodge to shoot 'em." He laughed again. This time Jotham joined him. "But back to the election," the bear hunter continued, "It's all settled and you're the new DA. I've been campaigning for you since August, and when I ask people for something, I usually get it. You and Roosevelt. I campaigned for him, too."

"Thanks Bear Hunter. I hope it works." Jotham looked around. "I take it those important guests you were telling me about don't like the cold Wisconsin weather."

"Nah," Chauncey chuckled. "Weather don't trouble them. I told them Bayfield county was electing a new DA and they all went on the lam."

"Too bad. I'd like to meet them some time, socially of course. I don't mean to pry, but what does Wildernest Lodge charge for a north woods vacation?"

"Charge?" Chauncey wrinkled his face pretending to be hurt by the question. "Ahmeek, my good friend, I don't charge my guests to stay here. Like I told you before, I don't believe in money. Good will is all I ask. I invite them, they come, and after they go home, always after, if they want to, they send me something. I'll admit I let them know what I want, but it's all voluntary. They are good people and very generous. They take good care of the Bear Hunter."

"I've got to ask, Bear Hunter. You know I've got to ask, not officially, just as an interested friend. Who are these people?"

"No secret, Ahmeek. When they send me something, it usually it gets in the papers. Some of 'em are the top dogs in American industry. Some just run a smaller company someplace. I don't give out names, but if you come up some time in the summer I'll introduce you to them."

"Thanks Mr. Bear Hunter. I'll try to do that."

Jotham spent about an hour talking to Chauncey. They talked about the weather, about the depression, which Jotham thought, had little effect on Chauncey's life style. They talked about cars, including the new Graham that sat in Chauncey's shed, the only building at Wildernest other than the lodge itself. On a more serious side, they talked about Roosevelt and the depression. "Why," Chauncey asked, "would anyone want to become president at times like these?" There were dozens of questions he wanted to ask, but this was not the time. He once before, asked about the structure on the top of the main lodge and got an evasive answer. He was sure it wasn't for hunting bear. It was more likely for security when some particularly security conscious guests were present. No law against that, but it did make him a little suspicious about who those guests might be.

Monday was a day for Jotham to hit the streets and shake hands with everybody he met. He found them in the stores, bringing their children to school and later picking up children after school. Of course no one got through the county building without a handshake. When he had covered every other place for a decent period of time, Jotham stood on the street corners. He felt a sense of shame, begging people for their vote, but Flynn said that was how it was done.

When the day was finally over, Jotham retreated to his office where he, Flynn and the office staff waited for the results to be phoned in from each town hall. The telephone had made getting the election results infinitely faster than they could only a few years previously, but to Jotham, it seemed like the election would never be over. Early returns from Bayfield and other townships along the south shore of Lake Superior were disappointing. His opponent had gained ground in those areas by emphasizing Jotham's relationship with Johnny Bearheart, whom he referred to as a killer. Jotham had been successful in the villages of Bayfield and Port Wing by taking the initiative and pointing out the advantages of a County Attorney being familiar with the Chippewa, but many commercial fishermen saw the Indians as competition for the walleye that provided so much of their livelihood. For them the "Indian Lover" label had an effect. Later when Drummond, Iron River and other townships in the southern and western areas phoned in their returns, Jotham began to build a large lead. The bear hunter was right and his friend Ahmeek was able to go to bed knowing he was the new District Attorney.

Chapter 16

While Jotham moved into his new office, he had only minimal help. The office staff, which consisted of a legal secretary and one law clerk, were busy preparing a party for their outgoing boss, Joe Flynn. Jotham made no objection to the loss of help from his staff. In fact, he had been the one to suggest the party. He knew, however, that his job would require more time than his predecessor. The depression was still causing severe pressure on the county budget. Members of the county board had voted to eliminate the position of Assistant to the District Attorney at their last monthly meeting. After moving the last file from his old office to the much larger space Joe Flynn had occupied, Jotham decided to take a break. He sat down at the desk with the placard that said "Jotham Marichetti, Bayfield County District Attorney, picked up the phone and ask the operator to connect him to Judge Burnside in Ironwood, Michigan.

After only twenty minutes, Jotham's phone rang and a pleasant voice on the other end of the line said, "Your call is ready, Mr.

Marichetti. Jotham thanked the operator and waited for the click that told him she had plugged the connection in. The next sound that came through the receiver pressed to his left ear was the voice of Oliver T. Burnside.

"Hello, Burnside here."

"Judge Burnside, this is Jotham Marichetti."

"Who?"

"Marichetti." Both men were talking much louder than the volume of a normal conversation, partly to try to override the line noise and partly because they were talking to someone all the way over in another state. "Jotham Marichetti," he repeated, "the lawyer that talked to you about the Johnny Bearheart case. You remember; he's the man Bob Norton in Ashland was planning to charge with second degree murder."

"Oh yes, of course, the Indian fellow," the Judge affirmed.

"I was wondering," Jotham said, "If you've been able to make any progress."

"That depends, Mr. Marichetti, on your definition of progress. I don't see any chance of getting him off without prison time, but I do believe I can get them to try him for something other than being an Indian."

"He's admitted that he hit the victim and that blow resulted in his death. I don't know how I could ask any lawyer to get him off without jail time. At the same time, I don't know how Bob could justify a murder charge."

"Bob Norton knows that," Burnside said. "He also knows he is between the rock and the hard place. I've given him a little more work to make it easier for him to do the right thing."

"Do I dare ask what that means?"

"Probably not, the election is over and Bearheart is still charged with murder two. I've filed a couple of papers that will harass

Norton a little. Help him kill time. Let it go a couple of weeks and I'll fill you in on the details."

Jotham hung up the receiver. He had a good idea what the Judge had been up to, but it was only a little bit comforting. The big question was: Would it work?

Jotham turned his attention to other matters. He had satisfied his suspicions about the guests that kept coming and going at Wildernest lodge, but that did not quell those of other Bayfield County residents. The suspicion by 1933 was limited to the few who lived in the smallest communities and received most of their information by rumor. Merchants did not like Chauncey because he "bought most of his goods mail order." Community leaders knew that he bought very little locally and, what others thought were mail order purchases, were gifts from some of the nation's wealthiest industrialists. To them Chauncey was a member of community organizations, service clubs and other philanthropic ventures. Jotham looked forward to hearing the complaints from those less informed because it gave him a chance to get out of the office and visit with an unusual friend who had invented his own myth of hunter and woodsman, but was really the most sophisticated and urbane person in the county, except perhaps, for Dan Koepp. Responding to the most recent complaint, Jotham promised another trip to the Wildernest Lodge as soon as spring came and the roads were better.

A more pressing matter was brought to him by several elders from Red Cliff that appeared in his office late on a Friday afternoon. Indians at Red Cliff were not well educated, particularly the older members of the community who could not read or write. They had heard from relatives and friends from the Odanah village that congress was considering a bill that would return much of their reservation land. They said the Odanah people had heard about it on the radio. They wanted to be ready when the bill passed. They asked Jotham to find out what they had to do.

Jotham had heard of the Wheeler-Howard act, but had little knowledge of the details. He promised to find out all he could and get back to them. First he wrote to Washington to obtain a copy of the bill. Two weeks later he received it by mail. The bill, which was also referred to as the Indian Reorganization Act, brought an end to the allotment policy enacted in 1887 and gave Indians funds to buy back portions of their former reservation lands and restore the sovereignty of the tribes. Jotham slid the letter into his brief case and drove to Red Cliff to meet with the tribal elders. He gave them the basic information about the bill.

"I think," Jotham said, "if the bill gets through congress without too many changes, it will be good for the Indians. It will help you buy back the old reservation lands and be in charge of your tribe again."

"The reservation is not good," one of the elders said. "When our grandfathers had the reservation, the government promised to give them all they would need, but it was never enough."

"That is true," Jotham agreed, "but that was the old reservation where they told you how to live and you could not decide for yourselves how you want to run the reservation. This law will let you establish your own government, not be governed by the people in the Bureau of Indian Affairs. It will let you elect your own leaders."

"Our elders have always chosen our leaders, even when we had no reservation, just a small village. How would new law change that? How would it make our life better?"

"You would no longer have to pay taxes to Bayfield County or the State of Wisconsin for the property you own as you do now," Jotham said. "Your leaders would set the taxes and the money would stay in Red Cliff to be used by your leaders to help the whole tribe. The law is also going to provide money for better schools for your children and doctors to help when someone in the tribe is sick."

"If we want to go back to a reservation of our own," an elder asked, "what we have to do?"

"You would have to set up a tribal government," Jotham said. "It would be a lot like the government of a town, like Bayfield or Washburn."

"But we do not know how to make a government like your town has."

"You would have to write a constitution. Our office can help you do that, and we can find a lawyer that would represent you when you send it to the Bureau of Indian Affairs. When that is done and it has been filed with the United States government, your own people will be in charge, not the BIA."

One of the oldest of the elders said, "I am very old and I remember the BIA, the agents. The agents never help the Chippewa."

"But now they will have to," Jotham said, "because with the new law, the US courts will watch over the agents."

That seemed to satisfy them. The one who had asked most of the questions said, "We will think about it and discuss it with our people and the people of other bands. If we agree, we will ask you to find someone to help us make the constitution."

Jotham left, feeling good about his discussion of the Wheeler-Howard act with the elders, but at the same time with a heavy heart. It was still too early for him to talk to Mourning Dove, to express his sadness at the death of Jimmy Little Wind and the arrest of Johnny Bearheart. He had looked to see if she might be outside, but did not see her.

Easter had always been Jotham's favorite holiday. His Aunt Sarah made sure Jotham knew the story of the resurrection when he was child in her Wausau, Wisconsin home. Aunt Sarah was a devout woman, but it was not the Easter celebration of the resurrection that moved Jotham. When he was a child the Easter vacation from school each year marked his first visit to his father's logging camp in the north. It was on one of these trips that he had first met Old Eagle Feather and began his journey into Native American culture and spirituality. It wasn't that he rejected the religious training his aunt had tried to provide, nor did he accept the stories Eagle Feather had told him, he simply questioned the idea that anyone could know the unknowable. He did not want to deny anyone else their particular faith, but he objected when that faith exercised control over the lives of others. Such ideas had been no more than fleeting thoughts until he had returned from Army Officers Training back in 1917 and, on the basis of Father Murphy's word alone, Rebecca Morgan had broken their engagement.

These were not Jotham's most salient thoughts on this weekend. They were merely memories that flashed through his mind as he drove from His house in Washburn to the farm house where his brother Dominic lived. This time the visit was not simply routine. The paper mills in central Wisconsin were going back into production. Dominic had received a letter from the Nekoosa, Edwards Corporation saying they were looking for pulp wood. This was great news for Dominic, who had spent three years voicing unnecessary apologies for "loading in on Jotham." He was now in the process of arranging to buy Jotham's farm, the one he had been living on, and go back into the logging business. He had talked to Jotham about his proposal and Jotham had agreed, now it was time to start the paperwork.

"Dominic," Jotham asked, "Are you sure this is the time to go back into pulpwood? The paper market isn't going to recover too fast. There are a lot of big corporations, the big consumers of paper products that haven't begun production again. Many of them never will."

"We won't need to sell much pulp at the beginning," Dominic said. "I'll keep the farm going. People still need food and we can sell quite a bit in the fall. By then we should have some wood ready to ship and most of the food we need for winter."

"Have you figured out how you're going to be able to run a camp if you're still living here and running a farm?"

"Logging isn't what it used to be, Jotham. The old logging camps with big crews and a cook's shanty an' all that are a thing of the past. The loggers that make the money now are going to spread out and use their cars and trucks to move from one small tract of timber to another, while two or three men, half dozen at the most, that do their own cookin' an' stuff, cut the trees."

"Really?" Jotham realized he had been out of the logging business for a long time. "You mean you can run a logging camp by splitting it up into two or three man crews scattered all over?"

"That's pretty much it," Dominic said. "Pulpin' is different. You don't find giant timber stands that stretch for miles like they used to. Even if you did it would cost too much to buy it from the land owners and the paper mills eat up the supply of wood pretty fast. You have to keep your workers movin' to be in the timber business now days."

"How are you going to haul all that pulpwood from so many different places?"

"That's the easy part, Jotham. The railroads crisscross the land all over now. Haulin' pulp wood is their main business up here so they've got spurs close enough that you only have to truck it a few miles, fifteen or twenty at the most. The other thing about the rail roads is that they own a lot of land and they sell it pretty cheap. Back in the nineteen hundreds, they bought land to put their tracks on and raced the other rail companies layin' the track. The one that won the race got the business. The ones that were too late to make a profit got out of the race and went someplace else. Now that land has a good crop of timber and a lot of it's for sale. I've got a bid in on a hundred and twenty acres just north of Brule. That's where I'm hopin' to start."

"I'll be damned! I guess I haven't kept up with the logging world. If you're sure you can run a timber business in Northern Wisconsin from here, you can have the farm."

"That's what I want. Jotham, but I'm going to pay for it."

That was Dominic's last word on the subject. He believed his brother had done too much for him and his family already. He not only intended to pay full price for the farm, a sum of over $2000, but he would pay the going rate of interest until the loan "was paid off". They had agreed on the phone that Dominic could pay in installments. Jotham knew it was no use to argue. He would let Dominic have it his way. Dominic did agree to delay the first payment until the logging business sold its first car load of logs. Jotham decided, without Dominic's approval, there would be no penalty for any payments missed and they would revisit the question of interest payments later.

As the spring wore on, Jotham remembered his promise to make yet another visit with the owner of Wildernest Lodge, but decided to give it another month or two. He really wanted to take advantage of Chauncey's invitation to come in the summer time and meet some of the guests. Until then, he had other things to be concerned about. There was a daily mountain of paper work and he was anxious to get to a final outcome of the Johnny Bearheart case. One afternoon in late May, he got the call he had been waiting for.

"Marichetti?" The voice on the other end was distinctively familiar.

"Yes, Your Honor," Jotham said. "I am talking to Judge Burnside, aren't I?"

"You are, but it's going to be a short conversation. I want to talk to you about your friend, but not on the phone. How about lunch? I'll pick you up at your office and you can choose your favorite local restaurant."

"Sounds good to me," Jotham agreed. "I'll be waiting in my office, Bayfield county building, second floor." He heard the phone click. He would like to have asked Burnside about the outcome of his efforts on Johnny Bearheart's behalf, but there was no such thing as a secure phone line. The local operator could monitor any call and Jotham knew, most of them did.

Promptly at twelve o'clock, the door to his office opened and his secretary let Judge Burnside in. Jotham stood, they shook hands, and immediately exited to Burnsides Cadillac. On the brief drive to the north end of town the only words exchanged related to Washburn eating establishments and directions thereto. When they entered the restaurant, Jotham asked the waitress for a table where they could talk privately. She led them to a table for two centered in an alcove somewhat separated from the other patrons.

"Well, Mr. Marichetti, the deed is done," Burnside said with a mildly dramatic flair. "Your Indian friend will be charged with manslaughter."

"Thanks. I was sure you could get the charges reduced after our last conversation. How did you get Norton to change his mind?"

The judge raised the forefinger on his left hand. "We will get to that presently, but I must tell you that is only the good news. The bad news is that he will have to spend a year at Waupun"

"The state prison," Jotham affirmed. "I am sorry to hear that. Johnny won't take that well."

"It will be only a year, but it had to be Waupun. It's the one thing I couldn't get Bob Norton and his staff to budge on."

"It's as much as I could have expected," Jotham said. "I couldn't even get Bob to drop the murder two charge."

"I'll take but a small amount of credit for that. All I did is help him do what he wanted to do in the first place. I said I would fill you in. Now is the time for me to keep that promise. All I did was to put on a convincing performance for everybody else. I enjoy playing the villain. They all hated me."

"What?"

"Oh I don't mean Norton. He was a part of charade and played his part admirably. It was the local press and part of Norton's staff that wanted to run me out of town on the rail. Norton and I agreed to the outcome before the opening curtain."

"So all you did was make it easy for him?"

"Oh, no." Burnside said. "I made it difficult. I made his life hell for several months, until we were well past the election."

"The election?"

"Yes, like you, Bob Norton was running in the election, except, of course, in his case it was for re-election. The public and the press were at this throat, as you said, looking for blood. As we agreed, he charged Bearheart with second degree murder, but we both knew he could change that charge right up until trial. All I had to do was make it look to the press like he had more pressure to change it than the pressure they were placing on him to hold to it."

"And how did you go about that?"

"First I had to get him to make the charge," Burnside explained. "So I filed a writ of Habeas Corpus. That had no meaning except to feign pressuring Norton. It made it look like I rushed him to judgment. Once charges were filed I began the normal delaying tactics. I asked for a bail hearing. Of course I was going to lose that, an Indian who killed a white man was not about to be released on bail, but the hearing took a few days. Then I filed a series of motions asking for delays while I prepared my defense. On each, Norton and I were called in to play our parts before the judge. I ran out of good excuses when they contacted me to agree on a trial date and nearly received a contempt charge on a couple of bad ones. When they finally did force me to agree on the date, I started on the Jury. I think I might have set a record in *voir dire*. I questioned every potential juror for as long as I could with Bob Norton showing immense exasperation at each question. Finally I moved for dismissal on the grounds that there were no Indians on the jury. I reminded them that congress had made Indians citizens with all the rights of any other citizen of the country. The judge called us both to the bench and an agreement was struck for a manslaughter charge. Norton's performance was one the Bard himself would have been proud of. The best part is that when Bob comes up for election again, the voters will hold him blameless and curse that bastard Judge from Michigan."

It looked like a wild party. Guests were enjoying the finest whiskey money could buy with hors d' oeuvres to match, all brought, of course, by the guests themselves. Chauncey the Bear Hunter was beaming. "You wanted to meet some of my guests, Ahmeek," he said with a broad smile, "here they are. You might have seen pictures of some of them in the newspapers and magazines, hopefully not on the post office wall."

"Not many," Jotham answered, "but I assume there important people for you to put on a spread like this for them."

"I put nothing on, Ahmeek. They brought all this stuff. They provide the cooks and bakers. I let them have the blue berries. They grow like weeds around here and the folks from the cities really love 'em. All I give them is the space and a little anonymity. It's a chance for them to just be themselves. No photographers from *Life* allowed. They all come by invitation and they are all part of the club."

"The club?"

"Yeah, the club. A few times every summer we have a members only week. Nobody gets a room at the lodge unless they belong to the club. Of course I can have a friend in, like you, if I want to. They know I won't give an invite to anybody from the *Post* or *Harpers*. Clubs are all the rage now. That guy Townsend, you know the one that wants the government to provide pension money for old people, has clubs all across the country to promote his idea."

"Sure," Jotham agreed, "Francis Townsend, the Townsend Plan."

"That's him. Somebody said his club has over a million members, probably will have at least two million in a few years. Then you got Father Caughlin, that priest over in Michigan with his *Union for Social Justice*. That's another club. I heard that Senator Long, you know, the one they call 'Kingfish' is tryin' to start a club to promote his political ideas. But the Wildernest club is strictly elite. I'm not looking for a million members, just fifty or sixty that will make the '400' look like pikers and light weights. You see that fella over there." Chauncey gestured toward a white haired man dressed in a tailored fishing outfit. "He's the top dog in the top flour mill in the country. We call him Tiddyboom, but I wouldn't advise you using that name until you get to know him very well."

"Tiddyboom?" Jotham stifled a laugh. "He's called Tiddyboom?"

"Only at Wildernest. I said I provide anonymity. Like Ahmeek and the Bear Hunter, nicknames, everybody in the club goes by a nickname."

"Who are some of the others?"

"Well." Chauncey's right hand stroked an imaginary beard. Jotham was not sure whether he was pondering whether to tell him the names or was simply grandstanding. "There's the Grand Knight and his Court, there's, the Melted Icicle, Mouse, Henry the Eighth, and The Princess of The Blood."

"I don't often read those magazines you were talking about," Jotham said, "but there's one face I might recognize. Is that guest over by the window with the blonde by any chance the one you call Henry the Eighth?"

"Very sharp, Ahmeek. You got the significance of the nick name. That's Tony Mansfield. His picture has been in the news a lot, usually for his marriages."

"That's who I thought it was," Jotham said, "and that fellow in the corner has a familiar face. I think I've seen him around the area, Hurley maybe. Don't tell me he's a member of the club?"

"Actually he isn't a member, but one of the members asked me to invite him. He's Johnny Pregnano. Has some interest in some hotels, not too big himself, but well connected."

Jotham thought he knew what Pregnano's connections were, but officially he was a guest at Wildernest Lodge, no more, no less so he didn't press the Bear Hunter for more.

Gertrude didn't bother with a "good morning," or even a "where have you been." Instead she stood mute as she handed Jotham two pages from her ever present note pad. Gertrude was a combination receptionist and legal secretary in the District Attorney's office. The two jobs were combined into one when state revenues were reduced and the state started paying in scrip. She was a buxom, mildly obese woman in her fifties who wore dark dresses, sensible shoes and, Jotham thought, a diamond studded crown that was invisible to everyone but her. He took the papers and thanked her. She ignored the gesture, obviously in protest of his absence the previous afternoon and thus beyond her control.

The first paper from Gertrude contained a short list of telephone calls that had come in while Jotham had been "investigating the potentially nefarious "going's on" at Wildernest Lodge. The second was a list of what would be coming later, the overnight arrest record and the papers that needed filing with the clerk of court. He set that in a prominent place on his desk and turned his attention to the phone calls, neatly listed time, name and number on each line. The first four were from Bob Norton. Jotham picked up the phone. As soon as he heard the pleasant voice of the operator on the other end of the line, he asked for a connection to the Ashland District Attorney's office.

"Hello, Bob Norton here."

"Bob! You answering your own phone now?"

"Who the hell is this?"

"What?" Jotham gave the phone a confused look. "Oh, Jotham Marichetti, You were trying to call me yesterday."

"Jotham, Sorry Marichetti, a lot of static on the line this morning. I didn't recognize your voice."

"You tried to get me four times yesterday. What's up?"

"Where were you all day?" Norton stopped short. "No. That's not important. I called to tell you about your friend, Johnny

Bearheart. You knew that we've been holding him for transfer to Waupun, didn't you?"

"Yes, Burnside told me. What about it, Bob?"

"We cancelled the transfer. Emile's deputy went to his cell with lunch yesterday and found him dead. He was hanging from a water pipe on the ceiling. He had ripped strips from his bed sheet to make a noose."

"Oh my God!" Jotham put the phone down and quietly, to himself said, "A caged animal."

"What was that?" Jotham didn't answer for several seconds and Norton yelled into the phone, "Marichetti, Jotham. You okay?"

Jotham picked up the phone and put the receiver to his ear again. "Yeah, Bob. I'm okay."

"What was it you said? I couldn't hear you, something about an animal."

"A caged Animal. That was the last thing he said to me. 'I can't live like a caged animal.' You know Bob, a long time ago when I knew Johnny Bearheart as a very young man, he and a party of Chippewa blew up a dam because he said, even a river has to be free."

Chapter 17

Jotham sat at his desk, stunned by the news of Johnny Bearheart's death. He had trouble sorting out his feelings. Guilt, he could not escape those strong feelings of guilt. *He told me,* he kept saying to himself. *I can't live like a caged animal.* He remembered when he was little more than a child, the day the loggers and the dam company stood, guns loaded and ready to fight. Johnny blew up the dam, not to take sides in the fight, but because even a river had to run free. To Johnny nothing should be caged.

That did not matter. He could not bring Johnny back with his feelings of guilt. What he had to do now was see Mourning Dove, tell her about her brother's death. It was still two months before the mourning period for her husband and her son would be satisfied, but she had to know and he had to be with her when she was told. It would mean leaving the office for another morning. Gertrude would not like that. Too bad. She worked for him, not the other way around. He was going to get up and walk right out that door past Gertrude, but suddenly it swung open. Without saying a word, Gertrude stepped aside, smiled, and allowed Mourning Dove to enter.

"Ahmeek," Mourning Dove called as she almost ran across the room toward him. "I have heard about my brother. I do not know what to do, so I have to come to see you."

"I am so sorry Mourning Dove. I tried to help Johnny. I got him a very good lawyer and tried to keep his time in jail short but for Johnny, even a short time in jail was too long for a Chippewa. Men like Johnny want to be free more than anything else. That was more important to Johnny, more even than his life."

"I know you tried to help, Ahmeek, and I know that nobody can help Johnny. He left his mother and me long time ago, when whiskey came to be his family and his tribe. You could not change that, nobody could."

"How did you know about your brother? I was gone from my office yesterday and I didn't find out until this morning."

"Word moves fast with Chippewa. Johnny's friends from Bad River come to see me late in the night. I knew I have to come to see you. You were my brother's friend. You were my friend and you were like family for my grandfather."

"And it was right for you to come," Jotham said. "I was just getting ready to come to Red Cliff. I know that we are still in the time of sadness for Jimmy Little Wind, but I was hoping you would see me anyway."

"It was long enough. My father has been gone many years, a few years ago, my mother. In the moon of first frost, it was my son and my husband. Now it is my brother. I have no more family. There is no place else for me to go. The family of Jimmy Little Wind will not think me a bad woman. They know you were his friend, too."

"How can I help you, Mourning Dove?"

"First, I thought you could help me go back to the village where I lived with my mother and my grandfather, by the big lake where we played together when we were children. But there is no village, only a few old people. Others have all moved to the north, some place in Michigan." Mourning Dove hesitated for a long time. "I want you to help me, Ahmeek. I want you to help me find a job."

"A Job?"

"Yes, a job. My mother, when I was very little, left me with my gramma and grampa and went to work for a white man. She cleaned his house. I know how to clean a house and I work very hard."

"But it is not like the time when your mother worked for the white man. Today there is a depression. That means a time when no one has money to pay for work like your mother did. There aren't any jobs to find."

"I need help, Ahmeek, and I can work hard. I can clean house, I can wash clothes, I can cook the food. Any kind of Job is good. *Anishnabeg* come to me when they need help. I am a Medicine Woman. I have learned how to get medicine from the trees and flowers to make sick people well again. I can not help them with other troubles, but they come anyway, mostly the old people. They think I can make troubles go away by singing a song or saying some secret words to Gitchi Manitou. I can not help them, but when David Walking Boy wife and children come, I have to help. I have to be ready to take care of my own."

"But why will they come?" Jotham asked. "Will David Walking boy's wife not take care of your grandchildren?"

"For a time they will live with their mother and her family, but they do not have much. They are a big family. No one in the village has work now. The men go fishing. Before, they could sell the fish but now nobody has money to buy fish. That family has fish to eat and sometimes venison, nothing else. Some days they have food, sometimes they have none. Soon they will ask me to take the children. I am a medicine woman. I do not get money to be medicine woman. When they come, I will need a job."

"I can not find you a job, but I can help," Jotham said. "I would like you to come to Washburn, to my place."

"Here, you want me to come to your house?" Jotham could not tell if the tone of her voice was an expression of elation or alarm.

"Yes. I want you to come here, to my house. You could stay as long as you want to and when your grandchildren need a different place to live, you can bring them, too."

Mourning Dove turned her head away but continued to look at Jotham through narrowed eyes. Jotham, again, was not sure how to interpret her look. Did she not understand the offer he was making or was she expressing some sense of shame at having asked him for help. Her eyes widened and a sheepish smile came over her lips.

"Yes. I would come. It would not be like a real job, I know, but I could clean your house, could cook for you. And I would not have to worry are my grandchildren eating, do they have a place to sleep, do they have a sickness? Thank you, Ahmeek. I will come to your house."

It was settled. That evening he drove to the Indian Village at Red Cliff and brought Mourning Dove and her few possessions to his house in Washburn. He showed her to a spare bedroom, the same one Dominic and Lillian had stayed in. She helped him move some of his personal things to another room.

"This will be your own bedroom," he said. "You can fix it up anyway you want it, and you're free to go into any of the other rooms when you want to, the Kitchen, the Parlor, even the library."

She smiled at this. Jotham knew she could read very little, if any. He returned the smile.

"Where do you sleep," Mourning Dove asked.

"I sleep in the other bedroom, at the other end of the hall." Jotham answered. This time he thought he was having no trouble interpreting the expression on Mourning Dove's face.

As soon as Jotham reached his office the following morning, he called Bob Norton to find out what Ashland County had done with Johnny Bearheart's body.

"We're holding it at Big John's Funeral Parlor," Norton said. "We hold any corpse that is victim of a crime or accident until we find the next of kin. Same thing with suicides. If that fails they get a county burial, not very fancy but it's our policy. You don't happen to know any of Bearheart's close family, do you? We notified the people at Odanah that he had been living with, but they're cousins. We ought to do better than that."

"He has a sister, Bob. That's his only close relative. Mother and Father deceased."

"A sister's good," Norton said. "Do you know where I can get hold of her, where she lives."

"Right now she's here with me. I got her from Red Cliff right after you told me about Johnny." Jotham didn't bother to tell Norton that she had come to his office nor that she was now staying at his house. "I'll make arrangements to get the body. I'm sure she'll want to have him buried at Lac Vieux Desert," Jotham continued. "That's where he came from and where all his family are buried."

"That'll be great. Get hold of John Doakes as soon as you've made arrangements with the tribe. I'll approve transfer to you, but don't wait long. There's a limit to how long he'll be able to keep the body."

"Thank's Bob. I'll get on it right away."

It took more than a little coaxing to get permission from the Lac Vieux Desert Band elders for Johnny to rest in the tribal burial ground. It was not that Johnny had a white father. That had prevented him from replacing Eagle Feather as Chief of the band, but it would not prohibit his burial there. Johnny's behavior had brought question on his worthiness, especially the things he had said about his own family and the elders who had refused to accept him as their leader when Eagle Feather had died. Jotham repeated for them most of the things he had said in his campaign speech in Bayfield, but pointed out at the same time how Johnny's war record was an example of Chippewa values of bravery, honor and trust. He blamed Johnny's behavior on his drinking and blamed his drinking on the war. Jotham told them that, for Johnny, learning to drink so much was like being wounded in battle. Jotham knew that Johnny had started drinking several years before he was sent to France by the army, but he knew that the specifics, the first time Johnny had turned to alcohol would no longer be clear in the minds of the elders, and he could make his bravery more important.

After Jotham spoke to them, the elders sat in a circle for a long time. Then they called Mourning Dove to tell her what they had decided. Jotham observed, with some impatience, how unlike a jury their deliberations were. They talked a long time with Mourning Dove, each one explaining how they arrive at their decision. He was too far away to hear any of their conversation and he couldn't make anything out of Mourning Doves expressionless face or their infrequent gestures. Even if he had been close enough to hear, the Chippewa would have been unfamiliar. All he could do was wait. Finally, Mourning Dove returned. She told him the elders had agreed that Johnny Bearheart had been a hero in

Chippewa tradition and they would permit him to be buried by the side of Eagle Feather and his mother.

Chapter 18

Mourning Dove turned out to be as good a worker as she said she was. Jotham came home to a clean house every day and their conversation was pleasant, usually reminiscing about the days they shared as children so long ago and events in each of their lives that had never before been shared. She told him about the "bad times" encountered by the Lac Vieux Desert tribe after her grandfather died. When the government abandoned the reservations, Eagle Feather had kept the village together. Once Eagle Feather was gone the former Lac Vieux Band began to move away.

When they ran out of things to talk about, they listened to the radio. Mourning dove was fascinated and a little concerned that hearing voices and music coming out of a box was not natural, but she soon began to enjoy and to understand most of the programs.

They celebrated many of the holidays on the farm with Dominic and his family. On some occasions they brought Mourning Dove's grandchildren with them. Mourning Dove was amazed at the gifts for the children at Christmas time. She remembered her mother telling about Christmas in the home of the white senator, but seeing the celebration for herself was a totally different experience. They were still feeling the effects of the depression but Jotham made sure there were gifts for John and Jane Walking Boy, who were close to the same age as Dominic's children.

By summer Mourning dove was adjusting to life in the white community and many of the people in Washburn had begun to accept her. She was in charge of grocery shopping and, Jotham thought, did a better job than he could have himself. In the evening they listed to the news broadcast on radio. When the announcer said that Adolph Hitler had declared the provisions of the Treaty of Versailles, which prevented Germany from having an army, null and void, it started a conversation about Jotham's service in the war. He told her about the ship that had been hit by a German torpedo and his experience in the life boat, but said little about his service in Europe other than meeting with Johnny Bearheart in France. He praised her brother's service during the war, but said little more about Paris. He knew she would have no reference to help her understand urban life in such a big city. He decided there might be a way to correct that problem.

"Mourning Dove, have you ever seen a movie?"

"No," she answered. "Why would I ever see a movie? Some of the men in our village went to see a movie one time. Of course the women did not go. They said movies were not for women. Jimmy Little Wind told me about it, how the picture was so big and how it moved. I thought it was a lot of foolishness. Jimmy did not go again, but when I hear talk about other movies the men go to, I think, maybe I should have asked him to take me."

"Good! Would you like to see one?"

"Now? Do you mean now?" She said. We just have supper. Now Mourning Dove got to wash plates and clean stove. No movie now."

"I didn't mean tonight," Jotham said. "I thought tomorrow night or the next night. There's a new theater in Ashland . . ."

"Theater," she cut in, "I thought you said we go to movie."

"Yes, a movie. A theatre is a house where they show movies."

Mourning Dove was wide eyed and shook her head from side to side. "No," she said. "Adam Running Deer went to theater one time in Hurley. Not a movie he saw there."

Jotham stifled an embarrassing laugh. "That was not the same kind of theater," he said. "The theater in Ashland is a movie theater. They have a movie there this week that is supposed to be very good. It has Clark Gable in it. He is one of the best actors making movies. It's called *It Happened One Night*. Some people that I work with saw it and said it's really good."

"You sure not like Hurley."

"I promise you it will not be like the theatre in Hurley."

She looked at Jotham and waited a long time. Jotham knew she was trying to decide if he was telling her the truth. Finally she smiled and said. "Okay. Tomorrow we go to movie."

The next afternoon, when Jotham returned home from a mundane day in the District Attorney's office Mourning Dove was dressed and ready for the movies. Jotham had told her not to prepare supper. He planned that they would go to one of the restaurants in Ashland before the movie. He avoided the places that served alcohol. Johnny Bearheart drank whiskey and he knew that would bring back unhappy memories for her. The meal was acceptable, but the beef did not taste good to someone who had been brought up on venison and it was obvious to Jotham that she found potatoes a poor substitute for wild rice. She cooked potatoes for Jotham at home, of course, but a night out was supposed to be something special. She did not complain, but she was anxious to get the meal over with and go to the movie.

"It is so dark. How you see pictures?" Mourning Dove asked as they entered the theatre.

"They make the picture with light," Jotham said, not knowing quite how to explain for her, the process used to project a movie onto the screen. "You'll see in a few minutes."

When Mourning Dove's eyes adjusted to the limited light in the theatre, she looked at the crowd that had filled most of the seats. There were people of all ages, a few children, but most of them were young adult couples. Then she noticed that the men and women sat together, usually one of each side by side. The men did not sit together in one place, while the women were gathered some place else as they would have at a meeting on the reservation. A few of the women appeared to take more notice of her than people did in Washburn or Bayfield when they saw her on the street, but she supposed not too many Indian women went to the movies. Instead of feeling self conscious, she felt a sense of pride. She smiled to herself, *Mourning Dove, going to the movie just like the white women,* she thought.

When the theatre lights dimmed and the movie started, she glanced over at Jotham. She had dozens of questions, but they would wait until after the show. She settled back in her seat to watch, but when the Characters projected on the screen began to speak, her gasp was loud enough for people in several of the rows near them to hear. It was followed by a few giggles from some of the people in the seats nearby and Jotham's embarrassed whisper to quiet her and explain that moving pictures also talked. Mourning Dove slid down in her seat as though she could make herself smaller and less visible. Jotham reached over, took her hand, and gave her a reassuring smile. Later in the movie, Mourning Dove again glanced around the theater and was surprised to see that the men and the women appeared to be even closer together than when they had first taken their seats. Mourning Dove put her hand on Jotham's upper arm and leaned closer to him.

As they drove back to Washburn, Mourning Dove was full of questions. "What is Walls of Jericho?" she asked, and "why did Clark Gable have the little horn?" Jotham told her the Biblical story of Joshua and the walls of Jericho, but stopped short of trying to explain the significance of that scene in the picture. In the movie, director, Frank Capra, had a blanket serve as the wall that separated the area in the hotel room where Clark Gable slept and the area where Claudette Colbert slept. When Gable blew on the toy trumpet at the end of the movie, he pulled the blanket away leaving them both in one room. The walls came tumbling down.

"And the little horn . . ." Mourning Dove stopped and thought for a moment, then said, "I think we should have a little horn."

The following Saturday, Jotham decided to take Mourning Dove for a ride in the country. His election campaign, two years earlier, had taken him all over Bayfield County, but she had seen little of it beyond Red Cliff and Washburn. To show her how vast and remote much of the county was, and also because he had not been there in almost a year, he drove to Wilderness Lake and the lodge of Chauncey the Bear Hunter. Chauncey and his wife greeted them warmly. They were the first visitors for the summer of '34.

After introductions Mrs. Bottum took Mourning Dove to show her the lodge while Chauncey and Jotham found a place outside to talk.

The Beaver and the Bear

"Ahmeek, my friend," Chauncey began jokingly," are all those displaced mobsters from Chicago keeping the District Attorney's office busy?"

"You know how it is Bear Hunter. I keep getting complaints; I have to keep checking up on them."

"I hope you haven't received more of those complaints about the Bear Hunter," Chauncey said. "I was just joking. If a DA is getting real complaints, he's more likely working in Iron County, not Bayfield. Be thankful you don't have to deal with all of those good folks who have moved into Hurley."

"I was just joking, too, Chauncey and I'm glad I don't have to worry about those newer residents of Iron County or Ashland County either for that matter. Speaking of those good people from the Hurley area, I heard Ralph Capone is out of prison and moved up to his place in Mercer, that right?"

"Bottles? Yeah, he's back in town, probably spends quite a bit of time in Hurley, but he claims he's legit now. He did three years at Leavenworth. They got him on a tax evasion charge. Ness wanted to try that in court before he went after Al with the same gambit. They got Al just two years after Ralph's conviction."

"You call him Bottles? Is that one of your Wildernest Club names?"

"No, Ahmeek. He came with his own nickname," Chauncey answered. "Been called Bottles as long as I've know him. That started back in Chicago when he went into the bottling business. Would you believe it? Brother Al was running white lightening in from Canada and Ralphie bought into a place that bottled Coca Cola."

"It sounds like he really is a legitimate business man, Bear Hunter."

"I think he is now that he' served some time but it wasn't always the case. When they were younger, back when I lived in

Chicago, a reporter for the Cicero newspaper was writing some pretty nasty stuff about the Capone boys. It was all true but nasty. Al and Ralph caught the guy and beat him to a pulp."

"Well," Jotham quipped jokingly, "Boys will be boys I guess."

"Right, Ahmeek. Al even paid for the guy's hospital bills. Then he bought the newspaper the guy was working for. Needless to say he lost his job, everybody that worked there did. Capone didn't want to run a paper. He just wanted to put the people who ran that one out of business."

"Well, Bear Hunter, I don't think Ralph is a problem for us or for that matter the people in Iron County. Prohibition is over and Ness and his G-men have brought about a change in the whole mob scene. They'll always find something to get into, but it's not likely to ever be as big again as rum running was. "

"I hope you're right, Ahmeek. I like the North Country quiet and peaceful. You're coming up for election again in the fall, aren't you? Are you planning on another term?"

"I have to. It's my only excuse for coming out here once in a while. I don't own a company that manufacturers anything."

"Maybe you don't have a case of anything to give me," Chauncey said with a more serious tone, " but I could use your help."

"I don't know how I could help a man of your means, Mr. Bear Hunter, but I'm sure willing to try. What is it?"

" Well Ahmeek, we live way out here in the sticks and I know the people in town think another ten yards and we'd fall off the end of the earth, but we like it. I've been reading about a lot of cities across the country that provide transportation for school kids who live too far from a school to walk. My little girl is going on eleven years old now. She would be in the fifth grade this fall. She should be in a public school, but instead my wife has been her teacher. My wife does a good job but she shouldn't have to. I've asked the county to start transporting the kids in the Barns area but so far they're dragging their feet. You deal with those guys on the county board. Maybe you could get them to do something about it?"

"I can't promise anything," Jotham said. "That board is made up of the people I work for, but I'll try my best."

"Good, I'll be campaigning for you. Last time it was for you and Roosevelt. This time Roosevelt isn't up for re-election. That's too bad because I'll have to wait two more years to campaign against him."

"You've changed your mind about Roosevelt?" Ahmeek asked.

"He's not for my people, the Wildernest clientele. If he keeps going with his damn new deal, he'll have the country in debt for the next century and there won't be any businesses left to pay it all off."

Before Jotham could follow up on this line of discussion, Mourning Dove and Chauncey's wife came out of the lodge. He decided he would wait to talk politics again with Chauncey until the next visit. He opened the car door for Mourning Dove, went around to the other side and climbed in. A quick good bye to the Bottum's and they headed back to Washburn.

The following weekend, Mourning Dove and Jotham went to the farm to visit his brother. When Jotham told them he and Mourning Dove had gone to a movie, Gino and Maria were full of questions.

"Did the pictures really move, Uncle Jotham," Maria asked, "or were they like the pictures in a book?"

"The pictures moved," Jotham said, "They even talked."

"Talked," Maria giggled. "Pictures can't talk."

"The pictures in a theater can," Gino said, "if you were older and a boy, you'd know that."

"You don't know any more than I do, Gino," Maria shot back. "You've never been to a theater."

"I do to. I read about it in a magazine. You don't even know how to read magazines yet. You're just a baby."

"I am not." Maria answered through clenched teeth. "I can read as good as you can. Girls can read better than boys."

"Let's not start a fight," Lillian said. "You two go outside and play for a while so Uncle Jotham and your father can talk. "Supper will be ready in about a half hour, so don't run off too far." Lillian and Mourning Dove returned to the kitchen.

"How's the DA business going, Jotham? Dominic asked. "I hear a lot of crooks from Chicago have been movin to Northern Wisconsin. Do you people in the court house ever run into any of them."

"I've run into a few that moved up from Chicago, but they're not part of the gangs. In fact the few I've met turned out to be pretty nice people. I think all the bad ones moved to Hurley. They're a problem for Dan Vigonallo, not me."

"Yeah, Hurley has a lot of people tied to the Chicago mob from what I've heard," Dominic said. "He's going to have a lot of trouble trying to check up on them."

"Not only Hurley, Dominic, a few other places in Northern Wisconsin, too There could be one or two in Bayfield County, but I havn't heard about it. Capone had a hide out down near Hayward for years, and you heard about Dillinger, didn't you? He escaped from federal officers someplace south of Mercer and they've asked law officers in most of Northern Wisconsin to be on the look out for him. Mike Flannigan got a notice last week."

"I read about that in the paper a while ago. Did you see the story about him today?"

"No, was there something else? Has he been caught?"

"Not caught, killed," Dominic said as he got up and retrieved the newspaper from the table. "Here's the story. I'll read it to you. 'Bank Robber John Dillinger, who escaped from federal officers at a restaurant south of Mercer, Wisconsin last month was shot and killed by police outside the Biograph Theater in Chicago. Dillinger had evaded a hail of gunfire and crossed the lake in a row boat, leaving law officers throughout Iron, Ashland and Bayfield Counties on alert for weeks. He returned to Chicago via Minneapolis, before police received a tip that he would be at the theater.' There's more, but that's the main part."

"Interesting year in Wisconsin," Jotham said. "When Al Capone went to jail and just a couple of years later, prohibition ended. I thought maybe things would be a little quieter in Hurley.

"I don't remember Hurley ever being quiet," Dominic said. "I remember the stories Frank and Stanley and some of the other loggers used to tell about Hurley back when we were kids."

"They never told me any of those stories," Jotham said jokingly.

"You were too young, but don't kid me. You got to hear the same stuff I did."

"It's time for you boys to quit reminiscing about Hurley." Lillian said as she entered the room. Why don't you call the children, Dominic? Supper's ready."

Conversation at the table took on a more serious tone. Jotham asked about the logging business. His brother said it was improving, but things were still slow. He apologized for having missed some of the payments on the farm. Jotham said not to worry about it. He knew it would take time for pulp wood sales to pick up again and he had no trouble waiting.

When supper was over and the women returned to the kitchen, Dominic asked about Mourning Dove. Jotham admitted that, while he took Mourning Dove in to help her after Jimmy Little Wind drowned, having her in the house was also consolation for his failure to cope with his failed relationship with Rebecca Morgan. It had been fifteen years since Rebecca had married someone else, but he had he never quite adjusted to her not being a part of his life.

"Mourning Dove's grandchildren spend a lot of time with us now," he said. "Her mother, David Walking Boy's wife has very little to take care of them. I'm beginning to love those children as if they were my own."

"Have you thought of you and Mourning Dove getting married," Dominic asked?

"To tell you the truth I have, Dominic. I've thought of it a lot more as time goes on, but there are a lot of things to consider."

"Keep thinkin' Jotham," Dominic said. "Keep thinkin'".

Chapter 19

"I wanted to talk to you about something" Jotham.

"Yes, what is it Gertrude?"

"Well, the election is coming up and like I said, I hear things in the café sometimes."

"And what did you hear this time?"

"It's a little hard to talk about, Mr Marichetti, It's your housekeeper."

"Mourning Dove? What could they be saying about Mourning Dove."

"Well, for one thing, she's an Indian. You already know Mickleson plans to use that against you. For another, he's planning to charge you with living together out of wedlock."

"He can't charge me with anything. Having a housekeeper, male or female is not a crime. It sounds like Roscoe is getting an early start. The election is almost three months away. "

"I didn't mean charge you like in court. I heard someone say he was going to make it a campaign issue."

"I've thought about that but I've also been thinking about something else relating to Mourning Dove that has little to do with the election, though it might take that issue away from him."

"You have?"

"Maybe," Jotham said. "You know Mourning Dove and I were friends when we were children, don't you."

"Yes. She told me about playing with you and her brother and how her Grandfather, who was Chief of the tribe, liked you," Gertrude said. "What kind of solution are you talking about?"

"Gertrude, would you be willing to act as witness for a small, private wedding."

"Oh, yes!" Gertrude said with a happy tone, "but wouldn't that make things even worse, I mean in terms of the election."

"I'm sure it could cost me some votes, but congress passed a law a few years ago now, that gives Indians all the rights of citizenship the white people have. I don't think he can make a big enough election issue to outdo the votes of the entire village at Red Cliff."

"Are you sure you're not thinking about marrying Mourning Dove because it might improve your chances for re-election?"

"Of course not Gertrude; Mourning Dove and I became very close friends when we were young. When she turned fourteen, she was expected that she marry one of the Indian boys in the tribe. In those days that was the Indian custom. Chief Eagle Feather told me she could no longer play with me and her Brother. Soon after that, she was married to Jimmy Little Wind. You know Jimmy Little Wind and his son both died in a boating accident on Chequamegon Bay. I asked her to live in Washburn as my housekeeper. I thought I did that because with her husband dead she had no means of support, but as time went on, I realized that it was because I was still very fond of her. Now, it's more than fondness. I really do love her and her grandchildren."

"Are you sure of that?'

"Yes I am Gertrude, very sure"

"Well, in that case I would be happy to witness such a union, Jotham. You can count on it."

Jotham's work was routine for the rest of the morning. He planned a trip to the florist on his way home. He wanted to get a large display of roses for Mourning Dove. He realized that he had asked Gertrude to witness the wedding, but had yet to ask Mourning Dove if she would marry him. It was the first time he had considered any possibility that she might say no. He kept asking himself questions but the answers came in ridiculous images. Should he kneel? He imagined himself kneeling in front of Mourning Dove and it became a picture of an Indian woman laughing hysterically. *I don't think Indians kneel,* he said to himself.

Morning Dove could not believe what she heard. Jotham wanted to get married. At first she thought it was some kind of joke and almost started to laugh, but Jotham looked dead serious. If she had laughed he might have changed his mind and she would not fulfill the dream she had nurtured since childhood. She had told her grandfather, Chief Eagle Feather, then, but he said it could not be. She must marry an Indian, someone like Jimmy Little Wind. That was almost forty years ago. Eagle Feather was no longer alive, nor was Jimmy Little Wind. She had grown children and, even grandchildren. No, they were both old now, no longer little children playing together in the woodland of their childhood. But deep down inside, she knew it was what she wanted. She turned toward Jotham and, sounding almost like that little Indian girl a long time ago, giggled, "Yes, Ahmeek. I think a good idea. We get married, yes."

The wedding was quiet, a few people in the court house, Dominic and his family and, of course, Gertrude, whose attitude toward the new District Attorney had changed dramatically since the first time Mourning Dove came into their office. From that time forward, Mourning Dove had become a cause célèbre for her which made Jotham, at least for a time, the hero.

The county judge conducted the ceremony at Jotham's house. It was over in a matter of minutes, but the party that followed lasted well into the night. There was no chivaree, but the pots and tin pans that accompanied wild songs after a lumberjack wedding were no match for the drums and dancing provided by members of the Red Cliff band of the Chippewa.

Jotham won the election for District Attorney in 1934 but it was by a much smaller margin than his first victory two years earlier. Being married to Mourning Dove was just as bad in the minds of some people as having her in his home as a live-in housekeeper. Either way his opponent was able to make it an issue that would resonate with the prejudice of many voters. The Red Cliff people were solidly in his corner, but unfortunately for Jotham, most of them had no inclination to vote. Some Indians were intimidated by prejudice, others by process. The written ballot, which many could not read, was confusing and choosing between two candidates who were both white failed to stir their interest enough for them to take the trouble to vote.

During the months that followed, Jotham was not sure running for a second term was such a good idea. He was well paid and a highly respected citizen of Bayfield County but he wondered if he could have selected a more boring profession. There were a lot of new laws the city passed to handle the traffic problems. Washburn established a speed limit of twenty five miles per hour and posted streets to designate parking zones as well as areas where parking an automobile would not be allowed. As a result, Jotham found his mornings filled with court appearances on minor traffic violations added to the regular list of charges arising from the growing number of drinking establishments. Such duties kept him busy, but did little to make the job more interesting. The good news was that with the depression moderating, there was less petty theft and fewer foreclosures for him to deal with. In the afternoons he usually found time to read the daily newspapers from Ashland and Superior that the Postman delivered in mid afternoon.

Though Jotham's work suffered from a lack of excitement, the first year of his second term was an exciting time for the world in general. In spite of Chauncey's misgivings he had to admit that the country was changing quickly under the administration of Franklyn Delano Roosevelt. Boulder Dam was completed on the Colorado River in May. Later, Roosevelt got congress to pass a law creating the National Labor Relations Administration. The President was not successful with all his initiatives, however. That same year, the Supreme Court declared his National Recovery Act unconstitutional. The Bear Hunter would be pleased with that item.

The news papers were also filled with interesting articles about things happening in other parts of the country. One especially intriguing to Jotham was the story about a new electrical invention called a lie detector which found its first use in a courthouse in Portage, Wisconsin. He thought one would be handy in the Wasburn court, but he knew they could not force anyone to subject themselves to it.

By mid-April, the dust bowl hit the Midwest and even as far north as Iron River and Washburn, lakes began to shrink and temperatures rose. No rain fell for weeks at a time.

News on the international scene was even more disturbing, especially for those who had served in the World War. Adolph Hitler was rearming Germany. In February of that year he had started to develop the Luftwaffe and by March, Herman Goering announced creation of a new German Air Force.

The same innovation that brought so much distressing news to people provided almost continuous entertainment that made the year pass quickly. Radio stations were blossoming like spring flowers and with the development of network broadcasting the airways were filled with programs that had audiences all across the country glued to their seats. Dominic particularly liked one of the new nationally broadcast programs. It was a program that featured the most popular songs of each week called *Your Hit Parade,* It made its debut on March twentieth. It was soon followed by Major Bowes and the Original Amateur Hour, The Bob Hope show and soon to become Mourning Dove's favorite, Fibber McGee and Molly. The networks were constantly introducing new programs and it seemed that there were more things to fill the time than there was time to be filled. The summer passed quickly.

When Christmas came, Jotham knew just the present for Dominic's two children. He made sure he did his shopping early to get the new board game that was sweeping the country. It was called *Monopoly* and its inventor, Charles Darrow, was soon to go from unemployed laborer to millionaire when Parker Brothers had agreed to buy the copyrights from him.

The summer of '36 was the hottest on record with temperatures in cities across the Upper Midwest hovering well above 100 degrees for most of July and August. On the fifth of July the thermometer read a state record 120 degrees in Gann Valley, South Dakota. It's neighbor to the north, Steele, North Dakota, had a reading that same day of and 121 degrees. Moorhead, Minnesota could only manage a meager 114.

When August approached, the temperatures had subsided only slightly, but even if there were no relief from the heat, Jotham would soon get relief from his daily boredom.

Chapter 20

"Jotham." The voice on the phone was that of Bayfield County Sheriff, Mike Flannigan. He sounded agitated. "We've got a problem."

"What kind of problem, Mike?"

"Hit and run with a car. It's an old Indian, over here in Iron River. A farmer found him lying on the side of highway number 2 this morning, just east of town."

"Are you sure he was hit by a car?"

"Not only that he was hit by a car, I'm pretty sure it was a fairly new one, 1932 or later," Flannigan said. "My guess it was a big Packard."

"How do you know all that?" Jotham asked.

"Part of a radiator cap imbedded in his hip," the sheriff answered. "It's shaped like a bird wing. That, along with the size of the tire tracks tell me it was no Model A. It was something a lot bigger, probably a Packard. I saw a picture of one in a magazine with a bird shaped radiator cap."

"Good work, Mike. Don't let anyone touch the body. I'll pick up the coroner and be right over there."

They rode in the county coroner's 1931 Graham that he had modified to transport a body. It was a large vehicle that he also used as an ambulance, quite handy at the time since most serious injuries required a vehicle of that size for the victim to have any chance of reaching one of the distant hospitals or even a well equipped Doctor's Office alive.

As soon as they arrived at the scene, Jotham asked Mike to show him where the car was when it struck the man. They looked at the tracks again. Jotham could not tell if Mike was right about it being a Packard, but he agreed it had to be a big vehicle. The body was lying in the ditch perhaps twelve feet beyond the point where the tracks veered suddenly to the left. The coroner joined them next to the body. He examined the piece of metal in the man's hip.

"That's a mean looking wound with a substantial loss of blood," the coroner said, "but not enough to cause his death." He moved to the deceased's head and lifted it. "This is the cause of death, a fractured skull. The car must have thrown him up into the air to result in a head wound like that. It probably happened when his he hit the pavement. Odd though, Macadam usually isn't solid enough to cause that kind of an injury. Of course he could have slammed his head on some part of the car as he went over it. Hard to tell without the car here to see what part of it was damaged."

While, Flannigan and the coroner filled out their reports, Jotham talked to the local residents. The sheriff also and made some sketches of the area and took pictures with the new box camera the county had provided, but he knew the detail would not be sufficiently helpful without the sketches. The Indian's name was Joseph Night Bird. He lived alone in a tar paper shack on

Jackman Lake, a few miles north of Iron River and worked for local residents for a day now and then when they needed help. When there was no work, which had been the case for most of the past three years of depression, he hunted, fished and gathered the wild nuts and berries. He was not known to drink and was liked by most of the town folks. They said it was not unlike him to be out on the road at night. When Jotham asked why, they said it was just his nature. The Indian had said he like the night time. That was how he got his name. Some of the locals had taken to calling him Joe Owl.

When they were through at the scene, Jotham had the coroner go back to Washburn alone. If the sheriff was right and Night Bird was hit by a big car, Jotham knew where a lot of the people with big cars hung out.

They parked the sheriff's car at the driveway leading in to Wildernest Lodge and walked from there. There was nothing written on the car that would label it as a patrol car, but Jotham was sure Chauncey would know. Most people might not notice the siren, mounted on the outside just in front of the door but the Bear Hunter was not most people. Not that Chauncey would have any objection to such a visit by Jotham and Mike Flannigan, but he might be concerned for the sensibilities of the Wildernes clientele.

There was no Packard parked in the wooded area of Wildernest Lodge. In fact there were no cars parked there at all. Chauncey had not provided a parking lot and those who came with automobiles had to pick their own spot where the trees were not too close together. Most guests arrived by train. Of course, Chauncey was a very accommodating host and drove his own car to Iron River to meet them. There was no Packard. In fact, when they got to the lodge, there was no Chauncey. After a brief look around the premises, Jotham and Mike Flannigan started to walk back to their car. About half way they were met by Chauncey driving a new Graham Page.

"Ahmeek," Chauncey called out as he stepped from the running Board, "I saw the car out by the entrance and thought I was in trouble," His always wining smile said it was intended as a joke. "When did you start driving a police car?"

"I haven't," Jotham answered. Let me introduce the driver. This is Mike Flannigan, Bayfield County Sheriff."

"County Sheriff? Chauncey asked with his smile slightly abated. Don't tell me you came with a warrant for the old Bear Hunter." He sounded tentatively serious.

"No trouble, unless you've got a Packard tucked away someplace around here," Flannigan answered with a broad smile. "So at last I get to meet the great Bear Hunter I've heard so much about. By the way, how did you know that was a patrol car?"

"Written all over the thing," Chauncey said, "siren on the left side, spot light on the right, what's this about a Packard?"

"Somebody driving a Packard hit the Old Indian, Joseph Night Bird last night," Jotham explained.'

"Night Bird?" That's terrible. He was really a nice fellow. He came out here a few times when I was first building, to help me with the heavy work. Of course he was younger then."

"Any of your guests drive a Packard?"

"Not that I know of. Most of them leave their cars in the city and come by train. The few that do drive, tuck their cars someplace in the woods out of sight. I don't often get a look at any of the cars."

"I thought maybe you'd know," Jotham said. "Not too many cars like that among the local people of Bayfield County ."

"I can tell you this, Ahmeek. If they came to the lodge in their own car, especially a Packard, they probably are local people, that is, if you consider the Hurley area local. A few folks from Hurley drive over sometimes. Almost everybody else comes by train. I have to pick them up in Iron River."

"I was surprised to see the place empty this time of year. All your guests leave?"

"Yep, all back in the cities," Chauncey said, "but most of them will be back. They'll be coming for the big party in September."

"A big party," Jotham said. "I thought every weekend in the summer was a big party at Wildernest."

"Let's just call it a gala event. This one is special," Chauncey answered with a smile. "You haven't been around for a long time, Ahmeek "We expect to have a new daughter to introduce to the club. Most of the biggies will be coming. Can you believe it? My first girl has already celebrated her thirteenth birthday. She's a teenager. My second daughter is in school already and after all this time, here comes number three, their little sister. I feel like Father Abraham. I got a great name for her, too, Ahmeek. Not the first name but the middle name. Landon, She'll be Nancy Landon bottom."

"Landon? I've never heard that used for a Girl's name."

"If it had been a boy, I would have used it for the first name, but this is the year for Landon. He's the one that's going to whip Roosevelt in November and become President. I want my little girl to carry the name, Landon. Maybe I should go all the way and name her Nancy Alfred Landon Bottom."

"Maybe she'll bring him luck," Jotham said.

"I sure hope so. You're welcome to come to the party, Ahmeek, you and Mourning Dove. I'm calling it a coming out party, either a sixteen years early or a few weeks late. Depends on how you look at it. Actually it's a pre-election party, but I thought she'd be a good addition. As a county official, you get in free, you, too, Sheriff Flannigan, if you want. The little girl is due to arrive early in September so we plan the celebration for the fifteenth. We might have to change that if she's late, but she should definitely be here by the election."

It became obvious that Chauncey and the Wildernest could provide no clue about who hit Joe Night Bird. Mike and Jotham bid the Bear Hunter good bye and returned to Washburn.

August brought little relief from the heat wave that had swept across the country in July. Washburn was unbearably hot and when the weekend came, Jotham and Mourning Dove looked for the slightly cooler temperatures in the country. When they arrived at Dominic's farm they found him and the children, not out in the yard where a light breeze cooled the air somewhat, but sitting in the warm living room listening to the radio. Dominic was dependent on the radio like his father had been on the daily paper. He rarely missed a news cast.

"Dominic, what are you doing here in the heat?" Jotham asked as he entered. Mourning Dove had stayed outside with Lillian.

"It's the noon news," Dominic answered. "There giving a report on the Olympics. They come in by telegraph from Berlin so the radio stations will have them for their next news program. Of course, it really all happened early this morning but because of the time difference the stations broadcast it later over here. Get this; Hitler wanted to have the Olympics in Germany 'cause he wanted to show the world the superiority of the Aryan Race and Jesse Owens just won his fourth Gold Medal. He's beat the Germans in every event he's entered." He turned the radio off. "Gino, Maria, why don't you go outside with your mother? I've got something I want to talk to Uncle Jotham about. Tell your mom we'll be out in a little while."

As soon as the children were out the door, Dominic changed the subject to more serious matters. He had heard about the old

Indian who had been struck by the car and was anxious to hear what Jotham knew and what his involvement was as District Attorney.

"Do they know who the driver of the car was?" Dominic asked.

"Not yet," Jotham answered. "He was hit by a Packard and that car isn't too common in Bayfield County. We checked with Madison for any car licenses for a Packard whose owners might live in the area and came up with only a few. One was a doctor in Ashland. There were a couple in Superior and two or three more in Hurley. I had law enforcement people in Ashland and Douglas county check on the owners. They found nothing but outstanding citizens driving undamaged Packard cars. Dan Vigonallo has a bigger job checking in Iron County because over there Packard drivers are harder to locate. A lot of people there have addresses on their registration that are in Iron County but, most of the time, they live someplace else.

"I hope you get whoever it was," Dominic said. A lot of people around here don't know the Indians like you and me and the other guys that worked with them in the old logging camps."

Jotham agreed with his brother though he remembered the time when Dominic couldn't understand why he wanted to spend so much time in the woods with Eagle Feather and his grandchildren.

The next morning, Jotham looked out the window of his office in the Bayfield County Courthouse. It was a bright, sunny, summer day' the kind of a day that caused him to envy his brother Dominic. Dominic spent his working days either cruising timber or overseeing the men who were harvesting it. It was his life, always had been, and he loved it. Jotham had always wanted to be a lawyer and especially liked his job as prosecutor, but on this day he would rather be with his brother Dominic looking for good timber stands or riding in the patrol car with Mike Flannigan, not stuck in an office. Some place in Northern Wisconsin there was a person who had driven the car that struck old Joseph Night Bird, then driven off without even stopping see if the old Indian was alive.

The driver of that car was still unknown and more than anything, on this beautiful summer day, Jotham would like to be out searching for that car.

He kept telling himself that it was people like Mike Flannigan, Emile Johanson and Dan Vigonallo whose job it was to apprehend the driver. His job was to make a case and prosecute whoever it was after they had finished with the investigation and arrest. That was fine when it was merely abstract theory, but that was a real person lying alongside Highway 2 in Iron River. It was also an Indian and he had heard about residents of the county suggesting that Flannigan need not work too hard on the case. Joe Night Bird was, after all, only an Indian. Not for this prosecutor. Joe Night Bird was a man, and according to those who knew him as a man, a pretty good one at that. Just as he was beginning to feel anger toward the people who would take the death of Joe Night Bird so lightly, the telephone rang.

"Hello. Jotham Marichetti here."

"Marichetti, this is Vigonallo. You busy?"

"I should be, Dan, but I'm stuck in my office."

"Well, how about getting your butt out of the office and making the drive to Hurley. I've got something to show you."

"Okay Dan. It'll take me close to an hour. What is it?"

"A bright yellow Packard sitting in a repair shop to get a new head lamp."

"Does it look damaged from an accident?"

"It sure does. Good sized dent in the fender. I want you to come over and have a look."

Jotham told Gertrude he would be out of the office for the rest of the day. She made no sign that she approved, but he left the office without her blessing. He drove slowly through Ashland, then pushed his Hudson Special Coupe to over a mile a minute past Odanah to Birch Hill. He had traded his Studebaker for the Hudson two years earlier and was especially satisfied with its speed and hill climbing ability. A series of curves and hills between Birch Hill and Kimball required slower driving, but he was able to pull into Dan's office in Hurley in a little less than the hour he had promised.

Dan drove his patrol car to a repair shop in the south end of Hurley. He and Jotham got out of the patrol car and walked inside. An auto body mechanic was skillfully hammering the dents out of the left front fender of a yellow Packard. Jotham and Dan watched as he placed a rounded brass die on the inside of the fender with his left hand, then tapped lightly on the face of the fender near the edge of the dent with his right. The tap hammer was made of a slightly softer brass to avoid putting dimples in the metal. The hammer sounded like a toy machine gun as the workman rapidly coaxed the dent out of the metal. Dan and Jotham waited until he stopped for a rest before disturbing him. Dan had warned Jotham that body work required concentration and they should not be interrupting the man, if they hoped to get any help from him. While they waited, Jotham glanced at the radiator cap. It held an image of a bird. Jotham thought it might be standard ornamentation for a Packard of that size. Both wings were intact.

"Whose car, Toivo?" Dan asked as Toivo Kempala lifted himself beside the vehicle and inspected his work

The Beaver and the Bear

"Whose car! How do I know whose car? Maybe, Sheriff, you think I'm the dry cleaners. I fix car, I take name and if they don't come get it in thirty days, I keep it. No, it don't work that way in body shop. Somebody bring a car like this and say 'fix', I fix. They come back, you bet. Nobody leaves a car like this for old Toivo."

"Toivo," Dan yelled with a hint of anger in his voice. "You got a name for the people who left this car for you to fix or not?"

"Sure, Sheriff," Toivo said with a hearty laugh. "I think so. Let's look, Ya." He walked over to a small writing table where several papers were spindled. "Sure, here it is, a Mister Samuel Rodello. He's listed as the owner, but another guy brought it in. I don't have his name."

"You got an address for this Rodello?"

"No. Like I said, he'll be back. I don't need address. If he doesn't pay, I hold car."

"When did he bring the car in?"

"Couple of days. I don't know. He said he hit a deer over the other side of Ashland."

"Any marks on the car that looked like it hit a deer," Dan asked, "You know, hair, blood, scratches like a horn hit it."

"No, he said it was doe. Car looked like it was just washed before he brought it in."

"That radiator cap," Jotham asked, "did you have to put that on?"

"Nope, It was there when he brought the car in."

They looked inside of the car for anything that might tie it to the hit and run, but found nothing. Jotham wrote the license number in his note pad. It was an Illinois license but there was nothing suspicious. Dan thanked Toivo for his help and they returned to the sheriff's office.

"Toivo wasn't much help, was he?" Dan observed.

"Afraid not. I don't think that was the car we're looking for anyway," Jotham answered. "The car that hit Joe Night Bird had a radiator ornament like a flying bird. One of its wings ended up in Night Bird's leg. That car had no damage to the radiator cap and it was a little different than the one on the car that hit the Indian. The wing didn't look quite the same as the one the coroner gave us for evidence. It didn't really look like a bird. To me, it looked like a female form with long flowing hair." Could Mike have mistaken a piece of that hair for a bird wing? When I get back to the office I'll take another look. Something isn't quite right. I am also a little curious about the guy saying he hit the deer someplace west of Ashland. How far west of Ashland? If it was close to Iron River I might still find it interesting."

Back at the Bayfield County Court House, Jotham went to the evidence locker and looked at the piece of radiator ornament that mike had taken out of Night Bird's leg. That wasn't hair. He could clearly see the texture of the feathers. He put the wing back in the box, then checked with Gertrude who had no pressing legal work for him to deal with. He told her he would be out of the office for much of the afternoon.

"Are you finding out anything about who ran into the old Indian over by Iron River?" she asked with a knowing smile. "I know that's what's keeping you out of the office."

"Yes it is," Jotham said, surprised at tone of Gertrude's voice. It was neither accusatory nor officious. She sounded like she actually wanted to strike up a conversation. "I spent the morning with the Iron County Sheriff, looking at a damaged car that he thought might have been the one that hit old Night Bird."

"Was it?"

"Probably not. The owner told the repair man that he hit a deer, but I'd like to know a little more about that and about him. The car had Illinois license plates."

"Most of the cars here have Illinois license plates. People who live regularly here can't afford a car, and even if they could, a horse and sleigh works better in the snow."

"That's true," Jotham agreed, "especially if they live in the country, which most of them do. Tracing the license number won't do much good anyway. We would still have to prove it was the same car and nobody was at the scene to see it. I keep hoping for some loose talk."

"Plenty of that around," Gertrude said. "I heard some people in the café talking about it. Some were wondering why we're looking for anybody. Just an old Indian, they said. Why does the DA's Office waste the time?"

"That kind of talk is what makes me want to take the time," Jotham said. "I think it's possible that comments like that in a tavern will get somebody else to take credit for killing Night Bird, or for knowing the person who did. There are more confessions made in taverns than in courtrooms."

"That's probably where you'd here it, but you'd have to be there. There are too many people who don't care enough about the death of an Indian to report something otherwise. What I heard in the café might have just been your opponent starting to work on the election that's coming up again."

"Might be," Jotham agreed as he turned toward the door. "I'm going to stop across the hall and ask the people in the highway department to check on the that plate number, then go to the Sheriff's office and ask Mike to go up to Bayfield and see the game warden. I'd like to know if any of them saw a dead deer on the road to Iron River."

"Jotham," Gertrude called as he opened the door. "Good luck. I hope you find him. Protecting Indians is part of our job, too."

Jotham thought about going back to the Wildernest Lodge, but decided against it. It would be a place where people who could afford a Packard might congregate and talk freely, but it would not be in the nature of the Bear Hunter to report any such talk. Those people valued anonymity. They came to Wildernest Lodge specifically to have private conversations. Jotham thought it better to regard Chauncey as he would another lawyer or perhaps a priest. Chauncey did not want to be a part of any criminal activity, but if something *extra legal* was going on around him, he just wouldn't let himself know about it even if he had heard it. Chauncey's, however, was not the only place where people had a few drinks and talked too much. Prohibition was over. Taverns had sprouted up all over the area and Gertrude was right. That's where people would engage in loose talk. He left a note in the Sheriffs Office for Mike Flannagan to come see him as soon as he returned from Bayfield,

It was late afternoon before Flannigan got back. Jotham and the sheriff exchanged reports on their afternoon activities. No one in the County Highway Department had reported seeing a dead deer between Ashland and Iron River on highway 2 and no sign that there had been one. The game warden told Mike Flannagan he had no report of a deer kill on the date in question either. They considered driving to Ashland, but decided it would make no sense. Even if there had been a deer killed on that stretch of the road, wolves, or possibly people, would likely have taken it. These were lean times in Northern Wisconsin and a fresh deer kill was a prime source of food for both species no matter what killed it.

"Mike," Jotham said, "I think we need to spend more time in taverns."

"What? Are you crazy? You've got an election coming up this fall."

"I'm well aware of that, but I believe sooner or later somebody in one of those establishments will say something. Not necessarily the guy who drove the Packard but somebody that knows a lot more about it than we do."

"But they're going to be quiet as mice if we show up. Everybody knows you're the District Attorney and I wear a star. All that loose talk will tighten up real fast when we walk in. Besides, I like to spend the nights with my wife and kids. I get called to those taverns too much as it is when a fight breaks out or something."

"We won't go to listen to the patrons talk," Jotham said. "We'll go in the morning, about nine o'clock and talk to the tavern keeper. Those fellows like us Mike."

"Sure they do," the sheriff chuckled.

"Okay, actually the hate us, but they want us to like them. It's really important for them to have us on their side. If they've heard something, I have a feeling they might tell us."

"Okay, when do we start?"

"Nine o'clock tomorrow morning. By then all the tavern owners should be in. I figure three or four days will take us to all the taverns in Bayfield County. I'll call Dan and Emile and see if they can cover Iron and Ashland counties for us."

"You know Jotham," Mike said. "This just might work, but whatever you do, don't take a drink. You're the DA, and you're going to find a lot of people will want to buy you one. If that gets started it will take four months instead of four weeks."

"I don't intend to let that happen." Jotham laughed. "But it should work. It was Gertrude's Idea."

Chapter 21

The door to the carriage house flew open. The burley man sleeping on the cot woke with a startled jerk. His right hand slid quickly under his pillow.

"Leave it where it is," the gruff voice barked. "It's just me. We need to talk."

"Sure boss, I didn't know it was you." The man was short but muscular with broad shoulders and a bald head. He instinctively took his chauffer's cap from the bed post beside him and slapped it on his head as if he felt naked and out of uniform.

"You're makin' trouble for me Frank. I told you to keep your mouth shut."

"I've kept quiet. I haven't told a soul what happened. You and me, we're the only ones that knows anything. I swear to ya."

"Frank, use your head. You threatened a DA. That's not smart Frankie."

"I didn't threaten no DA. I haven't talked to no DA. Honest boss."

"But you talked to a bar keeper down at the Silver Dollar. You told him to tell that DA that if he wanted to stay healthy to quit nosing around where he don't belong. You don't do that to a DA Frankie."

"This ain't Chicago, Boss. Some little hick town DA has been goin' to all the saloons and taverns askin' what they heard. So I tell them to let him know he's getting' in over his head. He's not going up against you."

"So what happens if they tell him?" Then, he starts asking about you and ya know what? They fold. So Mister DA wants to know who you work for. If they know you work for me, then what?"

"Then you got trouble?"

"No Frankie. Then you got trouble. They finger me, I give them you. If the barkeeps don't finger me, the DA will take you in and ask a lot of questions, then what?"

"Then I deny everything, right?"

"Wrong. You confess to everything, Frankie. Look at it this way. You can blame me, but if you do you're a dead man, or you can confess and only have to do a little jail time."

"But you was driving, boss. You was drinkin' and said you wanted to drive."

"Really, I must have had a lot to drink that night. I thought you were driving. Either way, Frankie, you take the rap, unless you can come up with something else."

It had been days since Mike and Jotham visited the bar owners in the county. If any of them had heard about the death of Joe Night Bird, none of them would admit it. As he walked to his office, Jotham tried to think of some other way in which they might get a lead on the case. If tavern keepers could provide no information, who else might have heard something? At this point he had to admit he was out of ideas.

Gertrude stood up the minute Jotham came into the office. It surprised him. It was something she had never before done and he knew she had bad news.

"Mr.Marichetti, I have to talk to you right away.?"

"Come into the office and sit down, Gertrude, What is it?"

"I got a call this morning that was very upsetting. I don't know who it was or even where it came from, but it was a warning. He said he was one of the people the sheriff talked to about the Old Indian. He said one of his patrons told him that if you wanted to stay healthy you should quit asking questions. Then he hung up. Mr. Marichetti, what's happening?"

"It's all right, Gertrude," Jotham said soothingly. "Mike Flannigan and the sheriffs of Ashland and Iron Counties have been asking tavern owners if they've heard anything about who ran into Joe Night Hawk. Apparently the questions got under somebody's skin. They're making idle threats. That's all."

"Are you sure they're just idle threats?"

"No, but phone calls like that usually are."

"Why were you contacting tavern owners?"

"You gave me the idea, Gertrude. You said none of the patrons would talk to Mike or me, so, I decided to go out in the morning when the taverns fist opened and talk to the people that might pass along what the patrons were saying, the owners. Actually this is good news. It could be the first break in the case. If they're making threats, they can also make mistakes."

"It's all kind of scary."

"Don't worry. When I've gone out to the taverns Mike has gone with me."

The Beaver and the Bear

Jotham tried to get his mind onto something else. He picked up the notes he had scribbled when he and Mike visited the Tavern owners, nothing provided a clue. He looked at the page of notes he had jotted down when he went to the repair shop with Dan. Something wasn't quite right, but he didn't know what it was. The car was freshly washed. Why would someone wash a car just before taking it to a shop for body work? And that hood ornament, it just didn't look right.

Jotham wondered which of the tavern owners made the call Gertrude told him about. Was it a friendly warning from one of the places they visited or was he just passing on a threat? If it was the latter, he thought he could probably narrow it down to one of the Hurley establishments, and if that was the case, it was something to worry about. But Dan made the calls in Hurley. How would that lead to a threat on the DA of Bayfield County? Jotham was so deep in thought and concern for his safety that he actually recoiled when the office door opened.

"Somebody to see you, Mr. Marichetti," Gertrude announced, looking a little bit too concerned. "He calls himself the Bear Hunter."

"It's Chauncey, Chauncey the Bear Hunter. Send him in."

Chauncey entered the office and took a seat across from Jotham.

"I was in the neighborhood and thought I'd stop to see my old friend, Ahmeek."

"You're always welcome, Mr. Bear Hunter, but you never really stop just to see an old friend, do you? What can I do for you?"

"No Ahmeek, I'll admit I usually have something on my mind when I visit somebody, but this time it's not what you can do for me. Maybe it's what I can do for you. I heard you and the sheriff have been out asking some of the businessmen in our county if they've heard anything about the car that hit Indian Joe."

"Yeah, but we didn't find anything," Jotham said. "We did shake somebody up, though. A call came in this morning suggesting we stop asking for the sake of my health, but I'm not taking it seriously."

"Take it seriously, my friend. Take it very seriously," Chauncey warned. "A call like that doesn't come from some farmer down the road. Did you visit any of the night spots over in Hurley?"

"Dan Vigonallo, the Iron County Sheriff, canvassed the places over there for me, but I wasn't with him, so I don't think the call came from Hurley."

"Don't make too many assumptions," Chauncey cautioned. "Those are the kind f people that go right to the top. They don't bother with a county sheriff. They want to make a threat, it goes right to the guy callin' the shots. When you went around to the taverns, why didn't you stop and see me?"

"I'd already seen you. Besides, you have a different relationship with your clientele. Your whole business with them is based on a kind of anonymity and privileged information. I feel I should respect that."

"Thanks, Ahmeek. I knew you were the right kind of guy for the job the first time I met you. I'd help you any way could, but betray one of my customers? I can't do that."

"And you said you came in to help me today. Without betraying any of your people, what can you do?"

"I'm offering a different kind of help, an Idea. I heard via the grape vine that you found part of a hood ornament at the scene."

"Yes, we did but don't spread that around."

"Well, I don't think a person who owns a car like that wants to drive around with a broken anything. I know a company in Chicago, the Warshawski Company that sells more, oddball auto parts than any place in the world, and it's mostly mail order. Any

The Beaver and the Bear

part, any kind of car, Warshawski probably has it. Now, if you wrote to him, you probably wouldn't even get an answer, but if I wrote to him?"

"You could find out if anybody up in this area ordered a new radiator ornament for a late model Packard?"

"It's what I do. I write letters to people when I want something. This time, I don't want a case of tomato juice or a new boat. I want information, and I think a good letter to the top man in the company, Isreal Warshawski, might do it, if you want me to."

"Do I want you to? That could be the key to the whole thing Chauncey. Yes, I want you to."

"Good, I'll get right to it," Chauncey said. "By the way, you gonna make it to the party for my new little girl?"

"I wouldn't miss it for anything, Mr. Bear Hunter."

"My wife and I will be happy to see you there." Chauncey started toward the door. "Come on out. I'll show you my new car. It was a gift from Don Juan. The Graham was getting a little old. Too may rough trips from Iron River to Wildernest. He commented on the worn upholstery last time I took him to the lodge, so I ask for a new one."

They reached the street and Jotham was awed by Chauncey's new Cadillac. His eyes locked in on the hood ornament. It looked like a female form with long flowing hair perched on a curved rod that rose up from the radiator, perhaps a Greek goddess. Jotham wasn't sure what that might mean to the Night Bird case, but of one thing he was sure. It looked like the one he had seen in the repair shop in Hurley, but that was on a Packard, not a Cadillac.

Jotham returned to his desk and tried to figure out what it all meant. Was Mike sure about the bird wing? Could it have been the flowing hair of a Greek goddess instead? But if so, that would mean it wasn't the Packard he saw being repaired in Hurley.

Chapter 22

The party for little Nancy was the social event of the decade In Northern Wisconsin. Wildernest Lodge was decorated with balloons of every color of the rainbow and crepe paper streamers extending from the center of the great room to every corner. Gertrude had taken Mourning Dove shopping and provided her with a pale pink evening gown that accentuated her dark complexion and black hair, with streaks of white that only added to the mystique. Jotham thought she was easily the most attractive woman in attendance even at more than fifty years of age. Her shoes were the only concession to her native background. She would have felt more comfortable in moccasins, but agreed to wear a moderately high heel. She had tried the high heels that had become the fashion for white women, but even with a week of practice she said she had the "walk of a she bear" and joked that Chauncey might think she was something to shoot.

Chauncey's wife was the belle of the ball, dressed in the finest silk gown money could not buy, donated by an importing company in San Francisco. She was an attractive woman, Jotham guessed, five or six years Chauncey's junior. She wore a single red rose corsage and a big smile that in combination with her long blonde hair, could light up the room. The introduction of the new daughter was presided over by Judge Burnside, who thrilled his audience with quotes from Shakespeare, Byron and Tennyson and only occasionally paused for a breath while Lester Lanin's band added music with a tasteful swing. The celebration that followed continued into the morning hours. Lester Lanin once said, "A debutante party that broke up before 5 A.M. was a bomb." To accompany Burnside's introduction, the band played primarily light classical music, but once the reception started it was strictly swing. As always Lanin's musicians appeared in full formal dress. Chauncey made a point of telling everyone this was the band that had played for the coming out party for Barbara Hutton, the Woolworth Heiress, as well as weddings for the Vanderbilts and Rockefellers. Jotham wondered which one of them was tagged for the band's appearance at Nancy's party. At one point Judge Burnside asked Mourning Dove to dance. She, of course, declined but the judge insisted. Jotham, knowing that for Mourning Dove a husband's permission was necessary, nodded his approval. On the dance floor she tried, but could not quite match the rhythm and, by force of habit, emphasized the first beat as she would have at a powwow. Lanin, noted for watching the dancers and adjusting his music to suit them, began to syncopate only the first beat of each measure and soon the whole house was dancing the Fox Trot with an Indian twist. After that set, some of the other men asked Mourning Dove to dance and each time the band adjusted the rhythm as soon as their leader saw her out on the dance floor.

While Mourning Dove was enjoying the dance, Jotham took the opportunity to move about and observe the crowd. He had a terrible temptation to start asking questions about Packard owners but that would be breach of faith. He did, however, catch bits and pieces of conversation that he thought interesting. Tony Mansfield was asking for a little help from a face Jotham thought had Chicago mob written all over it.

"Ya got too many wives, Henry, too much alimony. Couple of wives less and you could pay your workers a little more."

"Not my workers, your workers," Tony answered, "at least workers you control."

"So howzat?" the one they called the King asked. Jotham remembered Chauncey talking about him. He was the King because, Chauncey said, his court always followed close by whenever he entered a room. Jotham didn't know his real name, but he did know that a person with an entourage like that was likely to be either a movie star or a mobster.

"We're starting a new line of building products. We got the plant up and ready to go, but it takes a lot of raw material, asbestos ore. Our big supplier is in Quebec."

"So where do I come in?"

"Well, it's with the shipping. The raw ore, in Quebec they call it white gold, comes across the Great Lakes. Trouble is, I hear the Longshoremen are threatening to strike. A strike on the lakes would kill us right now."

The King sat quietly, elbows on the table with his thumbs tucked under his chin and his fingers laced together. His only response was "So?"

Jotham turned his back to them and took a couple of steps toward the dancers. The King looked a little nervous to have anyone quite that close and Jotham saw the eyes of one of the King's Court lock on him. Jotham waved his hand pretending he was trying to attract the attention of somebody across the room. The eyes looked back toward the King and Tony. Jotham heard

Tony say, "Danny, I need your help. You've got influence with those people."

"I'm the King, Henry. No names, remember. We're both Kings when we're here." The words were almost too soft for Jotham to hear. From that point the conversation got softer, so Jotham drifted away. He had a good Idea now, what attracted wealthy businessmen to Wildernest Lodge, nothing illegal, just business, shady perhaps, but business none-the-less and nothing that related to a Packard and dead Indian, which was really what he was listening for.

Jotham and Mourning Dove left the reception a little after one a.m. Mourning dove was bubbling with conversation about what a good time she had. She thought the band music was wonderful, just as pretty to listen to as Indian music, but she could not understand the meaning of any of it. Her only negative comment was all the drinking and how she had to keep saying no to the many drinks she was offered. All the whiskey reminded her of Johnny Bearheart. Whiskey was bad and she could not understand why so many white people liked it so much. Jotham turned the car onto the county road headed toward Iron River.

Only a few miles and Mourning Dove was asleep in the seat beside him. He didn't notice. Even at this late hour, his mind was still occupied with the crowd at Wildernest and his inability to get any idea who might have been there that owned a bright yellow Packard. He also had the advantage of not having spent near as much time on the dance floor as Mourning Dove had. It was not only the late hour that brought on her sleep, she was physically worn out. In her world men and women rarely danced together, but on this occasion at Chauncey's, she had been on her feet most of the night and all of her dance partners were men.

Jotham was rounding a curve where the road circled a small lake when he saw a pair of headlights behind him. "It looks like we're not the only ones to leave the party early," he said, then chuckled when he realized Mourning Dove was asleep. As he reached the top of a hill a quarter mile past the curve, he saw the lights again, this time much closer and approaching rapidly. Then he felt the car lurch forward as the bumper on the vehicle behind connected with the rear bumper of his own. The Hudson veered to the right, narrowly missing a giant white pine tree as it slid into the shallow ditch. Jotham looked ahead, expecting to see a yellow Packard, but instead, his eyes locked on a black delivery truck. He had never seen a vehicle like it before. It was much larger than the truck his brother Dominic used to haul pulp wood to the railroad loading dock and the oversized flatbed looked like it had a board fence built all around the outside. Mourning Dove was stirring. "What happened?" she asked sleepily.

"That truck bumped the back of our car," Jotham said. I suppose the driver had a little too much to drink at the party and clipped our back bumper when he tried to pass. Funny though, I didn't remember seeing a big truck like that at Chauncey's. I don't think anyone there would drive a truck like that."

Jotham shifted into reverse and inched the Hudson, wheels spinning, back on to the graded road. When he turned forward and shifted into low gear, he saw the truck backing off the road and making a y-turn to face him. Jotham spun the steering wheel to the right, and instead of continuing toward Iron River, headed back down the road toward Chauncey's. He depressed the gas pedal as much as he dared at night on a dirt road, hoping he could stay ahead of the truck. Mourning Dove was now fully awake.

"Ahmeek, what are you doing?"

"Hang on, Mourning Dove. That truck tried to run us off the road and it looks like he's coming back to try again."

For the first few miles the truck gained ground on Jotham's car, but on the steep hill, just before the turn off to the Wildernest Lodge, Jotham was able to pull away from the heavier vehicle. When they went down the hill on the other side, he shut off the headlights. He hoped the truck driver, assuming he too had come from Chauncey's, would think he had turned on Wildernest Road. There was just enough moonlight for Jotham to see where the graded portion of the road ended on either side. He had to slow down. Just before he reached the curve that would put them on the road to Drummond, he glanced in his rear view mirror. The truck looked like it had slowed almost to a stop. Then it made a left turn and stopped. That was good, Jotham thought. The truck driver could either decide they had returned to Wildernest or he could take a chance and continue the chase. Either way Jotham and Mourning Dove should reach the Drummond road far ahead of him. Should the truck driver continue that far he would be faced with another decision, He could only guess whether Jotham turned left toward Drummond or right toward the town of Barns. Even if he guessed right, Jotham thought he would be too far behind to catch up. Jotham turned left. A few minutes later, after having rounded enough curves and gone over several hills, he was sure they were they were no longer visible to anyone on the road behind them. He turned on the headlights and began to increase his speed.

"Okay Mourning Dove, you better stay awake." Jotham said. "We're going to see how fast this car can go." With lights illuminating the road ahead, he pressed even harder on the foot feed. Soon, they were traveling at speeds as high as a mile a minute in places where the road was straight and relatively smooth. On the curves he slowed only as much as he had to. Once they reached Drummond the macadam highway heading toward Washburn made the speed less frightening and Mourning Dove again went to sleep.

The next morning was Sunday and the county offices were not open, except for the Mike Flannigan's. Jotham drove to the Sheriff's office and told Mike what had happened.

"You're kidding. Are you sure it wasn't just an accidental hit?"

"I thought so at first, but when I saw him turn back, my first thought was to get the hell out of there. That truck was big, Dan."

"Maybe he was coming back to see if you were okay," Dan offered.

"Could have been, Dan, but if that was what he was doing why didn't he stop when he saw me back out of the ditch and head back toward Chauncey's? Not only that," Jotham added, "but he was picking up speed all the way. It's hard for me not to be convinced that he either wanted me dead or wanted to send me a pretty strong message."

"Did you get a license number?"

"Heck no, I was too busy trying to miss that big pine tree."

"That doesn't give us anything to go on, Jotham. If your Hudson took the hit without any more damage than a scratched bumper, I doubt there will be any marks on the truck. Any idea what kind of truck it was?"

"I couldn't even guess. All I saw was that fancy wood fencing on the flat bed. I might be able to get some help on that. There's a mechanic right here in Washburn that knows a lot about cars. Considering who he worked for in Chicago, I'd bet he knows everything about delivery trucks too."

"Who's that?"

"Don McCain."

"Oh, yeah," Mike acknowledged. "He's got a little shop down on the south side of town. He's a pretty good mechanic. He worked for a guy in Chicago that delivered a lot of bottled goods, right? And I'm not talking about Coca Cola."

"That's the one." Jotham agreed. "His boss's brother had Coca Cola."

Mike laughed. "I'll go down and see him. "I don't think we'll find out anything that will tell us who ran into you, but I'm curious about what kind of contraption you tangled with."

Jotham did not go with Mike. Instead he unlocked his own office. He had what seemed like a million thoughts going through is mind and he wanted to get them on paper. Of course Mike was right, at least in a legal sense. Finding out who owned a truck like that would mean nothing in a court of law. Even if there were only two such vehicles in all of upper Wisconsin, but evidence that would satisfy a jury wasn't what Jotham was looking for, not at this point anyway. If there were a dozen trucks and one owner who also had a yellow Packard, then the whole episode might be tied in with the death of Joseph Night Bird. It still would not make a case in court but that was not Jotham's immediate concern. Somebody had left a threatening message. The incident with the delivery truck could have been a way of emphasizing the threat. Why the truck and not a yellow Packard? It was obviously not an attempt on his life, not a light bumper to bumper hit with a vehicle big enough to flatten the Hudson. He was sure it was another warning. As soon as that thought struck him, he got up, locked the door to his office, and raced home.

Chapter 23

Jotham was relieved when he got to his house and saw that Mourning Dove was at the same place she would have been on any Sunday morning. She was in the kitchen preparing what he knew would be scrumptious dinner.

"Ahmeek, you are home so soon. You say you are going to work in office today. Why did you come back so early?"

"To see you, of course," he answered. There was no way he was going to admit that he was afraid, afraid for her. It made no sense to him that he should have been concerned. If there was to be another warning shot from whoever drove that truck, it was unlikely to be on a Sunday morning in broad daylight. He decided to wait before he told her what he wanted to do.

"Here," she handed him the Sunday paper and pointed to the living room. "You read the paper now. I will have dinner ready for you in little while."

Jotham was not interested in the newspaper. It was a Minneapolis publication and carried a lot of stories about Minnesota along with the national and world news, but his only interest currently involved what was happening in Northern Wisconsin. That wouldn't be in a Minneapolis paper. He thumbed through it anyway. One headline caught his attention and briefly took his mind away from his own problems. He read the article. Von Hindenburg had died and Adolph Hitler had called for a referendum, not only to make him the new Chancellor, but to give him *Fuhrer,* unlimited power. *So much for the war to end all wars,* Jotham thought.

Jotham could not stifle an audible chuckle when got to the next article. It said the president had appointed Joseph P. Kennedy, a "Boston born" Wall Street speculator as head of the new Securities and Exchange Commission. Jotham had seen articles about Kennedy before but in those days, the articles referred to him as a "bootlegger." He was about to put the paper down when he saw an article about the rash of strikes across the country including several called by the longshoremen, his interest again deepened. Tony Mansfield had express concern that they would hit Great Lakes shipping. He had heard one of the other guests at Chauncey's ask' "Why do we keep giving this guy all this stuff?" Jotham decided that Tony and The King had answered that question for him with the conversation he evesdropped on the night before. Other articles were about Dr. Francis Townsend's pension plan and Northwest Airlines contract to expand its mail service to the Dakotas, Montana and Washington State. He read enough of those articles to grasp the point story, then set the paper aside and concentrated on what he planned to suggest to Mourning Dove and how much he should tell her about the reasons for his concern. He had not so much as to decided how to broach the subject when he heard her call from the other room. His dinner was ready.

Before Mourning Dove had come to cook and keep house for him, Jotham had eaten most of his meals in the local café. The waitress considered him such a regular that, whenever he and Mike came in for their morning coffee, she joked about how close they came to going under without the District Attorney as a regular luncheon customer. He could no longer imagine himself eating meals in a restaurant. Mourning Dove had become adept at most dishes the white people ate including a good selection of Italian meals Lillian taught her. Jotham's favorites, however, were when she combined the two with traditional Indian food. Wild Rice and Chicken with vegetables from the garden and that is what she placed before him.

They talked about the night at Chauncey's. Mourning Dove was still repeating over and over how much she enjoyed herself and how surprised she was that dancing with the white man could be so easy. "Last night was much fun," she said, "but not the ride home. You drive way too fast last night, Ahmeek."

"I know I did," Jotham admitted. "I don't know what I was more afraid of, driving so fast without lights or that truck trying to run us off the road."

"He was a bad driver, the man in truck," she said.

"He was a very good driver," Jotham said, "but he wasn't a very good man."

"What do you mean?"

"I mean he knew how to drive, but he was a bad person because he was trying to hurt us. Mourning Dove, I want you to go back to the reservation, back to Red Cliff."

"Why, Ahmeek? Was I a bad wife because I dance with other men?"

"No. It was all right for you to dance with those men. It's just that I . . ."

"No, Ahmeek. I am sorry. I am Chippewa. I was trying to be like white woman."

"And that's okay Mourning Dove. Wives of white men do that all the time. You are my wife and I am not Chippewa. It is right for you to be like a white woman when you want to and it is right for you to be Chippewa when you want to. Last night we were at a White man's party. You did the right thing. I want you to go back to Red Cliff, just for a few days, because of the man in the truck. He tried to hurt us last night. He might come here."

"Last night I was white woman Ahmeek. Today I am Chippewa. I am not afraid."

"I know that a Chippewa woman is not afraid," Jotham agreed, "but I am afraid for you."

"You said I could be Chippewa when I want to." Mourning Dove stood erect and squared her jaw resolutely. "Now is when I want to."

Jotham smiled with admiration at the way she used his words against him. He was trying to think of a rejoinder when he heard a knock on the door. Mourning Dove, having made her point, broke into a smile, too, then turned and went to answer the door. It was Mike Flannigan.

"I need to talk to the DA Mourning Dove," Flannigan said as he crossed to Jotham. Mourning Dove followed him to the table, removed the dinner dishes and returned to the kitchen.

"Hi Mike. Did you find out anything?"

"Not about what happened to you last night but I found out a lot about the truck." The sheriff sat down across the table from Jotham. "You were right about McCain. That guy really knows his trucks. He wasn't working today, but he lives in that little house behind the shop. I just knocked on the door and told him who I was. He invited me in and gave me a lesson on motor vehicles like you've never heard."

"What about the truck?" Jotham asked.

"He said he couldn't tell for sure without seeing it for himself, but it sounded like a . . . just a minute. It's right here." Mike stopped and reached into his pocket for a small note pad. He looked at the pad intently, squinting to try to read what he had written. "He said it sounded like a Gotfredson."

"A what?" Jotham asked.

"A Gotfredson Delivery Truck, it's made by a small company over in Alma, Michigan. That is it used to be. They only built a few of them. They bought trucks from one of the bigger manufacturing companies in Detroit then, extended the frames and added extra leaves to the rear springs, they call them overload springs. That way they could build a bigger flat bed on it and add side panels to keep the load from sliding off."

"Can you find out who around here might have one?"

"Not a chance. All official records on motor vehicles list the original manufacturer, not some company that modifies the vehicle for a specific use. Nothing on record is going to say Gotfredson. Besides, the company only made a few of those trucks back in 28. When the stock market crashed in 29 they went out of business. Don said nobody knows where the owners are today. I could keep an eye out for one and if I happen to see it ask some questions, but that's about the only way we could find out and not a very likely one at that."

"Don't bother Mike. Even if you found it there's no way to prove what you saw was the same truck that ran me off the road. There is a favor you could do for me though if you want to keep you eye out for something. I'm concerned that what happened last night might be related to the threatening phone call Gertrude got. If it is, they might try something here at the house."

"So?"

"Well, I've got this recalcitrant wife that doesn't like my suggestion that she go back to Red Cliff for a few days. Maybe you could drive by occasionally to see that everything is okay."

"I'll do that, but I don't think you'll have a problem here at the house, at least not in daylight hours. Give me a call if you need me for anything else, I mean like something that deals with the Joe Night Bird case."

As the sheriff closed the door behind him, Mourning Dove came out of the kitchen and stood in front of Jotham, her hands planted on her hips. "I heard you talk to Mike about a re-recal-something wife. You mean me?"

Jotham smiled. "I said recalcitrant, and yes I did mean you."

"Re-cal-ci-trant." She paused as though letting the word roll back and forth over her tongue. "I don't know that word. That word mean good or bad?"

Jotham laughed. "Good, Mourning Dove, in your case nothing but good."

"That means I don't have to go back to Red Cliff?"

"That's right, beautiful lady, it's exactly what it means."

October started badly for Jotham. Gertrude kept him informed about the campaign his opponent was running. It ran all the way from criticizing Jotham for wasting so much time and taxpayers money pursuing the case of an Indian hit by a car to calling him incompetent because he hadn't solved the case of the Indian who was hit by a car. He knew he probably should be writing speeches and identifying campaign issues, but his heart wasn't in it. He and Mike still had not one solid suspect in the Joseph Night Bird case and he was still spending most of his time on the more mundane things that came into the District Attorney's office each day. Mourning Dove was still an election issue and Jotham had thought of no good way to combat it. The morality question was no longer relevant now that they were married, but she was still Indian and there were dozens of ways the other side could use that. Just as he was beginning to question whether he should put Mourning Dove through the troubles an election campaign would bring, the Bear Hunter walked into the office.

"Cheer up Ahmeek," Chauncey began, "I've got something that will make your day a lot better."

"Good morning Mr. Bear Hunter. I didn't know I needed cheering up."

"Are you kidding? You look like you just lost your last friend."

"Not yet, Chauncey, Not yet, but that might be what's coming next. What can I do for you?"

"It's not what you can do for me. It's what I can do for you. I got a letter back from Israel."

"From who?"

"Israel Warshawski, you know, the guy I told you about that sells car parts mail order. Well, I got a return. The Warshawski Company says they got an order for a Packard radiator cap from some car repair shop in Hurley."

"I don't know how much that will help, Bear Hunter."

"Maybe this will make it a little more helpful," Chauncey said. "Israel said that particular cap was not too common. Packard only put those on a limited number of cars and then only by special order. That radiator ornament is for the *crème de la crème*. It's rare."

That means we do have a fighting chance of locating it," Jotham said, "and I know just where to start looking."

"Good. I hope you can work it out," Chauncey said, "Stop and see me some time at Wildernest, Ahmeek. You know you're always welcome." He turned toward the door.

"Wait a minute, Mr. Bear Hunter." Chauncey turned back. "I want to thank you for the party. I enjoyed it and my wife really had a good time. Keep having fun Chauncey and thanks for the information on the Packard."

"Any time Ahmeek, Any time."

That afternoon Jotham and Mike Flannigan went to Hurley, back to the body shop where they had first seen the yellow Packard. They stopped at the Sheriff's Office to get Dan Vigonallo. Jotham remembered that the proprietor was not very anxious to help the first time. He knew he would be more agreeable with Dan there.

When he and Mike along with the Iron County Sheriff entered the repair shop, Jotham was not surprised to find that Toivo Kempala was as surly and uncooperative as he had been at the time of their first.

" I toll ya last time," Toivo said, "I don't write down the name of my customers. They want a car fixed, I fix it. They don't come back they don't get the car back. It's a lot easier than keepin' the books."

"But this is a little different, Mr. Kempala," Jotham said. "We're not talking about a situation where they left the car here for you to hold them up with. We're asking for the name of somebody that ordered a part from you."

"I'm not in the parts business Mister District Attorney," Toivo said with a sneer. "I'm in the fix it business."

"Come on Toivo," Mike said as he moved a bit closer, a mild threat, "you know what he's talking about. We know that you got a part from the Warshawski auto parts company. You ordered that part for somebody and if that person doesn't show up to get it, you got a fancy piece of high priced merchandise on your hands and nobody but you to pay for it. You know damn well who ordered that hood ornament."

"I don't talk about my customers to people like you. You ain't no policeman in this county. You're the sheriff here Dan. You gonna let these guys from Bayfield push citizens of your county around."

"Dan Vigonallo stepped in between Mike Flannigan and Toivo Kempala. As he moved forward, he reached back and unclipped a pair of hand cuffs from his belt. "No, Toivo," he said, "but I'll help them. You don't want to answer them, you answer me. You know it's against the law to interfere with a police investigation don't you?"

"I'm not interferin' with anything. I'm just not answerin' a bunch of questions they got no right to ask."

"Well, maybe that's the way you see it, but I see it as interfering with their investigation," Viganallo said. "Now you can tell me who ordered that ornament or you can spend the afternoon down at my place. You know where my place is, don't you? It's called the county jail."

"All right, I tell you."

"That's better." Dan said. "When Marichetti and I were here before you said that big car you were fixing belonged to Sam Rodello. Did Sam Rodello order the ornament?"

"No, it wasn't Rodello. It was that Frenchman, Frankie Courtier."

"Got an address?"

"No, I don't got his address, but I can find him. He hangs out at one of those clubs a lot.

"Okay then, what's he look like?"

"He's a little guy, maybe five foot six. He stays in the clubs cuz he likes to act big. He use to be a sailor, has an anchor tattooed on his arm. He always wears a cap cuz he don't want people to see his bald head."

As they drove down Silver Street to start looking for Frankie Courtier, Jotham posed a question for Dan Vigonallo. "Why do you suppose that guy is so reluctant to tell you anything?"

"This is Hurley," Dan answered. "Some of the people that have moved to Hurley in the past few years don't like anybody telling the police anything about them."

"I thought it was because he was a Finlander," Mike added.

Dan laughed. "Watch it Flannigan. Us Micks and Wops don't do so well in this North Country either."

"You back off, too, Vigonallo" Jotham chimed in. "I always preferred Dago myself."

They were still chuckling as they pulled up in front of the Silver Dollar Saloon.

It was only three o'clock in the afternoon but the Silver Dollar was already bustling with activity. Prohibition had ended nine months before and the clientele could not seem to get enough of the alcoholic beverages they had been deprived of for so many years. Jotham and the two sheriffs looked around for a short balding Frenchman, but no one they saw matched the description. They went to the bar, ordered three beers and asked the man behind the bar if he knew Courtier. He said he knew who they were talking about but hadn't seen him. They split up and began to mingle among the customers, asking the same question over and over again: have any of you seen Frankie Courtier, or some variation thereof? It was the same answer from each and, though they knew most were not honest answers, they declined to press the point. After a while, they sat down together at a table some distance from the clatter of slot machines to finish their drinks and watch the crowd. Soon, a waitress came to their table and asked if they wanted another drink. They all said no, but she lingered for a moment, then, bent down to speak quietly to Dan.

"I heard you asking about Frankie Courtier," she said.

"At close range Jotham thought he could see a black eye resisting her effort to hide it under a thick layer of make up.

"You know him?" Dan asked.

"Yeah I know the S.O.B., and I know where he is. He's in the back room." She gestured with her head toward a door behind them. "He's sleeping it off. Big Otto, the bouncer, punched him after he gave me this shiner." She placed her finger on her cheek below the swollen eye.

"He did that to you?" Dan asked with both anger and sympathy in his voice.

"He thought he wasn't seeing enough of me. I told him he better sober up if he had any ideas of seeing more. That's when he grabbed my wrist and smacked me in the face. I hope you guys want him for something big and put him away for life."

Dan, Mike and Jotham slipped through the door to the back room where they found a man lying on a camelback couch. They could see clearly the anchor tattoo on his left arm. Mike walked over to the sleeping man and yanked his hat off revealing a shiny bald head. The man stirred but did not fully wake up.

"It's gotta be Frankie," Mike said. He shook Frankie's shoulder. "Come on sleeping beauty, wake up. You're going for a ride, my friend."

"There's a door that looks like it goes outside from this room," Jotham said. "Dan, you get the car and we'll bring our boy here out the back. No use taking any chances going through that crowd in the Bar." Dan went back into the bar room and out the front door. Mike and Jotham pulled Courtier to his feet.

When they stepped out side, almost carrying the semiconscious Frankie, they were shocked to see an oversized delivery truck parked in the alley. Jotham reached over and lightly slapped the man between himself and Mike on the face until he began to stir and show some sign of consciousness.

"Is that your truck, Frankie?"

"Frankie shook his head and squinted. "My truck? I don't have a truck."

"No, but you drive one, don't you?"

"Ya, I drive a truck, but it isn't my truck."

"Is that the one you drive, over there?" Jotham grabbed Frankie's jaw and turned his head toward the delivery truck. This time there was no attempt to be gentle.

"Frankie squinted again. Uh huh, that's the truck I drive. So what? What are you guys doin' to me? What's goin' on?"

Dan pulled up with the patrol car and opened the door. Mike pushed the, by now fully awake man, inside. "We're taking you for a ride, Frankie. We're going to a place where we can have a nice long talk."

Chapter 24

Dan escorted Frank Courtier to a jail cell adjacent to his office then, went back where Jotham and Mike were waiting.

"Okay, our guest is comfortable," Dan said. "I don't think the surroundings are unfamiliar to him. What do we want to do?" He turned to Jotham. "I can't give him to you for buying a hood ornament. Even if we knew it was to replace the one Mike found in the Indian's leg, it would be pretty flimsy evidence for me to turn him over to you guys on."

"I think we need to talk to him here," Jotham agreed. "It's only probable that truck was the one that forced me off the road, but even if we knew for certain he could claim it was an accident. Do you suppose he was also driving the Packard that hit Night Bird?"

"At this point we can't even make a case that it was a Packard," Mike said. "The fact that Courtier ordered the new radiator cap doesn't prove a thing unless we can find the old one and match it with the broken piece we're hanging on to."

"That's the point," Jotham said. "We only have a case if Frank Courtier gives us one. And I think we can get him to do that, even tell us where to look for the broken ornament."

"Why's that?" Dan asked.

"Because I don't think Frankie was driving when the Packard hit Joe Night Bird. My guess is he did make those threatening phone calls and he did try to run me off the road, but a guy like Frankie doesn't make threats unless he's covering for someone who was at the wheel and is a lot bigger than he is. I'm thinking the guy he works for."

"Sammy Rodello," Dan affirmed.

"What do we know about Rodello, Dan?"

"Strictly legit, but it wasn't always the case. He ran a delivery business in Chicago, picked up most of his merchandise in Windsor, Ontario, same stuff he delivers now, but in those days it wasn't legal. He was small potatoes, but he never thought of himself that way. Just the kind of guy that would convince people like Courtier that he was a big shot in the mob."

"Okay," Mike said, "So we get him to give us a case. How do we go about doing that?"

"My guess is Frankie isn't as loyal as Rodello may think he is," Jotham said, "but we're going to need more time. Let's go out for dinner. Does the Silver Dollar serve food, Dan?"

"Sure they do, but I don't know how good it is."

"That doesn't make any difference. I want to give Frankie time to think about how much trouble he might be in, let his imagination work. While he's doing that, we find that waitress and, Dan, you get her to file a complaint, assault and battery. That will give us a few days if we need them to convince Courtier that he talks or he goes a lot farther up the river than the Iron County Jail."

After a meal, which they all admitted was better than they had anticipated, Mike, Dan and Jotham returned to the Iron County Jail. Dan informed Frank Courtier that he was staying over night and would appear before the Judge in the morning to be formally charged with assaulting the Silver Dollar waitress. In the mean time, Dan said, there were some other serious matters the Bayfield County Sheriff would like to talk to him about. He brought Frankie out of the cell and took him to a small conference room where Jotham and Mike were waiting. Dan seated Frankie at the opposite side of the table from the other two then, took a seat away from the table for himself.

"Frankie," Jotham began. "It is all right if I call you Frankie isn't it?"

"My name is Frank. Everybody calls me Frankie, it's okay."

"Good. We want you to be comfortable. We don't have anything to do with the charges Sheriff Vigonallo told you about, we're just looking for some information."

"You guys are always looking for some information. I ain't got no information."

"Well, we think maybe you have. Do you own a Packard Automobile?"

"What? Yah think, I'm made of money? I look like I'd own a Packard? I don't own any automobile of any kind."

"Then who did you order the fancy Packard hood ornament for?"

"I don't know what you're talkin' about. What hood ornament?"

"You know what hood ornament," Jotham said quietly in a friendly voice, "the one you got from Toivo Kempala."

"Frankie." It was Dan Vigonallo's voice from across the room. "These guys aren't charging you with anything, at least not yet. They're just looking for information. If I were you, I'd try to be a little more cooperative."

"I bought it for my boss's car. He hit a deer and broke the radiator cap."

Jotham rubbed his chin as though trying to remember. "And your boss would be Sammy Rodello?"

"Sure, everybody knows that."

"And while you were waiting for the new ornament to come, you took the car to Toivo's to get the fender fixed right?" Frankie didn't answer. "And while you were waiting, you found another radiator cap someplace so the boss's car would look good until the new one arrived, right."

"Right, how'd you know that?"

"Oh, we know a lot of things, Frankie. The one you found, the one you bought for temporary use came off a Cadillac instead of a Packard. Is that right?" Frankie didn't answer. It was obvious his nerves were shaken.

"Were you driving when you hit the deer?"

"Sure, I'm Mr. Rodello's driver. Who else would be drivin'?"

"Where did you drive Mr. Rodello that night, Frankie?" Courtier stared ahead and didn't answer the question. "Was it Iron River, Frankie?"

"Yeah, someplace around Iron River, it was out in the woods. I don't know exactly where. My boss told me where to go."

"Was it a resort on a lake near Iron River?"

"Well not so near, but yeah."

"Was it Wildernest Lodge?" Frankie's head jerked. How did these people know so much they weren't supposed to know? He remained mute, looking down where his hands rested on the table.

"Frankie." he continued to stare at his hands. "Frankie!" Frankie looked up at Jotham, a little bewildered. "Let's get back to that deer, Frankie," Jotham said.

"Okay, the deer," Frankie muttered looking a little relieved.

"When you hit the deer," Jotham asked, "did you know the radiator ornament was broken?"

"No," Frankie spoke more quietly than before, "we didn't see that or the fender until the next morning."

"And that's when you saw the ornament has a piece missing, right?"

"That's right."

"Do you know," Jotham leaned forward to make solid eye contact with Frankie, "that piece of the hood ornament was stuck in the deer's leg.?"

"Huh?" Frankie looked like he had been hit in the face with a pail of cold water.

"And do you happen to know where it is now?" Jotham continued. "It's in the evidence locker at the Bayfield County Courthouse." Jotham paused. "It wasn't a deer was it Frankie? It was an old Indian named Joseph Night Bird. It was a man who was killed and you know what happens when a man is killed? Somebody goes to prison. Now, once again, Frankie, were you driving the Packard?"

"No, No," Frankie shouted, "it wasn't me. Sammy was drivin'. He was drunk and told me he wanted to drive. It was him that hit the old man. Then when you guys started askin' questions about a yellow Packard, he said if you got close I had to take the rap for him. I ain't gonna take the rap for nobody. Not a rap for killin' somebody." Frankie looked up at Jotham and said, pleadingly, "You guys believe me don't you? You do believe me?"

"Yeah," Jotham said, soothingly, "We believe you."

Jotham sat up, moving his chair back a little. They gave a sobbing Frank Courtier time to regain his composure then, Mike moved forward. Thus far, the interrogation had provided the information they wanted. It tied up most of the loose ends, but it still failed to provide the kind of evidence they could use in court. Frankie did not look like he would be a dependable witness. Even if he were, they could end up with two people at the scene of the same crime accusing each other of being the perpetrator. Mike started questioning Frankie.

"I'm Mike Flannigan Frankie. I'm the Bayfield County Sheriff. I'd like you to add a few details for me. What happened then? Did you take over and drive the rest of the way?"

"No, not right away," he said. Then he began to sob.

"Frankie, tell me what happened then." Mike's voice was soft and gentle. "You can tell us the whole thing."

"No I can't. If I do I'm a dead man. I can't tell you, not the whole thing." He was on the verge of a breakdown,

"It's Okay, Frankie," Mike said. "We don't have to hear that now. Let's talk about something else. "Were you and Rodello at the Wildernest Lodge last Saturday night?"

"Last Saturday," Frankie affirmed. "Mr. Rodello wasn't, but I'll admit I was. There was some big party going on there and I was sent over to deliver some bottled goods."

"And you were driving that big truck of Rodello's?"

"Yes," Frankie answered in a quiet voice. He knew what was coming next.

"The same truck," Mike went on, "that bumped the back end of the District Attorney's car and forced him off the road and into a ditch."

"Yeah, that was me." Frankie turned to Jotham. "I'm sorry Mr. Marichetti, really I am. I didn't want you to get hurt. I just hoped I could scare you off the case. I really didn't want to hurt nobody."

"Are you saying you thought you could scare Mr. Marichetti and get him to drop the investigation into Joseph Night Bird's death?"

"I made the phone call to his office because I was scared. Mr. Rodello told me, if anybody found out about his car hitting the Indian, he'd say I was driving. Then after I made the phone call he said I screwed up and I'd have to fix it. That's why I was trying to scare the DA."

"Frankie," Mike said, "we thought you were just an innocent fellow that got caught between his boss and a crime. Now this comes out. What can we do Frankie? Running a car off the road with a big truck like that. We could consider that attempted murder. Maybe if you'd help us a little more, Mr. Marichetti might be willing to charge you with something not quite so serious. You might even avoid any jail time."

"I'll help," Courtier answered. "What do you want."

"I want to go back to when Rodello hit the Indian, okay Frankie? You said Sammy Rodello was driving. What happened then?"

"Sam told me to . . ." He began to sob again. "He said to me, 'make sure he's dead, Frankie, otherwise he's going to finger the car.'

"I said I can't do it. I never killed anybody. I just can't do it. Then he swore at me and said he'd do it himself and for me to get my coward's ass into the drivers seat and be ready to take off fast as soon as he was done." Frankie continued to sob.

"What happened then Frankie?" Mike's voice was reassuring. "What did he do?"

"He took a tire iron out from under the seat and hit the guy in the head. He got back into the car and told me to drive as fast as I could all the way back to Hurley."

Mike nodded toward Jotham then, sat back. Jotham again moved a little closer to the frightened man in front of them.

"I just have a couple more questions Frankie," Jotham said. Courtier looked toward him. "What happened to the tire iron? Do you know where it is?"

"Ya, I can tell ya. Sammy threw it out into the woods. He was still drunk enough that he couldn't throw worth a damn. It hit a big poplar tree and it bounced back toward the road. It landed in a bunch of brush next to a cluster of birches." Jotham glanced at the Sheriff. Mike nodded his head.

"Good, Frankie. That'll help. Now the other thing I want to know is about the hood ornament, the broken one you took off Mr. Rodello's car, what happened to that?"

Frankie almost smiled. He was ready for the question. "I saved it in case it might somehow help me if Rodello tried to accuse me of killin' the Indian. It's in my closet in the carriage house at Sammy's estate. I got a spare pair of boots that goes with my chauffer's uniform. It's in the left boot under some paper I stuff in there to keep the boot from losing its shape."

"Thanks Frankie. We'll see how your story checks out. If we get the tire iron and the hood ornament and we don't run into any other problem, I can probably forget about the charges for running me off the road. I don't think there is anything else we need to ask you."

Dan agreed to hold Frank Courtier for a few days until Mike and Jotham could look for the murder weapon. Both Jotham and Dan remembered the coroner saying that the cause of Night Bird's death was a blow to the head. At the time they assumed his head had struck some part of the car when the impact took his legs out from under him. They all agreed that what Courtier had told them made more sense. Sheriff Vigonallo also said he would obtain a search warrant for the carriage house on the Rodello estate and call them as soon as they were ready. The three of them planned to conduct the search together.

On the drive home Mike said he expected to have no trouble finding the tire iron.

"I don't know," Jotham said. "That brush is pretty thick this time of year."

"I'm counting on that," Mike answered. "That's why I'm pretty sure nobody else has found it and picked it up already."

"Then how are you going to find it? Frankie's description might not be quite a specific as it sounded."

"I've got a few tricks up my sleeve," Mike said. "I expect to have it in my hands by noon tomorrow. Then maybe I'll tell you how."

"You know Mike, if you're as good an investigator as you are an interrogator I have no doubt you will come up with it. If you find it, don't touch it with your bare hands. Put gloves on. That was a good job of questioning the suspect tonight," Jotham added. "You would have made a good attorney."

"You did alright yourself counselor. With a little practice you might qualify for sheriff." They both laughed. It was past ten o'clock by the time they had finished questioning Frank Courtier and almost fifty miles back to Washburn.

When Jotham quietly entered his house in Washburn, he was surprised to find a still wide awake Mourning Dove. She ran to him and threw her arms around his neck.

"Ahmeek," she said, "you are so late. I was afraid something happened. And I was afraid here alone so long. What if the man with truck came?"

"Oh, you would have been all right. You're Chippewa, remember."

"Don't tease. I mean it."

"I know Mourning Dove, but I knew you would be okay. We found the man with the truck. He's spending the night in Dan Vigonallo's jail."

"That is good, Yes?"

"That is very good and we found the man that killed Joe Night Bird, too. Let's go to bed."

Chapter 25

Mike Flannigan was on the road early Tuesday morning. He pulled his patrol car onto the side of the road where he remembered parking it the day they found the body of Joseph Night Bird. He glanced around and thought he saw the birch trees Frank Courtier had described. He looked at the poplar trees on both sides of the birches until he spotted one with a gouge in the bark about six feet above the ground. There was no other cluster of birches near it. Mike went over to the birch trees.

There was a thicket of hazel brush next to it. The grass was so matted under the brush that he could not see the ground. He reached in his pocket and took out a large compass. Holding the brush out of the way with his left hand he passed the compass over the ground about six inches above the surface. He moved a small distance between passes with the compass and repeated the process. After a dozen or so times, when he passed the compass over one spot the needle spun around to the South. *Funny thing for a compass to do* Mike muttered to himself with a satisfied smile.

He put the compass back in his pocket, as Jotham had suggested, put gloves on and began to dig into the matted grass with his fingers. In only seconds, he came up with the tire iron.

Mike looked at the iron Frankie said was the murder weapon, but found no sign of proof. There was neither blood nor any hair from Joe Night Bird to be found on it. That being the case, Dan wondered how it could be of any value to the prosecution, but Jotham said he wanted it so he carefully placed it in the car.

"I'm not sure this is going to be of any help," Mike said as he placed the tire iron on Jotham's desk. "I can't find anything on it that would serve as evidence of a murder or even corroborate Courtier's story."

"Frankie's story establishes it as the murder weapon. For corroboration, we've got the coroner's testimony. I expect this is the blunt object that will tell us if the story was true or a fabrication."

"How's that going to tell you anything with no sign of a crime on it any place?"

"The sign of a crime will be on it if the story is true, Jotham said. "It's just that we can't see it. The U.S. Bureau of Investigation provides fingerprint services. That's how they got a positive identification on the body of John Dillinger? I'll send the tire iron down to their Milwaukee office. If they can find a print on this tire iron, they can find out for us if it's Rodello or Courtier or neither one of them. With their equipment, they'll probably see blood or human hair that we can't see with our bare eyes, too."

"How will they know if it's Rodello's print?" Mike asked.

"My guess is both Courtier and Rodello have been in enough trouble that the Chicago office has the print from their fingers on file already. If they don't we can get a court order to have Dan Vigonallo's people get prints from them for comparison. Now, that's how we can find out who used that tire iron on Joe Night Bird. You tell me how you found the tire iron."

"It was easy, Jotham." Mike pulled the compass out of his pocket, placed it next to the tire iron, and smiled as Jotham watched the needle spin toward it.

Weeks passed before they got a report from the federal laboratory. They obtained a search warrant for the carriage house much sooner. Sammy Rodello was actually pleased to see Dan, along with Jotham and Mike, come to exercise the warrant. He had heard that his driver had been arrested and was in the Iron County Jail. Not knowing what Frank Courtier had been arrested for, he assumed his threatening Frankie and ordering him to take the blame for what happened had worked. Jotham stayed outside and talked to Rodello while Mike and Dan went into the carriage house. They found the broken hood ornament where Frankie had said it would be, in his left boot.

Mike tucked the metal object under his shirt and none of them said anything about what they had found. Dan, carrying an empty box to make Rodello think they had found evidence against Frankie, thanked the estate owner for his cooperation and the three of them left. When their car was well beyond the gate, Jotham took the broken wing he had brought from the evidence locker out of his pocket. It fit perfectly with the metal object Mike had retrieved from Frankie's boot.

A week later a package arrived at the Bayfield County District Attorney's office from the United States Bureau of Investigation, Milwaukee office. The package contained the tire iron they had sent and a written report of the test results. It stated that the laboratory obtained fingerprints for both Frank Courtier and Samuel Rodello from bureau files. It said the only clear prints on the tire iron were those of Samuel Rodello. It also said the surface of the tire iron had residue of blood and human hair, but there was currently no way to identify the source of those items.

After the trial, Chauncey came in to Jotham's office to congratulate him. Rodello's lawyer could come up with no defense against the physical evidence. A jury found Samuel Rodello guilty of murder in the first degree and sentenced him to life in the state prison at Waupun. In a separate proceeding in Iron County court, Frank Courtier entered a plea of no contest in the assault of a waitress at the Silver Dollar and served fifteen days in the Iron County jail. No charges were filed relating to his forcing Jotham off the road.

"Well Marichetti, my friend Ahmeek, like the Canadian Mounties, you always get your man."

"My thanks to you, Mr. Bear Hunter, without that letter from Warshawski we couldn't have gotten a conviction," Jotham said. "Sorry it had to be one of yours."

"I'm not. I should never have let Rodello in the club," Chauncey said. "That cheapskate thought his dues required no more than a bottle of Canadian Whiskey once a year. Not a case, mind you, but a bottle and cheap stuff at that. How is the electioneering going? Putting a Chicago rum runner turned murderer in prison going to help with the votes?"

"It will help some with a few people but there are still too many who have this idea that killing an Indian doesn't matter. Believe it or not I still hear about some folks who have more sympathy for Sammy Rodello than for Night Bird or his family. As for me, the vote count doesn't matter. Justice was served, and if people don't care about that, I can live without being DA. I only want the job as long as the people of Bayfield County care about justice."

"That's the spirit Ahmeek. You can always turn to my kind of work. I don't collect a salary, but I get the best of everything. You want to chat and have a good cup of coffee, my place is always open."

The press coverage on the Joseph Night Bird case was too much for Roscoe Mickleson to counter. In spite of his attempt at an early start in his campaign, when he saw the tide turn for Jotham, he withdrew from the election. Jotham did not have to give speeches or shake hands on the street corners. He ran unopposed. Jotham served two more years as District Attorney. During those years he encountered no other case like the Night Bird murder and for that he was thankful.

The presidential election shocked the news media experts and disappointed the Bear Hunter. This was to be a test for Franklin Delano Roosevelt who, some pundits thought, had an uphill battle for his second term as president. He had brought the country out of the great depression, but had done it with a variety of "new deal" programs some said called for an equally innovative variety of taxes. Alfred Landon, a fiscal conservative who ran against the new deal policies, which he said, wasted too much and gave the president undue power made few public appearances. The *Literary Digest* magazine, based on a survey taken with telephones across the country predicted Landon would win. Instead Roosevelt won by the largest landslide in presidential history and a short time later the magazine ceased publication. The pollsters failed to account for the limited availability of telephones among the rural population, who benefited the most from new deal programs and cast their votes for the incumbent.

It was one of the areas where Jotham and his brother Dominic disagreed. Jotham felt that Roosevelt, having lifted the country out of the depression, deserved another term. Dominic was afraid the new policies would be bad for business. Mourning Dove disagreed with both of them.

"Politics, politics," she said, one day when they were visiting the farm. "Why you argue politics. You can not fix and your brother can not fix. All you can do is read the papers and argue."

"You know, Dominic," Jotham said, "she's right. We probably should find something else to talk about. The country's getting so big now people like you and I don't have much of a say in how it's run."

"Maybe we don't have much say anymore, Jotham, but we gotta keep tryin'. Did you ever think about running for congress?"

"Okay, Dominic, you're right. We do have to keep trying, but I'm not planning to run for congress. That's too big a jump from Bayfield County District Attorney. To do that I'd have to get elected to some state office first. That would mean living in Madison and I have no desire to live in Madison. I got my fill of that a long time ago. I think I'm through with this District Attorney job though. I think, when my term ends this time, I will take a long vacation until the April elections. Then I'll run for judge."

As the depression eased, more and more of the people who had moved to the North Country from the Twin Cities and Chicago returned to their former residence. There were exceptions. Chauncey Bottum had left the city long before the depression and was determined to stay. Dan Koepp and Don McCain who had both found a more satisfactory life in the less populated environs of Bayfield County also remained. Don married a local woman from the Wasburn area. She had a small daughter out of wedlock and Jotham joked that he might have escaped marriage if he had not fallen in love with the little girl. Don came back quickly. "Same situation for you, my friend, but in your case it was her grandchildren." McCain continued to repair cars in his small shop on weekends, but during the week he drove truck for Jotham's brother Dominic.

By the end of Jotham's second term as District Attorney, the paper mills were buying as much pulp wood as available and Dominic had three crews cutting timber from Washburn to Port Wing. He had paid Jotham in full for the farm and continued to live there. He and Lillian maintained a minimal agricultural activity if for no better reason than to winter his draft horses. Though the truck replaced the rivers for transporting timber, the horse was still the only feasible means of getting the timber out of the deep woods. The logs, more often referred to by the loggers as sticks when used for pulp wood instead of lumber, were stockpiled next to a logging road where the truck driver and his helper could load them and haul them to the railroad loading dock.

Jotham and Dominic continued with their respective jobs but what was happening in Bayfield County seemed insignificant compared to the daily news for the rest of the world. In Europe almost every country was involved in modifying its alliances in an effort to escape the buildup of the Third Reich and the onslaught of Hitler's war machine that was already spreading its tentacles across the continent. On the other side of the world, the war between Japan and China had been brewing for years with a series of battles on the Chinese mainland. People of the United States were influenced greatly by an isolationist movement that assumed the Atlantic and Pacific Oceans provided protection from any threat arising from European and Asian conflicts. Jotham thought it ironic that a primary spokesman for the isolationists was Charles Lindberg, the first man to have crossed the Atlantic Ocean with an airplane only eleven years before.

The Beaver and the Bear

On August, 30, 1938, the invasion that had some residents of Eastern U.S. cities fleeing there homes for safety farther west came. It was not an invasion of a military force from Adolph Hitler's new formed Luftwaffe or the growing German Naval forces. It was an Invasion From Mars, that started in the fictional town of Grovers Mill, New Jersey. As a Halloween prank, the producer of the *Mercury Theater on the Air*, a radio program emanating from the Chicago studios of the CBS Network, thrilled listeners with a dramatization of H.G. Well's book, *War of the Worlds,* in which a supposed meteorite landing in New Jersey turns out to be an invading space ship from the planet Mars. Producer Orson Welles presented the story as a series of news bulletins which caused listeners, accustomed to hearing bulletins about the action in Europe, to believe the attack was really happening.

For the next few days, newspapers across the country reported the panic the broadcast had caused. Hundreds of people from New York City and nearby New Jersey cities and towns left their homes looking for a safe refuge. One person, they said, had contacted CBS asking for money to return to New York. He had taken a train to Detroit and did not have funds for the return trip home. Jotham read the article a second time to see, but it did not tell if CBS had provided him with return fair.

The panic might have been much greater except that most Americans, like Jotham and Mourning Dove, were not listening to the Mercury Theatre. They were hooked on Charley McCarthy, ventriloquist Edgar Bergen's popular dummy that was on the NBC network at the same time. Serious news, even if the Martian War had been serious news, came in a poor second to Bergen and McCarthy. That became clear, Jotham thought, just a month earlier, on the twenty eighth of August, when Northwestern University had awarded Charley, Edgar Bergen's dummy, and Honorary Degree.

A week later when the election came, Jotham's name was not on the ballot. He decided his off the cuff comment to his brother made sense. He planned instead to fill the three months between the end of his term as District Attorney and the Spring Election helping his brother in the logging business and working on his election campaign for a judgeship. His household had also become a little larger when, as Mourning Dove had predicted, her daughter- in- law could no longer care for her grandchildren and they moved in with Jotham and Mourning Dove. Jotham knew that, no matter what else he did, he wanted more time to spend with them.

When the spring election came, the six month old news of the Night Bird case was still fresh in the minds of Bayfield County residents. Jotham was elected Judge of the Circuit Court for Bayfield County.

Chapter 26

"December 7, 1941, a date that shall live in infamy." Chauncey Bottum listened intently to the words of President Franklin Roosevelt asking Congress for a Declaration of War against Japan. It was Monday, the day after the attack on Pearl Harbor. The aerial bombardment had destroyed most of the US Naval Fleet. Chauncey had spent as much time as he could in front of his Atwater Kent radio since the first bulletins were broadcast Sunday afternoon. The radio was a Model 967 Atwater Kent Console that was capable or both standard and short wave reception. One of the guests at Wildernest had offered to buy him a newer one but Chauncey declined. He said his five year old Atwater was the best radio ever built and he would wait until someone built one that was as good. Atwater had ceased production in 1936.

When the President finished his speech, Chauncey shut the radio off. He hadn't liked Roosevelt, but now he was not only the President he was the Commander and Chief of the Armed

Forces in a time of war and the Bear Hunter new he needed the support of every citizen. Chauncey pondered what he could do. He was too old for the military. Even if he could join one of the services, it would shatter his heart to have to leave Wildernest for an extended time. Little Nancy was only five years old and her older sisters were still children. Surely, he thought, somebody can tell me what I can do that will help the war effort without leaving them. Chauncey sat down at his desk and did the one thing he did best. He wrote a letter asking what he could do to help. He addressed it to *Henry L Stimson, Secretary of the War Department, Washington, D.C.*

Within a week, things at the Bayfield County Courthouse were buzzing. Changes were taking place as county workers implemented new programs established to meet the needs of a wartime government. The Draft Board had to be activated. A food ration stamp distribution program had to be developed. Ration stamps for gasoline required totally different criteria. The rationing board had to differentiate between the needs of people based on pre-established categories. Fuel distribution had to accommodate transportation of goods and materials needed for the war effort; therefore Dominic had a stamp placed on the windshield of his truck simply marked T. "T" was a gasoline rationing category that gave him an unlimited supply without the presentation of ration stamps. Rural mail carriers had a similar stamp. Others whose automobiles were assumed to be used primarily for pleasure and convenience were given books of stamps with a specified number of gallons per month.

Items that were imported by ship, such as coffee and sugar, had severe rationing quotas. They might have been in large supply in Cuba or South America, but the country needed its ships to transport troops and machines of war. People on the home front would have to do without such luxuries. The regulations came down from Washington, but their administration was in the county offices throughout the country. The County Board Chairman was responsible for implementation and the County Judge was required to assist in the interpretation of regulations and legal oversight.

The first few weeks after December seventh were chaos but by Christmas everyone was catching on to their new responsibilities and the function of the court house became smoother. Assisting the townships with work caused by mobilization became a greater problem than county functions. In addition to people being required to step into unfamiliar jobs in each town, the most capable people moved out to take advantage of better salaries paid by the ship yards in Superior, Wisconsin. The railroads needed more section hands to maintain tracks that were carrying more traffic than ever before. To maintain the large crews, they provided rail passes to workers so they could commute by train from their homes to the nearest work site. The railroads also paid for the commute as regular work time which made such jobs very attractive.

Early in January, Jotham found himself with a clear docket and an opportunity to take part of the afternoon off. Just as he was getting ready to walk the few blocks to his home, he heard a knock on the door of his chambers. "Come right in," he called, expecting some sudden emergency involving the translation of yet another federal regulation. Instead he saw Chauncey Bottum come through the door.

"Good afternoon Bear Hunter. What brings you all the way to Washburn?"

"No business this time, Ahmeek my friend. I just came to see you. "I wanted to tell you I'm going to be away for a while. I'm going on extended trip"

"Bear Hunter, I thought you said you never wanted to leave Wildernest?"

"I said that and I meant every word, but this is different. My country is in trouble and I've got to join in the fight."

"You're joking, right? The Army will only take enlistments by men under thirty-eight. I know you're a few years younger than I am, but you've got to be well beyond that."

"That's why a wrote to Henry Stimson."

"Stimson?" Jotham asked. "You wrote to the head of the War Department?"

"I did," Chauncey affirmed, "the day after Pearl Harbor. I got this answer back yesterday." Chauncey handed Jotham a letter. He read the letterhead, *The Secretary of War, United States of America, Washington D.C.* "You told me you go right to the top when you ask for something. You weren't kidding were you?"

"I've done a lot of kidding, but not about something like this," Chauncey said as he took the letter back. I told the secretary about myself, my, let us say unique qualifications, and he said I should sell War Bonds. He suggested I go on a tour all across the country and raise money for the war effort. That's what I'm going to be doing. I got some people in Industry, head of a couple of railroads to cover my train fair."

"That's great, Bear Hunter." Jotham reached into his vest pocket and removed his checkbook. "Let me be your first sale. I'll start with a five hundred dollar bond. How long do you expect to be gone?"

"Sorry you can.t be the first. Tiddyboom offered to buy a thousand, but thanks. I don't know how long it will take, but I set a goal for myself at fifty thousand dollars."

"I wish you luck, Bear Hunter," Jotham said. "I wish I could do as much, but I'm stuck here being a judge for a while anyway. Keep in touch and let me know how it all works out."

Morning Dove's grandsons, like their great uncle, Johnny Bearheart, served in the army during the war. They all returned to their wives and the families they had started a few years before the war began. Dominic' son Gino enlisted in the Marines and served three years in the Pacific before returning home safely in 1945.

Chauncey exceeded his goal in war bond sales. When he last saw Jotham he said the one thing he wanted people to remember him for was raising more than sixty thousand dollars for the war effort. Stories of his success were carried in all of the area newspapers, but were dwarfed by the coverage of Richard Ira Bong, from nearby Poplar, Wisconsin, receiving the congratulations of Eddie Rickenbacker for besting his record of twenty six aerial victories in World War I. By the end of the war Bong had extended that record to forty.

After the war, Jotham retired from the bench and moved to a heavily wooded tract of land near Bayfield. He wrote articles on politics and law for both the Ashland and Superior daily newspapers and on rare occasions he represented a client in court but only in tort cases. He refused to serve as an attorney for the defense in any criminal preceding. He hunted and fished frequently with his brother, but as the logging business grew Dominic had less time for those activities.

One day Mourning Dove noticed that Jotham was spending more and more time out of the house. She knew he only liked to hunt when he was with Dominic and she could see him from their kitchen window when he worked in their little garden so when he returned that day, she confronted him.

"Where have you been so long today, Ahmeek?" She asked.

"I went for a walk in the woods," Jotham said.

"All morning in the woods?" She held a neatly folded copy of the Ashland Daily Press. "You didn't even read your newspaper." Then with a familiar twinkle in her eye she added, "I think maybe you get tired of a Chippewa wife. You look in the wood for a new, white wife?"

Mourning Dove could not hide the fact that she was teasing. Jotham decided to play along. "How did you know? Did you follow me? Did you send one of the children to follow me?"

"Now you are making jokes with Mourning Dove." She swung at him with the newspaper. Jotham caught the paper, tossed it on a chair and pulled Mourning Dove close to him. He kissed her then, held her in a tight hug.

"You know that could never happen," he said.

"Yes," she said with a smile, "and I know what it is you have been doing in the woods. My granddaughter told me." Those grandchildren Jotham had become so fond of by this time had children of their own, but Mourning Dove thought of all of them as her grandchildren. "You are playing Eagle Feather. She said you call her *Opechee*. Why?"

"Because it's her name," Jotham said. "Her mother calls her Robin, the English word. When I was a little boy your grandfather, Chief Eagle Feather gave me the Indian name Ahmeek. When I went to school I had to use the name my mother gave me, Jotham, but when I was in the woods with Eagle Feather, Johnny Bearheart and you, I was always Ahmeek, the Beaver. When Robin goes to school she is Robin, but when she is in the woods with me and the other children, she is *Opechee*."

"Not why do you call her *Opechee*." Mourning Dove protested, "Why do you play Eagle Feather with the children?"

"Because they have no one else, no one to tell them the stories and show them the old ways of the Chippewa. They go to public schools now and the older Chippewa don't teach them like your grandfather taught us. Soon all of that will be forgotten."

"I know that is true," Mourning Dove agreed. "I heard some of the men say they have enough to do to find food without trying to teach the children whose minds were being filled with useless things like arithmetic and spelling words in the English language."

Several children had started to join Jotham in the woods but there were two that he especially liked. They were Robin, who was ten years old and a boy named Robert, perhaps two or three years younger. Jotham thought they could have been a Mourning Dove and Johnny Bearheart had they lived fifty years earlier. He sat patiently with them and told them the stories Old Eagle Feather had told him when he was their age. As he had been given the name *Ahmeek* when he first met Eagle Feather, he called each of them by a name that he pretended to think was more appropriate. He teased Robert, by saying his name sounded like Rabbit, and then told him when they met in the woods for learning about the Indian way, he would be called *Wabasso*, the Chippewa word for Rabbit. The older sister of *Wabasso* Jotham called *Opechee*, because that was the Chippewa word for Robin. Then he told them how he had been given the name of *Ahmeek* because Eagle Feather had thought he looked like a beaver. When he said this he twisted his jaw to accentuate an overbite and show his front teeth. The children all laughed.

In addition to simple words of the Chippewa, mostly nouns, Jotham told them stories. How little *wazhushk*, the Muskrat saved Sky Woman and the earth from the great flood by bringing a small amount of earth from the bottom. He told them how the bigger animals laughed at *wazhushk* when he said he would dive to the bottom but Sky Woman said, "Only Gitchi–Manitou can judge others." He told them how Sky Woman put the small amount of earth on the back of a turtle and as she did, it grew to be a giant island that became the land where they lived. Beyond the stories he had learned from Eagle Feather, Jotham told the children what he had also learned from others who wrote about the Chippewa. He told them about the daughter of Sky Woman, Nakomis, who according to Indian legend he had found in the writings of Henry Roe Schoolcraft, was the mother of Hiawatha.

Each day that he spent with the children, after the story telling, he would teach them a game or one of the crafts that Eagle Feather had taught him along with Mourning Dove and Johnny Bearheart. He showed them how to make baskets from the wood of the birch tree and *baggataway*, Lacrosse nets, from the bark of the bass wood. He taught them how to make a toy drum and a feathered headdress the way Eagle Feather had shown him. Jotham thought there was little he could have done in retirement that would have been more important and nothing that would have been as much fun.

Author's Comment

Historical fiction is a blend of fact and fantasy. It is a story placed in a real historic setting and therefore often includes a mix of real characters and events of the time intermingled with fictional characters and events that have no foundation in reality. In *The Beaver and the Bear* I have tried to present the major events of the years following the "great depression" accurately with modifications only to accommodate the fictional characters and their story. Jotham Marichetti and Mourning Dove, were fictional characters in my first published novel, *Rivers Must Run*. Judge Barns, on the other hand, was the Wisconsin Supreme Court Justice in the time period referred to in this story, but that Jotham was his law clerk is a part of the fiction. The battle of Belleau Woods, including the heroic account of a handful of American soldiers capture of a large contingent of German troops, is true but one of them was not Johnny Bearheart. Johnny is a fictional character who first appeared in *Rivers Must Run* and is a featured character in *The Beaver and the Bear*.

Many other names, both familiar and real, can be found in this book. Some of the fictional characters are modeled after real residents the author knew during the time period but appear in this work with names and other identifying information changed. There was a mechanic and truck driver who had worked for Al Capone and moved to the North Country when his former employer went to prison. There was at least one tax accountant who, while he had no direct connection with the Capones nor any other figure in organized crime, moved from the Chicago about the same time. While their real names are not in the book, some of the stories they told are.

One character, too well known to need or permit a fictional identity is an exception and deserves particular attention. He is remembered by the name he gave himself, *Chauncey the Bear Hunter*. His is a name that has faded with the passage of time, though in 1941 he was well enough known to be featured in an article in the *Saturday Evening Post*. As a character in a fictional story, we have drawn him into circumstances that he, in real life, probably never encountered, but in so doing, we have described a persona as true to his life as we possibly could.

Other Books by Paul Kending

Rivers Must Run

In Wisconsin he was called Jotham. In Michigan's Upper Peninsula he went by the name of *Ahmeek*. A boy's upbringing in two cultures is at the heart of this historical, all ages novel. The mix of Italian and Native American cultures becomes central as Jotham grows to manhood and must try to resolve a bitter dispute between loggers and construction workers who have come to dam the river for electric power.

Rivers Must Run provides a slice of 19th century history in an engrossing story of cultural contrasts.

Survivor's Paradise

When Leon Cloud rescues Janet MacAlpine from drowning, the near disaster is the beginning of a spiritual journey through time and space guided by the White Buffalo Woman of Sioux legend. Leon, a Lakota Sioux, is an administrator in the computer industry while Janet is a free lance environmental writer. After their harrowing experience each tells the story and their reactions in their own medium.

Survivor's Paradise is fantasy style, future scenario in which readers see a possible result of human failure in dealing with the environment.